PLEASURE PALACE

Also by Marian Thurm

Floating
Walking Distance
These Things Happen
Henry in Love
The Way We Live Now
The Clairvoyant
What's Come Over You?
Posh (pseudonym Lucy Jackson)
Slicker (pseudonym Lucy Jackson)
Today Is Not Your Day
The Good Life
The Blackmailer's Guide to Love

PLEASURE PALACE

NEW AND SELECTED STORIES

MARIAN THURM

DELPHINIUM BOOKS

Library of Congress Cataloging-in-Publication Data is
available on request.
ISBN: 978-195300204-4
21 22   LSC   10 9 8 7 6 5 4 3 2 1
First Edition

"Winter," "Floating," "Still Life," and "Lovers" first appeared in *The
New Yorker*; "Ice" in *Ms.*; "Flying" in *Mississippi Review*; "House-
cleaning" in *Michigan Quarterly Review*; "Kosta" in *The Southampton
Review*; and "End. Of. Story." in *Narrative Magazine*. "Today Is Not
Your Day," "Hasta Luego," and "Kosta" were included in *Today Is Not
Your Day*, a collection published by
SixOneSeven Books. Their permission to reprint these stories is
gratefully acknowledged.

Artwork and Cover Design by Colin Dockrill, AIGA

In memory of my dear parents,
Judy and Leon Thurm,
who loved books
and inspired me to love them as well

And with gratitude to Lori Milken and Joseph Olshan

Contents

WINTER (1979)

Everyone said Harte would hardly remember a thing, that it would all be a blur in her mind and that she would need an album full of pictures to show her the way it had been. But six months after the wedding the details are still fixed firmly in her memory: the dry rustle of her gown against the carpet as her father guides her down the aisle, past her mother's friend who leans out from her seat and hisses, "Smile, this is a wedding, not a funeral!" the staccato clicking of the photographer's equipment all through the ceremony, the sweet look of contentment on Brian's face that makes her want to drop kisses beneath his cheekbones as they dance their first dance together as husband and wife.

It had been a hot, damp night and the first thing she did when she got into the car was take off her pantyhose, slinking down almost to the floor as Brian kept watch from behind the steering wheel. Then they had driven to a hotel in Manhattan. In a small, square, green-and-gray room, which would have been a disappointment to anyone except a salesman in town on a business trip, they stayed up past dawn counting the checks that had been tucked inside the pockets of Brian's tuxedo—checks for fifty, seventy-five, and less frequently, one hundred dollars.

By now the checks have all been spent on tuition for Brian's third year in medical school, and Brian and Harte are living in a university town in Florida, in a garden apartment ten minutes from the hospital where Brian does his clinical training. Harte finds the smallness of the town intolerable, and hates the dull, hot days that are easily wasted away. After a half year of marriage she doesn't know what there is to say for her life. Every week her mother calls long-distance from New York and asks questions, and Harte feels like weeping. She doesn't know how to explain that nothing is happening to her, that her days are as motionless as the water in the neighboring swamp.

Three years ago, when Harte first met Brian, he seemed· the only person she knew who was confident about his future. He was in his last year at Harvard, with four applications filed for med school, and every weekend he waited for her at South Station in Boston with a rose wrapped in waxy green paper. One night, late in April, as she sat curled drowsily in his darkened dorm room, he played "Suzanne" for her on his guitar, sounding just like Leonard Cohen, and convincing her that it was all somehow connected with love.

Immediately after his graduation, Brian drove home with his parents, who had retired and moved from Ohio to a suburb of Miami. Because he was now an official resident of Florida, Brian's med school tuition would be as low there as it could possibly be anywhere. And that, he explained to Harte, was the one good reason for putting a thousand miles between them. He called her every Sunday night that summer and wrote her two or three times a week, though as soon as school began, the letters became postcards and he occasionally forgot to mention how much he missed her. Harte kept his letters and postcards in a shoe box, but only the romantic ones—the rest she stuffed into the compactor under the kitchen sink in her parents' house.

She started school in the fall, enrolling in a graduate program in English at NYU, which was what she had planned to do before she met Brian. Sometimes she wondered why he hadn't asked her to alter her plans and come down south for grad school. He never even seemed close to suggesting it, and if the subject of her going to NYU came up, he always said that it was an excellent school and that he was glad she had the opportunity to go there. Whenever she heard him say these things, it seemed to her that the balance of love was tipped in his favor, and she began to feel uneasy. But each time she went through the letters in the shoe box, the evidence showed that she had no cause to worry.

Thanksgiving vacation of her second year at NYU, Brian came to visit Harte's family, and he finally admitted that he was tired of carrying on a long-distance romance, that marriage seemed like a good idea to him. They both agreed that once Harte got her master's, she would try to find a teaching job in one of the community colleges near the town where Brian lived. But even as they made plans, she didn't tell him how often she had imagined herself marking her students' papers with a red felt-tipped pen as he lay beside her on their double bed, reading the *New England Journal of Medicine*, his hand resting gently at her neck.

Harte's mother and father did not want her to marry Brian. They said it was because he was self-absorbed and didn't pay as much attention to her as he should, but Harte (who knew these accusations had very little truth to them) was sure it was only because they didn't like the way she and Brian looked together. She is tall and sturdy-looking, with big, wide hands and feet that are larger than Brian's. When she and Brian stand side by side, it's clear how tall she really is, how broad across the shoulders. Her father even tried to convince her that small men were a breed of their own, saddled with inferiority complexes that they covered up in predictable ways. After that, he said nothing further to dissuade her.

The wedding plans were made and carried out, and Brian's new Fiat got them all the way to Florida without overheating once.

In Florida, they settled in the apartment Brian had rented for them, and Harte waited to hear about the teaching jobs she had applied for and tried to get used to the burning summer heat. One afternoon during their first week in the apartment, she nearly blacked out while crossing a parking lot.

On weekends the two of them walked the malls of the handful of small shopping centers nearby, looking at all the things they couldn't afford. Together they went through the racks in the Better Sportswear department of the one decent department store in town, and assembled outfits for Harte—pale silk blouses and corduroy skirts and matching jackets with leather buttons. Each time she came out of the dressing room, Brian stood alongside her in front of the mirror in the middle of the floor and adjusted the collar of her shirt or smoothed the shoulders of her jacket and finally grinned at her in the mirror and told her she looked terrific. After she changed back into her jeans and T-shirt and returned the clothing to the racks, she and Brian would walk over to Baskin-Robbins for frozen chocolate-covered bananas, which came on an ice-cream stick and cost a quarter. Now and then, they went to the movies, though the only films playing were violent ones starring Clint Eastwood or Charles Bronson, or had titles like *The Stewardesses*. "This isn't New York," said Brian when Harte asked where all the good movies were. Later, he said she was suffering from ordinary homesickness and culture shock. He was positive she would feel much more settled and at home as soon as she found a job.

When it was clear that the schools hadn't any openings, Harte began reading the tiny column of want ads in the local paper and convinced herself that working in Burger King or Pizza Hut or as a clerk in a discount drugstore would be better than not working at all. She dressed up in a skirt and tried to look eager as she filled out one application after another for jobs that she couldn't imagine anyone ever wanting. At the end of her first week of interviews, the man who took her application at Uncle Jerry's Family Restaurant told her that what he was really looking for was someone who would fit in well with the rest of his employees, who were mostly kids from the high school in town. "We're like a family here," he said, "and I just can't picture you as one of our relatives."

Then, one afternoon in October, Brian called from the hospital with the news that he had found Harte a job as a shelver in the medical library. That night they decided to celebrate and baked a quiche for dinner—their first joint project in the kitchen. They kept laughing and bumping into each other along the narrow length of linoleum, and Harte spilled a frying pan full of sautéed onions into the sink, but the quiche came out perfectly. When they sat down to eat, Brian lit a candle shaped like an ice-cream sundae and turned the lights off for the rest of the evening.

Harte's "poor attitude and general lack of enthusiasm" got her fired from the job six weeks later. After that she couldn't even go to the public library in town and take out books for herself without being reminded of her failure.

It is a sultry January day and Harte is on her way to the supermarket. She drives with the windows rolled all the way down in the dark-blue Fiat that has already turned purplish in the Florida sun. Her hair blows across her mouth in the hot wind. She tries to remember the sound of a shovel scraping snow from the sidewalk outside her parents' house and her father in a red-and-white-striped ski hat, knocking off the row of icicles that hangs every winter under the roof over the porch. In the car, perspiration dampens the creases of her arms, and her hands stick to the hot plastic of the steering wheel.

She quickly fills her cart at Pantry Pride with cans of SpaghettiOs, boxes of frozen pizza, and several kinds of cookies for her friend Sam, the only friend she's made since moving to Florida. Sam, who lives in the apartment above theirs, likes to visit when Brian is at the hospital. Brian does not approve of Sam. He regards him as a bad influence on Harte.

She joins the express line, ten items or less. A man directly ahead of her and a woman directly ahead of him are having an argument. The man accuses the woman of pushing her shopping cart in front of his.

"But you weren't here," the woman begins reasonably. "You left your wagon. Why should I have stood here like an idiot, wasting my valuable time?"

"What a hustler!" the man says. "You're a real asshole, you know that?"

Reaching into her wagon, the woman grabs a bunch of broccoli and brings it down over the man's head. "See what you get for opening up your filthy mouth like that?" she hollers.

The man stretches his thumb and index finger across his forehead like a visor. "Using a vegetable as a weapon is a felony in the state of Florida," he reports. He tells the woman that his brother-in-law is a lawyer. "You're in big fucking trouble," he says. Harte is about to laugh when he turns on her. "What are *you* looking at?" he says. "Haven't you ever seen anyone assaulted in a supermarket before?"

The cashier at the checkout counter shakes her head slowly and goes off to get the manager, and Harte abandons her wagon, slipping past the man and his assailant, hugging her arms to her chest, unexpectedly packageless. She drives more than halfway home; then, realizing that it is their six-month anniversary and she has forgotten to buy Brian a card, she heads back to the shopping center.

All the cards in the stationery store are extravagantly sentimental, with photographs of young lovers posed next to the ocean, or close-ups of roses in bloom and rhymed couplets about a love that is deep and true. Finally she chooses one that says "For My Grandson on His Confirmation Day."

In the apartment she finds Brian waiting for her. He leans against the kitchen counter, one small bare foot on top of the other, a stethoscope drooping from the pocket of his white coat like the dark stem of a wilted flower. He kisses Harte's shoulder and the back of her neck. "Come and lie down with me on the couch," he says. "I've gotta relax for a while."

Harte looks at her watch. "Just in time for a *Leave It to Beaver* rerun," she says, and she turns on the television before sitting down. Brian rests his head on her stomach and sticks his legs over the arm of the couch.

Beaver is having dinner with his family. His mother orders him to eat the brussels sprouts on his plate, but instead he tucks them into the pocket of his shirt as soon as she turns away. The laugh track goes wild. Brian makes a face at Harte and closes his eyes.

"Why don't you go to sleep?" Harte says. She helps him take off his white coat, pulling his arms from his sleeves like a mother tending to her drowsy child. Brian settles down into the couch, his shirt riding up his back, exposing a sweet pale square of skin. The skin is miraculously soft; Harte draws circles around it with her finger as Brian falls asleep.

"I'm so hungry," he says later when he wakes up. "Did you go to the supermarket today?"

"Went to Pantry Pride," Harte says, "but I had to leave without buying anything."

"What's *with* you? How could you come home from the supermarket without any food?"

"I'm sorry," Harte says. "Do you want me to tell you what happened?"

"Never mind. I don't think I want to hear about it. Listen, we had a cardiac arrest on the ward today. The resident had me go out and break the news to the patient's wife. The first thing she said was 'Oh God, who's going to do my income-tax returns this year? I'll never be able to do them myself.' " Brian rubs his eyes. "I'm not sure I can deal with all the people out there, Harte," he says.

"Sure you can. You can deal with everything." Harte takes

the confirmation card out of her bag and gives it to Brian. "Happy six months," she says.

He reads the card, his face solemn. "Everything is a joke with you," he says quietly. "Can't you take anything seriously? Did your friend Sam tell you to buy this card?"

"What are you talking about?"

Brian studies her for a moment, then runs his fingers along the underside of her arm. "Look," he says, "I think we should do something to celebrate our anniversary. We could drive out to Fat Boy's and have drinks and steak. I have to be back at the hospital by eight, but at least we can celebrate for a couple of hours."

"I don't feel like going anywhere or doing anything. I did a little while ago, but I don't anymore."

"It's the heat," Brian says. "You miss the change of seasons down here. I bet you feel like you've been cheated out of a fall and a winter this year."

"Listen, please don't talk down to me. Sam says that was the first thing he noticed about you. He could tell you were planning to specialize in psychiatry just by the expert way you talked down to me."

"I apologize," Brian says. "And we won't talk about Sam anymore."

Harte prepares a tuna-melt sandwich for Brian's dinner and places a delicate pink birthday candle through the layer of American cheese.

"That's a very nice-looking sandwich," Brian says, and blows out the flame after a moment of hesitation. Then he snaps the candle sharply into two pieces and throws them into the sink.

"What did you wish for?" Harte asks him, looking at the sandwich, which suddenly seems meager on the big yellow plate.

"Nothing too extravagant," Brian says.

*   *   *

In the apartment complex where Harte and Brian live there are tennis courts and a Laundromat that are open twenty-four hours a day, but there aren't any married women Harte's age who don't have at least one child. Without Sam, Harte doesn't know what would become of her. Sam lives upstairs with Dizzy, his lover. Dizzy sells expensive running shoes in a shop on the main street, which divides the town in half; actually, he is the manager of the store and works long hours six days a week, returning home to Sam too tired to do anything except sit with a pair of headphones on, listening to a tape of the music from *Saturday Night Fever*. The two of them own a borzoi, which Sam walks in the field of tall, bleached grass behind their apartment. Harte met Sam for the first time one afternoon when she was out in the field with her butterfly net, watching the borzoi run in long strides through the grass like a lean and fragile horse, while Sam stood smoking a cigarette, his head tipped skyward. They watched the borzoi together and Sam told her about himself: that he was a medical school drop-out, that after one four-hour session of gross anatomy he knew he had made a terrible mistake. Harte laughed and said she knew *she* had made a terrible mistake when she realized she was living in a town whose finest restaurant was called Fat Boy's Bar and Grill.

Tonight, after Brian leaves for the hospital, Harte climbs upstairs to Sam's apartment. He calls out to her from the bedroom and says, "I'm back here cleaning. I'll be out in a couple of minutes."

There is a record playing on the stereo: Gertrude Lawrence whistling a happy tune on her way to Siam. The record is from 1951 and is full of scratches. Sam stole it from his mother's collection when he left home. He also stole the original Broadway cast recordings of *Pal Joey*, *Oklahoma*, and *Carousel*. His mother writes him letters twice a month. On the bottom of every letter she writes, "P.S. What about my records? P.P.S. Pardon me for being such a nag." Sam has told Harte that his mother might get her records back if she wised up and stopped begging him to get psychiatric help for his "condition," as she calls it.

Harte gets herself a can of Pepsi from Sam's refrigerator. The soda foams in the glass, sprays her nose and mouth as she takes the first sip. She wonders if Brian is right and that her teeth will actually soften and fall out one by one because of all the soda she drinks. Brian has already warned her that if they ever have children, he'll make sure their house stays free of carbonated beverages. "So if you want a fix, you'll have to leave the house to get it," he said, looking so earnest that Harte leaned forward and turned up the corners of his mouth with her fingers.

Sam drops down on the carpet in the living room. He is large-boned and slightly overweight and is wearing a T-shirt with a subway map of New York City on it. In his lap he holds a dispenser of Fantastik, a sponge, a rag, and a plastic bottle of ammonia.

"If you had one word to describe the look in Brian's eyes, what would it be?" Harte asks him.

"Determined," says Sam immediately.

"Determined to finish med school, anyway."

"He's lucky he's got the stomach for it," Sam says.

"Do you know what the third-year students are doing now? Tracheotomies on dogs and cats."

"All right, that's enough." Sam goes back to his cleaning. He cleans in places Harte has never even contemplated: across the glass face of the clock on the wall, on the molding that runs below the windowsills, behind the filter in the air conditioner. He is a skillful and energetic housekeeper, moving from one task to another only after he's sure he's done all he can. Love dominates his life; it is love that propels him to keep the apartment in the perfect order that Dizzy needs to come home to every night.

Sam knows that running shoes figure most prominently in Dizzy's life, that Dizzy will always be a businessman with not much time for love.

Harte wishes that Sam would give up on Dizzy. Once she dreamed that she and Sam ran away to New York City together and got an apartment down in the Village. Brian showed up right away with a court order that gave him the power to take Harte back to Florida. The worst of it was that Sam, who stood at the doorway grooming his mustache with a tiny comb, kept repeating "It's all for the best," as Brian tied her up with string and placed her in the back seat of the Fiat.

As the second side of *The King and I* comes to an end, Yul Brynner gets a dancing lesson from Gertrude Lawrence. Harte, sitting with her ankles crossed in front of her, knocks her feet together in time with the music.

"*The King and I* is my favorite show," says Sam. "Even the happiest songs in it have something mournful about them."

The record is over; Sam flips it back to the first side and starts it again. Later he puts on *Pal Joey* and finishes off two white-wine spritzers. When his second glass is empty, he tells Harte that Dizzy will be home any minute. Harte says that she has to get back to her apartment anyway, pretending that Brian will be calling to make sure she's not feeling lonely.

Brian is on at the hospital every third night in February, and when he's not, he likes to be in bed by ten with Harte lying next to him. He says that he can't fall asleep without her, that he panics if she's not within easy reach.

One night, as Brian pulls back the sheets and gets into bed, Harte says, "You know what, before I married you, I never heard of adults going to sleep at ten o'clock at night."

"I'm exhausted," Brian says. "Today was awful."

"What happened?"

"I had to tell a patient he had lung cancer. He was a nice middle-aged guy, very quiet, very polite; he just kept nodding his head to everything I was saying."

Harte switches off the light and stretches out on her back along the edge of the bed. "Why do you have to tell me stories like that?" she says.

"The guy was so polite. He thanked me for talking with him. He shook my hand."

"Don't you know when to stop?" Harte says. "I can't listen to this, it's just too depressing."

Brian turns toward her. He covers her face with small, soundless kisses. Then, in a moment, it seems, he is asleep. Harte closes her eyes tightly and pushes them with her fingers, two fingers on each eye. It is an old game: first black becomes red, then there are perfect rows of geometric shapes, silver ones with violet centers. Upstairs, in Sam's apartment, the floor creaks. Something is thrown against the wall. Harte sits up in bed, strains to hear what it is the voices are saying. She thinks she hears her name; a door slams and there is nothing more to listen to, except the sound of Brian breathing evenly beside her, his arm bent across his forehead, his fingers clenched into a fist so small it might belong to a child.

It is early spring, and Harte and Sam have secretly taken up tennis. Several nights a week, while Brian is at the hospital and Dizzy lies on the couch with his headphones on, they spray themselves with insect repellent and head out for the courts. Harte and Sam play very badly. They wait until after midnight to start their games so that no one will see them. Even so, Sam dresses in proper whites and plays with an expensive racquet and a sweatband around his hair.

Their nights on the courts are always the same: the air

as warm and damp as the night Harte was married, and the two of them clowning around and calling each other "spastic" and "klutz" as they play. One night, though, they are surprised to see two people, a guy with a waist-length ponytail and his girlfriend, whom Harte recognizes from the Laundromat, playing on the next court. They have a nice rally going between them as Harte and Sam approach.

"I'm not going to play with them here," says Harte. "We can come back later if you want."

"I don't mind making a fool of myself. Why can't we just go ahead and play?" Sam says.

"Wait," Harte says. In a little while, the guy with the ponytail and his girlfriend end their game and come together at the net. The guy bends over his side of the net to embrace her. When they break apart, the girlfriend raises her arm and points overhead to an unimpressive sky, empty of stars.

"What are they looking at?" Sam says. "There's nothing to see up there."

"They're in love," Harte explains. "People in love watch for signs."

Sam takes three tennis balls out of a can and tries to juggle them. He drops them all and they roll away in three different directions. He goes after them, and when he returns to Harte, the couple is walking off the court, each with an arm over the other's back.

"They're so happy," says Harte. "I see them doing their laundry together all the time, and he folds her shirts and nightgowns for her in a way that lets you know there's really something between them."

Sam serves first. He keeps hitting the ball into the net. In the swamp nearby there are frogs jeering at him. A tiny band of them leaps brazenly onto the court. Sam swings at them with his racquet. "Time out for a cigarette," he says.

Harte listens for the sharp metallic click of his lighter. She can smell the smoke that hangs in the air in front of him. "What's the matter?" she says, and walks up to the net.

"I'm so depressed," Sam says.

"Your serve will get better if you keep at it."

"It's my hair." Sam leans over the net. "Feel the top of my head. Can you see how thin it's getting?"

His hair is soft and fine beneath her fingers. She smooths it in place with her knuckles, moving her hand slowly across his head, thinking of the couple embracing over the net, of the romance of their posture.

"So what do you think?" Sam says.

"Your hair is nice to touch."

Sam snaps his cigarette onto the court.

"All right," Harte says. "From now on we're going to try and play a real game. No more fooling around. You're going to run up to the ball when I hit it. You're not going to stand there and wait for it to fall at your feet, okay?"

"I'm a slow-moving guy," Sam says. "I've never been fast on my feet."

"Get ready to run," Harte says. She serves the ball as powerfully as she can. Sam rushes toward it, a luminous streak of white across the court.

Later, they collapse in their sweaty clothes in Harte's apartment, savoring their shared exhaustion, drinking Pepsi straight from the bottle, passing it back and forth between them like a pipe full of hash.

Sam turns on the radio. He switches from one station to another until he finds an old Beatles song, melancholy and slow. "Dance with me," he says, and pulls Harte up from the floor. His hand rests at the small of her back. "You're tense," he says with surprise. "Just go with the music."

Harte leans her head on the hard shelf of his shoulder and feels her bones go loose. "See how easy it is," she hears Sam say, and then she closes her eyes. She is dancing at her wedding, without her shoes on, hoping that she and Brian are nearly the same height. Her feet are slipping on the waxed parquet floor. "Easy now," says Brian, and he presses her to his chest, trying to steady her. But she loses her balance anyway, and slips through the circle of his arms around her and out of his reach.

FLOATING (1982)

The radio claims it is ninety-one degrees, but probably it is hotter. Even the twelve-year-old black-and-white mutt, Oreo, is in the pool, swimming quietly near the diving board. Lynne is lying on her back on an inflatable raft shaped exactly like a giant open hand. The hand is pale pink, except for the transparent blue fingernail on the third finger, which you can use to look straight through to the bottom of the pool if you want to. Lynne is wearing maternity jeans that she cut down into shorts at the beginning of the summer, and a red T-shirt, extra-large, which says "Coke Adds Life" in white letters that have turned pink from the chlorine. She is twenty-three years old and eight-and-a-half months' pregnant. She isn't sure she wants a baby, doesn't have a preference about its sex, just wants to give birth to it and work her way back into size-five jeans and skirts. After that, who knows? Sharon, her stepdaughter, loves babies; maybe she'll take care of Lynne's baby instead of going back to high school in the fall, and then Lynne will be able to get into an executive-trainee program at Macy's, where she used to work in the perfume department, or go for an MBA at some place like Columbia or NYU. Neither possibility seems likely, but Lynne finds herself fantasizing a lot in the pool.

In high school, in Boston, where she grew up, Lynne earned straight A's except for math, and ran around with the theatre crowd. She was in the chorus of *Annie Get Your Gun*, and of *West Side Story* and *Fiddler on the Roof.* She went to college in Maine, and for a year after graduation she stayed near campus and gave piano lessons and cleaned houses. Thinking she'd had enough home-grown small-town living to last her forever, she came to New York and got the job at Macy's. It was at Macy's where she met Daniel, Sharon's father. He had been trying to decide on a gift for his secretary and, instead, had ended up taking Lynne to dinner at a vegetarian restaurant called The Seasoned Vegan. Over dinner, he told her his wife had died three years before. Daniel works for a PR firm in the city, but he wants to be a songwriter. Last year, he recorded a demo in a studio, and hired a trio of women for backup. His voice is pleasant, or at least inoffensive, his songs forgettable. Lynne wishes she could tell him to quit while he's ahead, but on the other hand, she thinks Daniel's entitled to his pipe dreams just like everyone else.

For her, marriage and pregnancy have been like something in a dream. She feels no kinship at all with the women who sit alongside her in the waiting room of the obstetrician's office, exchanging stories of backaches and swollen ankles and breasts that are suddenly marked with streaks of violet. And she feels only a distant connection with the baby who is treading water inside her, who stretches its arms and legs a dozen times a day to let her know it's there. She and Daniel had been driving back to his house from the city one winter afternoon, fighting heavy rain all the way, when she told him she was pregnant. She had deliberately kept her voice neutral, not wanting to lead him in any particular direction. Mostly because she'd decided she couldn't bear to have an abortion, she had talked herself into going ahead with things, but she wasn't prepared to do the same with Daniel. At the least sign of ambivalence from him, she would have retreated. But what happened was that he pulled the car off to the side of the road. "Are you serious?" he said, and then he said it again. His mouth stretched toward an unambiguous smile that made Lynne ashamed of her own uncertainty. A few weeks later, she gave up her apartment in the city and moved into Daniel's split-level home with a swimming pool in the backyard. They were married shortly afterward, and a month ago she finally quit her job, mostly because she couldn't stand riding the Long Island Rail Road and the subways anymore.

As she drifts toward the shallow end of the pool, Lynne's eyes are closed against the sun. Without warning, the baby shifts its weight; a wrist or ankle seems to be struggling to poke its way through. But by the time Lynne's hand reaches her stomach, the little knob of bone has gone deeper underwater and there is nothing to feel.

Sharon is calling to her from the diving board, where she's sunbathing, but somehow Lynne misses most of what she says.

"Are you hungry yet? It's almost three o'clock," Sharon says again.

"Are *you*?"

"I'll be right there," Sharon says. She dives off the board and surfaces next to Lynne. After she shakes the water from her eyes and adjusts the straps of her bathing suit, she raises Lynne's T-shirt and squints at her belly button, pretending it's a window on the baby. "Hey, you down there," she says, and pulls the shirt back over Lynne's stomach. "I'm making us mushroom omelets. Is that all right?" she asks.

"Thanks," Lynne says. "Actually, I thought I was hungry, but I guess I'm not."

Sharon puts her hair up into a ponytail without taking her eyes off Lynne. "How about if I fix it for you anyway, and we'll just see what happens?"

"You're such a little mother," Lynne says, and makes a face, although really she is pleased by all the attention she gets from Sharon. Her stepdaughter is six years younger than Lynne; after lying around the pool together all summer, they have come to think of themselves as the closest of friends. They tell each other things they would never tell Daniel: Sharon knows that Lynne sucked her thumb every night in bed until she was twelve. It is Daniel's presence that reminds them that they are not two classmates who just happen to be amiably wasting away a summer together, but that they are linked to each other by something more complicated than the mere fact of their having been born in the same decade. Every night when Daniel gets home, Sharon disappears into her bedroom, emerging later for dinner, then disappearing again for the rest of the night. Lynne understands that Sharon does not want to be seen being treated like a daughter, nor does she want to see Lynne being treated like a wife.

In the kitchen, butter hisses in a frying pan. Sharon beats the eggs expertly as Lynne pours diet soda into two glasses filled with ice. The odor of eggs cooking in butter is making Lynne sick. The whole house smells of it, and she has to go outside. She lies down on a chaise longue on the patio and calls out to Oreo to keep her company. She whistles for him three times, tosses him his rawhide bone and his squeeze toy shaped like a Popsicle, but he won't come out of the pool. "Go to hell," Lynne says, and then she begins to cry.

Holding the door open, first with her foot, then her shoulder, Sharon backs out onto the patio carrying a large tray with two plates of food, glasses, napkins folded into triangles, silverware, and a bud vase with a miniature pink rose in it. She puts everything down on a wrought-iron table that has an umbrella rising from its center and hands Lynne a glass. "What's wrong?" she says immediately. "You're not feeling well?"

"What could be more pathetic than being rejected by the family dog?" Lynne says, laughing and crying at the same time.

"What are you talking about?"

"Nothing," Lynne says. "I'm crying about nothing."

"I bet it's hormones," Sharon says. "Aren't they all screwed up when you're pregnant?"

Lynne shrugs, and drinks from her glass. She wipes the tears from her face with the backs of her hands.

"I thought you were reading up on everything. Didn't you take a whole pile of books from the library?"

"That was Daniel. He reads out loud from them every night before he goes to sleep. He thinks it's all fascinating."

"I bet it is," Sharon says. "Miraculous, really."

"Miraculous." Lynne mouths the word. She raises her arm over her eyes and hides her face. She is weeping into the crook of her arm, very quietly.

"Is the sun getting to you? We can move into the shade," Sharon says.

Lynne stands up, and when she is able to talk, she says, "Have your lunch, and then I'll take you out for a driving lesson. We'll go out to Sunrise Highway and you can practice changing lanes."

"Only if you feel up to it. Otherwise, you can just—"

"Call me when you're ready," Lynne says. "I'm going inside to cool off."

"Me too," Sharon says. She brings the tray into the den and turns on the television set while Lynne settles into a reclining lounger. "Let's be morons and look at cartoons," Sharon says cheerfully. They watch in silence as a dog and a cat and a mouse do their best to wipe each other off the face of the earth. Half an hour later, they go into the garage and get into the front seat of Daniel's Chevrolet. (Lynne feels safer in a smaller car and much prefers the Jetta Daniel leaves at the Long Island Rail Road station every morning.) Sharon is dressed in a dry bathing suit and Lynne in white pants and a green T-shirt that says "I'M INFANTICIPATING!" She hates the shirt but feels obligated to wear it because it was a gift from Sharon.

Behind the wheel, Sharon waits for instructions. "I've never backed out of here before," she explains.

"Just take it slowly and watch out for the hedges when you're in the driveway," Lynne says. A few moments later, when the rear fender is scraping loudly against the privet, she says, "Jesus, watch what you're doing!"

"Sorry," Sharon says, but she sounds insulted.

It's a delicate business, teaching someone to drive, Lynne thinks. When she was Sharon's age and her father took her around the neighborhood to practice for her road test, it usually ended badly—with both of them in a rage. Her father was always telling Lynne that a car was a weapon and that this was the single most important thing she had to know about driving. When she passed her road test on her first try, he hadn't seemed pleased. "Just remember that a car is a weapon that can kill," he said gloomily as he handed her the keys for her first solo trip. "If you're not careful, you can wind up in serious trouble." It took her a long time to fully recover from his teaching methods; for months, she was uneasy behind the wheel, expecting trouble at every corner. This spring, when she wrote her father to say she was pregnant and married, he responded with a check for two thousand dollars. With the check was a note: "Who would believe a girl with such an expensive education could get herself into a mess like this?"

A block from home, Sharon eases the Chevy to a full stop at a blinking red light.

"Very nice," Lynne says. Wherever she looks, there are children playing in the street, roller-skating and tossing Frisbees and riding bicycles. Already she can imagine blood on the fender. She wishes there were a seat belt that would fit comfortably around her.

Soon they are on the highway, which is cluttered with gas stations and fast-food restaurants and strip malls. Sharon is driving well, changing lanes carefully and keeping up with traffic. Lynne switches on the radio and sings along with an old James Taylor song. One spring when she was in college, his voice was everywhere, drifting through open dorm windows out onto the quad, where she had sat typing papers under an oak tree a century old. Where had Daniel been then? Probably riding the Long Island Rail Road back and forth to work, still grieving for the wife he had lost, silently composing his love songs while the rest of the commuters were reading their newspapers.

At their first meeting, Lynne had been very impressed with Daniel. He had just returned from a week's vacation in St. Croix, and he looked as handsome as a model in a magazine ad, she thought. (She is always surprised at how poorly he photographs; the only expression he can manage is something caught halfway between a smile and a smirk.) She had guessed Daniel was in his mid-thirties, and was stunned when he said he had a sixteen-year-old daughter. He appeared to be very articulate, and everything that he said was slightly self-deprecating and ironic—a manner she felt comfortable with immediately. It turned out they were both interested in music and in the theatre, and even before they finished their dinner, she made up her mind that she would sleep with him. Afterward, in her studio apartment in Washington Heights, they took a long shower together, and made cinnamon toast in the tiny windowless kitchen that was hardly wide enough for the two of them. They spent the hours until dawn going through her Cole Porter songbook, Daniel singing while Lynne played the piano her father had shipped down to her from his house in Boston. The next morning, there was a note under her door from the man who lived beneath her. The note said, "One more noisey night, you bitch, and I'm calling the cops for sure." Daniel corrected the misspelling and circled the word with a red pen. He and Lynne went down to the neighbor's apartment and taped the note to his door, the two of them laughing so hard they could barely stand straight. During his lunch hour that afternoon, Daniel showed up at Macy's with a gift for Lynne—a two-record set of Cole Porter singing and playing his own songs. After that, he could do no wrong in Lynne's eyes. (Her first and only other lover, a teaching assistant in the history department at school, had persisted in buying her little ceramic animals, each one with the same dopey, lovesick look on its face.)

It wasn't long before she was certain that what she had with Daniel added up to something close to love, though neither of them ever called it that. She was uncomfortable with the word anyway; it seemed to make too many promises that couldn't possibly be kept.

She was the first of her friends to marry, and when they asked her what it was like, she didn't tell them that even thinking about the subject made her go numb—all she did was smile. The truth is that her friendship with Sharon is more real to her than her marriage and pregnancy. She loves Daniel, but living out her life in his house as a wife and a mother and a stepmother is something else entirely.

They are in one of two adjacent left-turn lanes when she hears Sharon say that she thinks she's had enough for the day. The light changes and then suddenly the Chevy is turning wide and carelessly into the rear end of a gleaming burgundy Mercedes. Lynne's arms immediately cradle her middle, though the impact is slight. The Mercedes pulls over into the parking lot of a big sporting-goods store, and Sharon pulls the Chevy in behind it. Once they are out of the car, they see that no one is hurt, but the Chevy's front end is dented and one headlight shattered. The other car has nothing worse than a few dents and some cracked plastic. The driver, a woman, comes toward them, pulling a girl about Sharon's age by the arm.

"Do you see?" the woman says. "This is my daughter—the one who had a three-thousand-dollar nose job last month. If that nose isn't as perfect as it was before this accident, you'll be paying for it the rest of your lives, ladies."

"Mom," the girl says, her face bright with embarrassment, "I'm all right, I'm fine."

Sharon clings to Lynne.

"We need the name of your insurance company," Lynne says.

"So what do we have here?" the woman says. "The unwed mother and her teenybopper sister?"

"Mom," the girl says again. She turns to Lynne. "It's her new car. She wouldn't even let me or my brother drive it around the block."

Lynne nods. "We're really sorry." She touches the back of Sharon's head.

"I hope your baby's all right," the girl says.

"What about you and your nose?" her mother says darkly. "What about *that*?"

"I said I was okay. We're all okay. Why do you have to act like such an idiot?"

Swiftly her mother grabs her wrist. "Like it or not, I'm the only mother you've got, kiddo. I'm sorry you think I'm an idiot, but that's the way it is." Turning to Lynne, she says, "It's no picnic, let me tell you."

"I think I ought to give you the name of our insurance," Lynne says.

The woman says, "Once they hit their teens, you've lost them forever." She closes her eyes. "I was in labor with Bonnie for over thirty-six hours. Back labor, too. The worst kind."

"Could you please just shut up!" Sharon yells.

"Another one," the woman says, and rolls her eyes. "It's a little late to start thinking about protecting your sister, don't you think?" she tells Sharon. "Why weren't you thinking about your sister five minutes ago, when you came crashing into us?"

"She's not my sister, she's my stepmother," Sharon says.

The woman's mouth opens wide. "Jesus Christ."

A police car with its siren on is headed their way. In a few moments, two cops pull into the parking lot. "Anyone need an ambulance?" one of them asks. "You?" He points a finger at Lynne's stomach.

"I'm fine," she says.

"We're all just fine," Bonnie says.

They are back in the pool when Daniel gets home. It is after seven, and the air is as hot as it was all day, the water in the pool as warm as bathwater. Lynne is on the raft, her hands clasped over her stomach. Sharon is doing a handstand near the shallow end, her legs perfectly straight and still above the water. Daniel kneels at the edge of the pool and yanks the raft toward him. He kisses Lynne's stomach, then her mouth.

"Hard day at the office?" he says, and laughs.

Sharon is swimming underwater now, close to the floor of the pool. "We had an accident—nothing too serious," Lynne says. "Broken headlight, dented fender—that kind of accident."

"Were you thrown forward? What about the baby?"

"Nothing happened. And anyway, babies in utero are well protected from the outside world. I could be shot in the stomach right now and the baby would be fine."

Daniel flinches. "Maybe you ought to go see the doctor anyway."

Lynne shakes her head. She is watching Sharon at the bottom of the pool. "Poor kid," she says. "She's been kind of spaced-out since it happened. Why don't you take her out to dinner or something?"

"We'll all go," Daniel says. "All three of us."

"I'm not very hungry. And the two of you should spend some time together alone," Lynne says.

"What about tomorrow? I'll make us some omelets tonight," Daniel says.

"When are you going to take a look at the Chevy?"

"Later," Daniel says. "After the sun goes down and it's too dark to see anything."

It's oppressively hot the following afternoon when Lynne and Sharon drive the Chevy over to the service station. The manager promises it won't take more than an hour to replace the headlight, and he offers to let them wait in his office—the only part of the station that's air-conditioned. For nearly two hours, they sit on molded plastic chairs reading year-old copies of *Reader's Digest*. Twice, Sharon goes out front to the soda machine and returns with paper cups of lukewarm Fresca and a progress report on the car. "They'll be getting to it shortly, whatever that's supposed to mean," she tells Lynne. To pass the time, Sharon goes through one *Reader's Digest* after another and reads aloud from "Laughter, the Best Medicine" and "Life in These United States" and searches for the dumbest things she can find. After a while, Lynne settles back in her chair, her mouth open slightly. When the car is finally ready, Sharon has to wake her. They drive straight home.

That night, Sharon and Daniel eat at the Bacon Brothers Diner. Lynne is too tired to go out; for dinner she has a large bowl of mocha chip ice cream, which she eats very slowly with a demitasse spoon. Wearing headphones, she listens to most of her Cole Porter album, then goes to sleep around nine, without Daniel, who still hasn't come back from dinner. At two, she is awakened by a cramp in her abdomen; then suddenly the mattress underneath her is flooded with warm water. She turns on the reading lamp over the bed and Daniel begins to stir.

"What?" he says.

"My water broke," she says, and slides toward the edge of the bed.

"Don't move!" Daniel yells. He races from the room and returns carrying newspapers, which he opens and spreads all around the bedroom floor and out in the hallway. "You can get out of bed now if you want to," he says, and as Lynne stands, water spills onto the paper. "Just didn't want you to wreck the carpet," Daniel says.

Lynne stares at him. "Call the doctor," she says.

She goes into the shower and washes her hair, forgetting

that she washed it after she got back from the service station, not many hours ago. Her mind is a perfect blank, but her legs are trembling on the tiled floor of the stall shower. She dries her hair in the bedroom with a dryer that looks just like a Colt .45, watching Daniel in the mirror as he gathers her bathrobe and toothbrush and some nightgowns together in a canvas bag for her. In his hand he holds a checklist from the hospital. "Cards," he says. "We need a deck of cards."

"We don't *play* cards," Lynne says. "What are you talking about?"

"Well, if it says to bring cards, we should." Daniel pauses. "Shouldn't we?"

"Why don't you go wake Sharon?"

"We can leave her a note," Daniel says.

"I want her to come with us."

"She's just a kid in high school. What do you want from her?"

Without answering, Lynne gets dressed and goes downstairs to Sharon's room. The first contraction comes as Lynne calls Sharon's name. In the dark, Sharon sits up against the headboard. "I'm so afraid," Lynne whispers as Sharon reaches for her.

Riding in silence on empty parkways to the hospital, Lynne can't stop thinking about something a friend of hers who was in medical school told her—a story about a baby who was born with one eye in the center of its forehead, a full set of teeth, and shoulder-length hair; when it was wheeled down to be X-rayed, the radiology tech fainted.

"Perfect parallel park," she hears Daniel say as he backs the car neatly into a space on York Avenue. "I hope you were paying attention, Sharon."

"I'm not getting out of this car," Lynne says. "I'm in the mood to ride around a little."

"In the mood?" Daniel says. "You're supposed to be in

the mood to have a baby."

"Not right now," Lynne says. "In a little while, maybe."

Daniel turns to Sharon, in the back seat. "Will you talk to your friend, please?" he says.

"When she's ready, she'll go," Sharon says.

"Listen, I'm trying very hard to understand what's going on here, but it's just not working out," Daniel says.

Lynne says, "You know, I've never actually seen Gracie Mansion. Why don't we take a ride over there?"

Daniel sighs. "One quick look, and that's all."

There's a color TV in the labor room and together Lynne and Daniel watch the best of late-night programming—a Troy Donahue surfing movie that was filmed on location in Hawaii and seems to go on forever. Toward daylight, just as Fred Flintstone is being berated by his wife for never taking her anywhere interesting, Lynne is rushed to the delivery room across the hall, where she propels her child into the world with a final push that distorts her face unrecognizably. Moments later, she asks for Sharon, who is waiting downstairs on a wooden bench in the lobby.

"Go down and get her," Lynne tells Daniel.

"Why would they let her into the delivery room?" Daniel says. "That's crazy."

"I want her here," Lynne says. "Get her. Please." She raises her head and watches Daniel and the obstetrician whispering at her feet.

Afterward, with Sharon standing shyly against the door, the doctor congratulates them all, and says to Daniel, "You may now kiss the bride." Then Daniel is leaning over her, a green paper mask still covering his mouth, and in a voice she's never heard before, a voice belonging to someone else, Lynne says to her husband, "Don't."

STILL LIFE (1983)

At his ex-in-laws' thirty-fifth wedding anniversary party, Brad is the only guest to arrive in faded corduroy pants and a sweater that has seen better days. All the men are in ties and jackets, and most of the women are wearing dresses and lots of jewelry. But in a crowd of fifty people, it is doubtful whether anyone will notice him, and anyway, he's not planning to stay long. He's only here because Nina followed up a written invitation with a phone call begging him to come. Nina, his ex-wife, has a new husband and a new baby and is the happiest person she knows. When she told all this to Brad over the phone last week, he immediately fell silent, though he knew that she was waiting for him to congratulate her on having achieved with someone else what had been only a painful subject for discussion when she was married to him. Listening to her go on about her happiness had exasperated him, and he cut the conversation short, perhaps was even the slightest bit rude, telling her the timer on the toaster oven had just buzzed with his dinner and that he couldn't talk anymore. To make up for his rudeness, he bought her parents a pair of carved wooden candlesticks that cost him more than he'd intended to spend. And for the baby he settled on a bear dressed in a blue hooded coat, red rubber boots, and a broad-brimmed yellow felt hat. The bear came in three sizes; he quickly decided on the largest, wondering later just whom he'd been trying to impress.

When he was first married to Nina, Brad had done very well at the large corporate law firm he worked for. But working for what seemed to be a thousand hours a week on what he was sure were the most unworthy cases in the world made him miserable. Understanding this, Nina encouraged him to quit. Given a choice between misery and happiness, it would be crazy to make the wrong decision, she said.

They left the city and moved up the Hudson to a tiny rented house in Garrison so Brad could be a country lawyer with Nina working as his secretary in an office they shared at the front of the house, just off the kitchen. At lunchtime they went into the living room and ate their sandwiches on a black suede couch while they laughed at ancient reruns of *I Love Lucy*. The couch had been borrowed from Nina's parents and it was the one where she and Brad made love every Saturday night before their wedding. Brad found himself remembering their whispered conversations and the time Nina had said she loved him, her voice so soft he hadn't caught the words. "You *what?*" he'd asked her more than once (probably sounding a little cranky), but Nina was too embarrassed to repeat it. Later, whenever one of them mentioned love, the other always answered, "You *what?*"

They'd been in Garrison almost a year when the transmission in their VW Rabbit died, and their stereo system and TV set needed major repairs, all in the same month.

"I just can't live like this anymore," Nina said one afternoon in the office, laying her head down on the typewriter so that her mahogany-colored hair streamed over the edge of the desk dramatically. "It kills me to admit it, but I was brought up to want things." Her voice was apologetic, even embarrassed. None of the things she named seemed unreasonable: a house with rooms larger than closets; vacation trips to interesting places; and most important, children.

When he came around to her and caught her hair in his hands, Brad could see that she was crying. "Our marriage," she said, lifting her face to look at him. "I can't imagine letting it go."

That night, in bed, they talked about Nina's wanting to

have a child, both of them trying hard to see how a baby might fit comfortably into their life together, but they came to the same conclusion: there wasn't any way they could manage it in the near future.

"It's only a matter of being patient," he soothed her, "of waiting for things to fall into place." For Brad, what mattered most was that he loved his work, that he was actually providing a useful service to a handful of ordinary, honorable people.

The following year, which turned out to be the last year of their marriage, Nina had an accidental pregnancy which ended in an early miscarriage. She insisted on showing Brad exactly what they had lost. Looking at a book of magnified photographs of an eight-week-old fetus with pudgy hands and fingers and an indistinct face, Brad felt nothing but confusion—the photographs were like a display of abstract paintings. He wasn't as patient with Nina as he ought to have been, he realized. He was disappointed in her for having all but given up on their small-town, small-time life (her words), for having convinced herself that neither of them was adventurous enough or romantic enough to live from hand to mouth with any degree of grace or pleasure.

He waited for her to leave him, and when she did, he could make no sense of her explanation. She just didn't want to be married, she said, to a man who showed so few signs of ever being happy. Refusing to meet his eyes, she said, "I fantasize about some kind of happiness for you, but I can't figure out where it's going to come from."

"You're talking about yourself," Brad told her, staring at the little opal ring she twirled around her finger. "You're the one to whom everything looks imperfect, impossible."

Now, nearly two years later, as he eases his way through Nina's parents' crowded living room and discovers Nina waving to him from a high-backed satin chair that looks like a throne, he has to smile. But his smile is vague, as if he were approaching someone he knew only slightly and couldn't remember from where.

"Didn't I get you that sweater for Hanukkah about a hundred years ago?" she asks him, but pleasantly.

He bends to kiss her, and as he does, the baby against her shoulder grabs a fistful of his hair and pulls so hard, tears spring to Brad's eyes. Holding his breath, he unfolds the baby's tiny damp hand, saying, "Is this what they call love at first sight?"

"Don't feel special," Nina says, laughing. "She does that to just about everyone."

The baby, a little bald girl in a knitted white dress and white tights, looks at Brad with wide-open eyes and then yawns.

"It *is* kind of a boring party," Nina says. "Lots of fourth cousins I've probably seen twice in my life. I'm sorry Kevin's not here. I think you guys might have been able to strike up a conversation or two." Hearing this, the baby hiccups. "Well, maybe not," Nina says. "Maybe it's just as well."

"He's at the hospital?"

"His beeper went off the minute we got here, and that was that."

"It must be hard, never knowing when your plans are going to be disrupted."

"Not so hard. You make the best of it, that's all."

"Unbelievable," Brad says. "Is that your new philosophy of life I'm hearing?"

"Baby doll," a voice says. "Brad!" He turns to see Nina's grandmother smiling in his direction. Approaching him, Evelyn puts a hand over each of his ears and kisses him on the forehead. "You know, I'm very disappointed in you," she says. "Come over here so I can talk to you." Leading him into a spare bedroom full of coats, she closes the door behind them and leans against a plastic-mesh playpen.

"I should have called you," Brad says. "I'm sorry I dropped out of sight like that."

"You know, when Nina told me she was going to marry this other young man, I just felt sick," says Evelyn. "It makes you sick to your stomach to hear a story like that. 'What's so terrible about Brad,' I asked her, 'that you couldn't make an effort to keep your marriage in one piece?' "

Nina's grandmother is five feet tall, but broad and fleshy. She is wearing black leather Space shoes, the only shoes that fit her at all, and a fancy silk dress with swirls of magenta and gray. "How do you like these new cataract glasses they've got me wearing?" she asks Brad. "They keep slipping down on my nose and all day long I'm annoyed with them."

"I didn't even know you'd had the surgery. Nina and I haven't really been in touch." He hangs his head, feeling bad that he's neglected her. When he was married to Nina, her grandmother used to send him a soft, battered-looking ten-dollar bill on his birthday, slipped between a large index card folded in half. Front and back, the index card said, "With 'love'"—no signature. He and Nina had never figured out what the quotation marks meant, though near the end of their marriage, Nina admitted she'd always assumed her grandmother was mocking him, letting him know that in her eyes he would forever be an in-law, never the real thing. Brad, who was touched by her gifts (which he could never bring himself to spend), considered that ridiculous. There were four bills in all, one for each year of their marriage. He kept them in a coffee mug on the top of his dresser, along with some loose buttons, a set of tarnished cuff links, and a torch-shaped National Junior Honor Society pin that he'd given Nina as a joke when they got engaged.

"At the end of my life, I'm seeing things differently," Evelyn tells him. "I look through these dumb glasses and everything is bright and glittery, like diamonds." She says this with a mixture of amazement and disgust, shaking her head slowly. Now her voice has softened to a whisper. "Do you want me to tell you about Nina's new husband? I see things there that keep me up at night, if you understand what I'm saying."

Sitting at the edge of a bed piled with coats, Brad trails his hand through someone's mink. "She claims to be very happy," he says.

"For some people, women especially, the loneliness is too much. They'll do anything to avoid it," says Evelyn. She looks up at Brad, her eyes exaggerated and blurred behind the lenses of her glasses. "And you?"

"I work very hard," he says quickly, feeling defensive. "And after work, I'm usually in the basement, puttering around, refinishing furniture—that kind of thing." He stands up, sticks his hands in front of her face, lets her see that his fingers are stained a reddish brown.

Evelyn takes a step back from him. "So you're down in the basement all night. So that's what you've been up to."

"There's more," he says, but won't elaborate. There are friends he occasionally drinks with, women he occasionally sleeps with; there's no point in telling her any of this. Still, he hates it that his life sounds so stark, so needy. "I'm getting by," he says. "Sometimes it seems almost enough."

"This new husband of hers," says Evelyn, "is a toothpick of a man. All sharp bones and about ten feet tall. Do you want to see a picture of him?"

"Are you kidding?" Brad says. "Not even a snapshot."

"He doesn't talk nicely to her. Even before they were married, he was speaking to her the wrong way, as if she were a salesgirl in some department store wasting his time, showing him all the wrong things."

"Listen to me," Brad says. "You can't contradict someone when they say they're happy. It just can't be done."

"You stubborn mule," Evelyn says sadly. "I could just kill you. I could put my hands around your throat and ... "

*   *   *

At Nina's suggestion, she and Brad are going to take the baby for a walk around the block in her carriage. Outside in front of the house, one of Nina's cousins is washing his new car, a Datsun 280ZX with a red leather interior. The cousin, Bobby, is dressed in a zippered jumpsuit, despite the cold. Underneath a mimosa tree across from the Datsun is a portable tape deck playing David Bowie songs.

"Perfect day for a car wash," Bobby says, pointing to the cloudless sky with a dripping sponge.

"I just love your jumpsuit," Nina says. She winks at Brad. "Ideal for any occasion, no matter how formal."

"Did you get the invitation to my wedding?" Bobby asks.

"We're looking forward to it."

"Well, tear it up," says Bobby. "The wedding's off."

"That's a shame. I don't know what else to say."

"Yeah, well, to thine own self be true and all that jazz," Bobby says. "From now on, it's just me and my Z."

"Beautiful car," Brad says.

"You bet." Spinning around and facing the hood, Bobby opens his arms wide, as if in an embrace.

Brad and Nina walk slowly along a sharply curving street past houses set close together on frozen, gray-brown lawns. "Cousin Bobby's clearly a man who knows his own heart," Brad says after a while.

"Pathetic," Nina hisses. She stops the carriage and leans in to look at the baby, who's already asleep. An angora hat with two small, peaked mouse ears covers the baby's head. "Am I prejudiced, or would anyone in the world agree this is one spectacular three-month-old?"

"Oh, I'm sure," says Brad.

"Of what?"

"Wait," he says, "watch out," and he lifts the carriage over a large patch of swollen concrete, then sets it down gently.

"You're so funny," Nina says. "What a father you'd make."

He assumes she is being ironic, and feels insulted. "You're always doubting me, hinting that I'm incompetent. Even now, when you have no stake at all in anything I do."

"Sweetie pie," Nina says, and grabs his arm urgently. "That was a compliment back there. I was very moved, thinking what a devoted father you'd be. And actually, I've missed you," she says, leaning her head against his coat sleeve. "Though I guess not our life together."

"In another setting I'd be very desirable, is that what you're telling me?"

"I don't know *what* I'm telling you."

Rushing toward them from the other side of the street, a gray-haired man in a long tweed coat yells, "Do I see a baby?" He takes a large, awkward step over the curb and looks into the carriage.

"So what do you think, Dr. Berkowitz?" Nina explains to Brad that Dr. Berkowitz was her childhood dentist. "One year I had seventeen cavities and spent a whole summer in his office, clenching my fists and staring at the plaid curtains he had up over the window," she says.

"To be clear, that's not seventeen *teeth* we're talking about, just seventeen *surfaces*," Dr. Berkowitz says. "Now tell me about your wonderful baby. Am I looking at a boy or a girl?"

"Her name is Amanda," Nina says, and pauses. "And this is Seymour."

Dr. Berkowitz shakes Brad's hand. "I congratulate you on your lovely little family, Seymour. And my professional advice is that you enjoy to the fullest these years as a young family. It all passes like a dream; in the blink of an eye it's gone."

Brad nods. He feels Nina's hand slipping into his own. He is light-headed, thinking of his secret life as a husband and father. Soon his child will be grown and he and Nina will be middle-aged, comforting each other in the silence of their empty house.

"Seymour," Nina is saying.

"I'm right here."

"Don't you think we ought to be heading home?"

"Home?"

"Let me just suggest that you wipe the baby's gums with a wet washcloth at least once a day," Dr. Berkowitz says. "Even at this age." With his back turned to them, he raises a hand high over his head and waves goodbye.

"I'm feeling very lonely all of a sudden," Brad says, and sighs, watching Dr. Berkowitz disappear into a silver Cadillac parked not too far up the street.

"What's the matter?"

"It's the empty nest syndrome, striking a little early."

"You must think I'm a Looney Tune," Nina mumbles, "trying to pass you off as my husband."

"Don't you know you're talking to a man who drove ninety miles to a party he'd been dreading all week?" And he is imagining, with astonishing ease, the two of them as lovers, their affair stretching effortlessly over a lifetime, accommodating her marriage, his marriage, children, grandchildren— every obstacle thrown (or carefully placed) in their path. As he envisions it, they won't ever be free to marry each other; really a very romantic notion, he thinks—just what is needed to keep things passionate. Not that he would want to be married to Nina again; he wouldn't dream of altering his life to suit her expectations. But at this moment, looking at her small, round winter-pale face, her eyes large and grave as a child's, he sees that what he has missed most these past two years is the thrill of desire. It seems incredible now that he's managed so long without it, indifferent to nearly everything except his work: women, friendship, the food he prepares for himself, the music he listens to as he falls asleep at night.

"Ninety miles," he says, and puts a hand over hers on the velvety roof of the carriage. He rubs his palm back and forth across her knuckles, no farther. Toward the end of his trip today, crossing the Throgs Neck Bridge, he'd been in such a panic that he missed the outstretched hand of the toll collector entirely, his quarters and dimes falling to the ground and rolling in all directions over concrete. The toll collector, a woman about his age, looked on with amusement as he jumped from the car and on his knees gathered the coins together breathlessly, as if his life depended on it. "You one desperate son of a bitch," the woman said, taking the money from him with both hands. Her hair was in dozens of little braids, decorated with beads and leather and thin gold coins. She shook her head at him, and the braids made a tinkling sound, like wind chimes. It was only later, when he arrived at Nina's parents' house and got out of the car, that he noticed his knuckles were bleeding slightly, the skin scraped in layers so delicate they were almost imperceptible.

Drinking champagne punch from clear plastic cups, Brad and Nina sit close to one another on a couch in her parents' den, their knees touching. On the other side of the room people are crowded around an aluminum folding table filled with platters of food. The room is uncomfortably warm. Too many people, too many chairs wherever you walk, too many hanging plants blocking your view out the jalousie windows.

A little girl, about four or so, wearing a long flowered skirt and white patent-leather clogs, is crouched on the step that leads into the den. She stares at Nina. "Where's your baby?" she says. She puts a cocktail frankfurter into her mouth and chews on it for a long time. "My mother told me I could play with her."

"The baby's asleep in a bassinet in one of the bedrooms," Nina says. "And you know, the last time I saw you, Janey, you were a baby yourself."

"You have milk in your bosoms?" the little girl says.

Nina and Brad think this is very funny (they look at each other and smile), but Alicia, Janey's mother, who comes along at just the right moment, does not; she yanks her up from the step and says, "Watch your mouth, Lady Jane." Then she taps Brad on the knee, saying, "Terrific to see you."

"If you have any influence at all with your brother," Brad says, "maybe you could get me a whirlwind tour of the neighborhood in his new car."

"Oh, sure." Alicia rolls her eyes. "You came to just the right person."

"What happened to his girlfriend?" says Nina. "Or can't you tell us?"

"Wait—" Alicia looks startled, as if she can't believe what she's just seen. "Can I talk to you for a minute?" she asks Nina. She pulls at Nina's hand. "It's absolutely imperative."

As Nina rises from the couch and turns so that she is facing him, Brad sees what it is that has unnerved Alicia: two wet stains are spreading across the front of Nina's shiny, off-white blouse. She is leaking milk, he realizes and then, unexpectedly, he is overwhelmed by a longing to shelter her, to shield her from the husband who speaks to her in a voice that has nothing to do with love.

"I have an announcement to make!" Nina's grandmother hollers from the middle of the dining room. "The bride and groom will now cut the cake. I'd like everyone at the table right now. And that includes all those men who locked themselves away to watch football on TV."

Nina has disappeared. From all directions people begin moving toward the dining-room table, which has been cleared of everything except a white sheet cake decorated with pink roses set in green-gray leaves, and stacks of dessert plates and silverware. Brad finds himself almost directly behind Nina's

mother and father, to whom he hasn't said a word all afternoon. The candles are lit and blown out, then Nina's father
is asked to make a speech. So what does he have to say after
thirty-five years of marriage, Nina's grandmother wants to
know.

"Ah, well," Leo says, and clears his throat theatrically. "Life
has its little disappointments." A few people, mostly men,
laugh uneasily. Then there is silence. "A joke," Leo says, raising
both arms in the air. "A *joke*!"

"You'll hear from me later, you stinker!" Nina's mother says, but of course she is teasing him, her voice light and
friendly as she guides cake into his open mouth with an ornate
silver fork.

Leo has just spotted Brad and is motioning to him to
come closer to the table. "Hey, buddy," he says. "Are you friend
or foe?"

"Happy anniversary," Brad says. Nina's father seems slightly drunk. His smile is goofy, his face flushed and shiny. Brad
doesn't like the feel of Leo's hand clamped on his wrist.

"Happy anniversary," says Leo. "And many more."

Nina's mother passes a plate of cake to Brad. "I'm going to
cry," she whispers, tipping her head so that it's nearly resting
on Brad's shoulder. "If anyone wants to know where I am, just
tell them I'll be hiding in the bathroom for the remainder of
the party."

Leo sighs as he lets go of Brad's arm. "Can I ask you a personal question? Yes? Did I invite you to this party? And if so,
why?"

"It was Nina."

"Nina," Leo says, snapping his fingers in front of his face.
"Who else." He blinks at Brad. "She's not a happy person,
buddy. I don't know how she got that way, and I don't know
what to do about it. I spend a lot of time thinking about it,
though." His eyes are closed now. "Do you think I'm wasting

my time?" When he doesn't get a response, Leo says, "At least there's a baby this time. That's something, I suppose."

Brad says, "I don't think you want to talk to me now. I think what you want to do is slice up the cake and pass it around to your guests, don't you?"

"The thing is," Leo says, "I don't think of it as a waste. There's no such thing as wasting your time when it comes to your children." Accepting the wedge-shaped knife Brad offers him, Leo runs his finger over the serrated edge. "When she was a little girl," he says, "Nina always had to have a rose."

Brad reaches for the knife and skims it along one side of the cake, collecting a row of perfect pink roses. Slowly, with a second knife, he transfers them to a plate that Leo holds solemnly in his hands.

Walking along the narrow hallway that leads to the bedrooms, his fingers curved around the thin china, Brad can feel his hands shaking slightly. Amazed, he stares at his strange coppery fingers, stained, he realizes now, the color of Nina's hair. He presses the rim of the plate into his middle, hugs it delicately, his elbows stiff at his sides.

He finds Nina in her parents' room, nursing Amanda in a blond bentwood rocker. Late-afternoon sunlight falls in narrow bands across Nina's thighs. The baby is asleep. Nina raises a finger to her lips in warning to Brad. She smiles at him, at the roses, but says nothing. The smile hasn't yet left her face as Brad settles on the floor with his back against the edge of the rocker. In his mind, they are a still life; a mother nursing her child in a sunlit room, while at her feet a man waits patiently, motionless, with a plate of bright roses.

ICE (1985)

Helen has understood for a long while now that Vivienne has flipped out, that she is losing her marbles one by one. It's been a painful thing to witness and sometimes Helen cries over it, but discreetly, so that Viv won't notice and say, "*Now* what are you crying about?" Viv is her live-in companion, and her salary is paid by Helen's sister, who had the good sense to marry a rich man and hang on to him forever. Helen's husband sold apples on street corners during the Depression and was never quite the same after that, never quite able to recover from the loss of dignity. He lived uneasily for another twenty-five years and then he fell sick and died, without giving much advance warning.

"Cancerous," Helen says out loud, but Viv ignores her and goes on with what she's doing, which is hurling handfuls of ice cubes from a five-pound plastic bag to the living-room floor, then smashing the ice with the bottoms of her thick-soled walking shoes. This is to exorcise the smell of evil that Viv claims has permeated the apartment. According to Viv, ice cubes are the only thing that will do the trick. That and the ammonia she has poured all over the lovely parquet flooring. Watching her, Helen says, "The landlord's going to have our heads, yours and mine both, I guarantee it."

"The evil," Viv says, "is everywhere in this apartment."

"Don't you know what all this ammonia is doing to you?" Helen says. "It's destroying your lungs, that's what." She picks herself up from the couch and wanders into the kitchen, where she fixes two bowls of Frosted Mini-Wheats and milk, and adds some sliced banana. She is a small woman with surprisingly long, beautiful legs. Her hair is thick and white, cut short with bangs, like a young girl. ("A pixie cut," Helen calls it.) She spent most of her life as a bookkeeper and was furious when, long ago, she reached seventy and was forced to give up her job. ("A clear case of anti-Semitism," she still insists.)

"This is the Lord's work I'm doing here!" Viv shouts. "So don't give me any lectures about lung tissue."

"Are you too busy doing the Lord's work to have some dinner?" Helen asks. No response. She flicks on the radio next to her cereal bowl and listens to a call-in show that is hosted by a psychologist with a PhD. She loves listening to this show, which makes her feel as if she is right out there in the middle of the world, missing nothing. The caller speaking now is a woman with three grown children, two sons, and a daughter. Her sons, the woman says in a trembly voice, are both in prison for selling cocaine, and her daughter, who was clinically depressed from the time she was a teenager, is now in a mental health facility. "It's a difficult thing," Helen says. The woman begins to weep as she talks about her children. The psychologist, also a woman, advises the caller that tears are sometimes productive. "Go ahead and cry," she urges. The caller weeps on the radio for a moment or two longer, and soon there is a click: She has hung up. Helen is crying, too. She thinks of calling the psychologist and saying, "My friend is losing her marbles." Of course, she'd make an effort to put it a little more delicately: "My friend is so busy doing the Lord's work that she forgets about eating and doing the grocery shopping. Not to mention the laundry." Helen looks down at her housecoat. It's a paisley pattern against a dark background and doesn't show much dirt. She brings a sleeve up close to her face and sniffs the fabric. "Viv!" she yells. "If cleanliness is next to godliness, I'd advise you to hop to it and get a laundry together."

Viv appears in the kitchen, tracking slivers of ice onto the linoleum. She is dressed in a short white uniform, white stockings with runs leading straight up from her knees, and white oxfords. Above her breast pocket is a plastic name badge that says "Vivienne." For years she worked at New York Hospital as a nurse's aide, until one day she felt too old and cranky for the job and decided to quit. (Or else it was the patients who were too old and cranky; Helen could never remember which.) Viv has four children, all boys, who send her flowers on Mother's Day—hearts and horseshoes covered with carnations, and once, a single white lily that Viv dumped immediately into the trash. ("The flower of death," she hissed, as Helen went right into the garbage and retrieved the lily, saying, "Even the flower of death has got to be better than no flowers at all on Mother's Day.") The rest of the year, Viv doesn't hear a peep from any of them. "Once they've grown, you can forget it," she tells Helen. "Children need you like a hole in the head and that's okay. Anyway, what can you do with four big tall men who get tangled up in your furniture and mess up your house with no regard for how much effort it takes to keep things in order?" Helen understands. Her daughter, Elizabeth, has lived in Los Angeles for several years now. She complains on the phone every week that it's a city full of shallow people but at least the weather is good. "Catch a plane and come visit," Elizabeth always says. "My treat. And, of course, bring Viv with you." Helen and Viv find this hilarious. Neither of them has ever been on a plane and they have no interest in risking their necks for a little good weather. Whenever she thinks about it, Helen has to admit that she enjoyed Elizabeth more as a child: all that kissing and hugging and open declarations of love. Still, she wishes she weren't afraid to travel across the sky like the rest of the world. On bad days, she misses Elizabeth with an ache that settles under her skin and will not budge, like Viv when she mopes in the Barcalounger, contemplating the evil she's convinced is thriving right under her nose. ("Why here?" Helen wants to know. "What's so special about this broken-down rat trap, anyway?" But Viv's not giving any answers.)

Viv sinks down into a seat at the table now and takes Helen's face in her hands. "Oh, Jesus," she says, squinting at her. "Jeepers."

"Eat your cereal," says Helen. "Notice that there's some banana in there, plenty of potassium for you." Viv is smaller than Helen and thin, growing thinner all the time, it seems. Helen worries that one day she'll slip right out of her uniform and just disappear, leaving behind only a puddle of white.

"You've got whiskers growing out of your chin," Viv announces. "Just like a man." Her fingers against Helen's face smell strongly of ammonia; Helen pushes them away.

"Hormones," says Helen. "Too little of one kind, too much of the other." She tries to make light of it, but brushing her fingertips over her chin, she feels herself blushing.

"Don't you move from that table, Miss," Viv says. Soon Helen hears her making noise in the bathroom, fooling around in the medicine cabinet. Bottles of pills tumble into the sink; something made of metal clatters to the tiled floor.

"Easy there!" Helen yells. "One of these days you're going to destroy this place altogether. Raze it right to the ground."

Then Viv is standing over her with a pair of manicure scissors and a small bottle of Mercurochrome. Helen shoves the back of her chair against the wall, covers her face with one arm. "Not today, thanks," she says.

Smiling, Viv says, "We've been together for what, three, four years now, and all of a sudden you're backing away from me?"

"Seven," says Helen. "Seven years."

"Imagine that," says Viv. "I must have lost track of the time somehow." Slowly she lowers Helen's arm from her face, squeezes her hand in a friendly way.

"Somehow," says Helen, shutting her eyes as Viv comes toward her with the manicure scissors. Then she tells Viv, "You remind me of my mother-in-law. She didn't care much for me and I didn't care much for her, and one day she sneaks up behind me and cuts off a piece of my hair just for spite."

"A deranged woman," Viv says. She snips cautiously at Helen's chin. "My poor baby doll," she says. She dots Helen's chin with the Mercurochrome, to prevent infection, she says.

"How about a mirror?" says Helen, and immediately changes her mind. "Not a pretty picture, I'm sure," she says.

"Don't be so hard on yourself. You're cute as a button," Viv says. "For an old lady, anyway."

"Old old old," Helen says, tapping a spoon on the edge of her glass cereal bowl. "What's the point?" Rising and walking to the kitchen window, she rests against the blistered ledge and stares two stories down to the street corner. Lights have just been turned on in the dusk below. It is nearly April now, nearly spring. She watches as some teenagers strip a long black car parked in front of the apartment house: first the hubcaps, front and rear, then the antenna. A radio and two small speaker boxes are next. The thieves are thin boys in their shirtsleeves.

Helen raises the window. "Why do you work so hard to make your parents ashamed of you?" she hollers to them.

"How about an Alpine radio, cheap?" one of the boys yells back.

Helen goes to the phone, dials 911, and is put on hold. Eventually, a woman comes on and takes down the information. She is clearly bored with the details, bored with Helen. At the end of the conversation she says, "Have a nice day."

"This neighborhood," Helen says, rubbing her chin with two fingers. When she takes her hand away, her fingers are bright orange with Mercurochrome.

Viv lights a cigarette and tosses the match into one of the cereal bowls, where it sizzles for an instant, then floats between two slices of banana. She smokes without speaking, leaning one elbow on the table, her head propped against her palm. "There's nothing wrong with this neighborhood that a few bombs couldn't cure," she says finally.

Nodding, Helen says, "I'm going to watch my boyfriends, Mr. MacNeil and Mr. Lehrer, on the television."

"Boyfriends!" Viv hoots. "Any minute there's going to be a knock on the door, right, and the delivery boy will be saying, 'Flowers from MacNeil/Lehrer!' right?" She laughs in that choked way that Helen doesn't like, soundlessly, her feet stamping hard under the table.

"Well, at this point, they're the only boyfriends I've got," Helen says, but she has to laugh at the thought of those flowers arriving and the miniature card tucked inside the miniature envelope that says, "To our sweetie pie."

"Got any money?" Viv asks when at last she stops laughing.

"You finally decide to do the grocery shopping?"

"Just going out for ice," says Viv, and Helen is amazed at how utterly ordinary and innocent the words sound, as if she had said, "Just going out for a pack of cigarettes." It's the ordinary sound of it that gives Helen a chill, along with Viv's round eyes, wide-open with alarm.

"What do you see?" Helen asks for the hundredth time. Not that she expects to get an answer. On the subject of "the evil" (as Helen thinks of it), Viv is resolutely inarticulate.

Abruptly, Viv shrugs her shoulders and says, "Can I have two dollars?"

Helen breathes through her teeth. The shrug makes her feel desolate, as if Viv were already far away, striding down the block toward the supermarket, a tiny dark madwoman with the moon shining on the shoulders of her hooded corduroy coat.

Viv is holding out her hand, palm upward. "Ten dollars, please," she says patiently.

"Beggar," says Helen, but not loud enough for Viv to hear. She tears off the month of February from a small calendar perched on top of a low glass-and-wood cabinet. On the back she makes a list: 99% fat free (one qt.), cottage cheese (California style), Hydrox cookies, toothpaste (anything but Crest). "This is an act of faith, Vivienne," she says, handing her the list and a ten-dollar bill.

"That February was something else," Viv says. "I must have had to use about thirty pounds of ice, maybe more." Out into the hallway she goes, hood up around her face, a large pair of men's canvas work gloves covering her hands.

In the living room, Helen turns on the TV, but the tenant in the apartment directly overhead has decided to vacuum. Helen gets a broom and bangs bravely on the ceiling; all she gets is more static on the TV screen. She shuts off the set and calls her sister Elsie on Sutton Place.

"Oh," says Elsie, "hello and goodbye. You caught me in the middle of a Great Books night. A few of my lady friends are over and we're doing Dante's *Inferno*."

"The *Inferno*?" says Helen, and laughs. "You ought to invite Viv to join your group. That's right up her alley these days."

"Vivienne?"

"I'm worried sick, to tell you the truth."

"Is it money?" Elsie whispers into the phone. "I can write you a check in the morning."

"She's destroying my living-room floor," says Helen, "but that's the least of it."

"Do you need wall-to-wall carpeting?" Elsie says. "I'd be glad to send somebody over from Bloomingdale's—"

"It isn't that," Helen interrupts. "It's something unearthly, I think."

"Well, I have to hang up now," her sister says. "You can let me know about the carpeting later."

Sitting in the Barcalounger, her feet tilted toward the ceiling, hands folded into fists in her lap, Helen says, "Damn." She remembers the years of her life that were spent at an adding machine, getting things exactly right, making sense of things. Tiresome work, though she has to admit she was good at it. But what does she know of unearthly things? She doesn't have much patience left. Ice storms in her living room, shards of melting ice everywhere; the sharp, unpleasant scent of ammonia lingering on her skin, her clothes. But in all the world there is only Viv calling her *baby doll*, cupping her face in her hands, painting her delicately with Mercurochrome. At the end of your life, you're no fool; you take what is offered.

Later, past midnight, long after Viv has come back with her bags of ice, Helen dreams of a carpet of shattered glass spread shimmering over the floor. In her warm bed she shivers, and slides deep under the covers.

FLYING (1986)

Alice's grandmother's funeral happens to fall on a sweet spring day that would have been perfect for a tennis match or a slow ramble through Central Park. At the cemetery, Gates of Paradise, Alice takes her father's hand and looks over her shoulder to smile faintly at the twenty-five or thirty mourners clustered behind them. The rabbi begins to speak. "According to the one closest to her," the rabbi is saying, "this was a woman who did not inspire much love, a woman who was difficult, if not impossible, to warm to." He pauses, and squints in the glaring sunlight at his audience. "Selfish, argumentative, unforgiving," he continues in a monotone. "Ungrateful—"

Alice lets go of her father's hand and kicks him hard in the shins, several times.

"Give the old lady a break," someone calls out in a deep voice, then is shushed into silence.

"Now what, you may wonder, can we learn from a person like this?" the rabbi asks.

"Will you kindly stop kicking me?" Alice's father says into her ear. "I think you may have fractured my ankle."

Alice bolts from the gravesite and runs back to the hearse in her high heels, with Drew, her fiancé, right behind her.

"Well," Drew says, as he and Alice lean against the hearse, both of them breathing hard and pushing their long hair from their eyes. "You know what they say about the truth setting you free."

"I'm speechless," Alice says. "Can you believe my father told the rabbi to say that crap? I mean, it's true that you couldn't quite love a woman like that, but even so..." She slips off one shoe and wiggles her toes in the warm grass. She thinks of her grandmother, chronically and incurably cranky and argumentative, who always enjoyed a good fight with her son, her eyes glittering as she accused him of failings so numerous it was hard to keep track of them. Once, a couple of years ago, Alice had come through the doorway of her father's apartment just in time to hear her grandmother yell, "And in addition to everything else, Victor, you're too short!" After that, it seemed to Alice, her father fought back only half-heartedly, without much enthusiasm. He no longer had the stomach for it, he claimed. As proof of this, he would stick his hand into his pants pocket and come up with a palmful of Tums, each one chipped at the edges and speckled with lint. "This is what the old lady has driven me to," he'd say, and flip a couple of pills into his mouth, not bothering to inspect them for lint. "This!"

Victor is a dentist specializing in adult patients terrified at the thought of walking into a dental office. All day long he soothes his patients' fears, talking to them with great empathy and gentleness. His patients love him, and regard him as a miracle-worker. He speaks to them as if they were children, which suits them just fine. Often he talks to Alice the same way, especially when the conversation turns to Drew. Since his mother's death, Victor seems exhilarated and full of energy, most of which he spends on trying to convince Alice that the world is overflowing with interesting men, men far more interesting than Drew. "The guy works in the garment center," her father says, and shivers. "What am I *supposed* to think of him?" If she marries him, Victor insists, she'll awaken disappointed every morning for the rest of her life. ("With the taste of disappointment on your lips," is how he puts it.)

"I love him," Alice says calmly.

It's been several months since the funeral, and her father

has come to her apartment one night after dinner so that Alice can model her wedding dress for him. She spins around in her bare feet in the middle of the living room, taking care not to trip on the gown, which is floor-length and trimmed in lace.

"Don't give me that," Victor says. "You're twenty-five years old and already you're on husband number two. Don't you know how nervous that makes me feel?"

Alice collapses on the couch next to Victor, lays her head on her father's lap. He is wearing tan Bermuda shorts, a button-down shirt, mint-green, with the sleeves rolled up, and loafers without socks. (Her grandmother used to call him "a snappy dresser," the only compliment she ever offered him.) The skin over his knees is smooth and shiny; Alice can't resist whamming her hand just under his kneecap, so that his leg shoots out comically, uncontrollably. "What about the dress?" she asks.

"You're a beautiful girl. Anything you wear looks great on you," Victor says, rubbing his knee with both hands.

"The truth," Alice says.

"Fine. The truth is, the man you're in love with is an unimpressive guy. He's good-looking—I'll give you that—but he's a wimp nevertheless. Besides, you've only known him a day or two."

"Six months," says Alice. "As I've repeatedly told you, the best six months of my life." She can't help smiling, thinking of the icy winter night when she first met Drew. It was in a supermarket, in the frozen food section of a narrow-aisled, brightly lit A&P. Alice was there with her therapist and a group of nine men and women, all of whom were on the lookout for love. According to Lorna, the therapist, the A&P was as good a place as any for the group to try out their social skills. They were supposed to approach a person of the opposite sex and make small talk the best they could, no matter how depressed it made them feel. "Confidence is the name of the game," Lorna reminded the group as they trooped slowly past a row of sleepy-looking cashiers. "Feel good about yourself and the world is your oyster."

"Is this a dream?" a freckled, overweight cashier asked. He peeked out over the top of the *TV Guide* he was reading and rolled his eyes at the group.

The cashier at the next register had a tiny gold cross pierced through his ear, and three larger crosses hung from a chain around his throat. "No, man, this is real," he said. "This is New York City, land of opportunity." He hoisted himself onto the empty checkout counter and stood up, raising his arms toward the ceiling theatrically. "Pick me and I guarantee you won't regret it," he said. "Johnston Livingull Seabird: MFA, Yale Drama School, New Haven, Connecticut. Not a school for dopes by any means."

Eyes looking downward, Alice made her way to the rear of the store, thinking ungenerously of Roger, her ex-husband. Roger had dropped out of graduate school at Cornell to join a community of Sikhs in Tucson. He had asked Alice to go along, but the thought of herself as Hindu, her arms and legs tightly bandaged in white, her hair hidden under a turban, seemed as impossible as their marriage itself, which had gradually and mysteriously been emptied of affection, generosity, and patience. All that remained was a sentimental attachment to one another, an attachment not easily broken, she discovered. She and Roger had been high school sweethearts in New York and had married while they were still in college. In the year since their marriage had ended, Alice had moved back to Manhattan and found a job in the editorial department of a magazine for businesswomen. Most important, she had made a daily effort to think of Roger as someone who had simply disappeared, like a leaf that had been carried off by the wind. A few weeks before Christmas, she had sent him a season's greetings card. Under her signature, she wrote, "Trying unsuccessfully to savor the pleasures of solitude and independence," but nothing came of it.

Shivering at the frozen food counter, she buttoned up her down jacket and stamped her feet a few times, as if to clear them of snow. There was no one in view except a guy in a camel's hair coat studying some packages of Lean Cuisine, and a small child in a stroller whose head and face were almost completely covered by a thick, furry raccoon mask. The child was holding a plastic gun cocked to his head.

"Believe me, I know just how you feel," said Alice.

"Kill kill kill," said the child, but listlessly.

"You say that word one more time, Jeremy, and I'm going to take our TV and pitch it straight through the window as soon as we get home," the guy warned. He turned to Alice. "Can I interest you in the sale of a three-year-old? A dollar eighty-nine and I'll throw in the stroller for free." Then his expression changed and he was winking at her.

"If you throw away the TV," Jeremy said, "you won't be able to watch the Eyewitness News Team ever again."

"Watch your step, wise guy."

Jeremy leaned over the side of his stroller. "How're you doing, sir?" he said to Alice. "Slap me five." Alice struck his palm lightly and introduced herself. "Slap me ten," Jeremy said. This time Alice ignored him.

"I'm Drew," said the guy. "Overworked and underappreciated, as you can see." He looked at least five years older than she was and very tired. His hair was curly and reached his shoulders; there was an odd, bright patch of silver above one ear. Alice was startled by his face, a beautiful, brooding face that reminded her of Alan Bates in *Women in Love*. She noticed that the rawhide lace of one of his deck shoes was untied. "You're going to trip on that," she said, and immediately had a vision of herself bending over to tie it.

She put her hands in her pockets.

"What time is it?" Jeremy said. "I have to watch *Who's the Boss?* tonight."

"I hate to break it to you, buddy," said Drew, "but it's already more than half over. You're going to have to wait until next week, kiddo."

Jeremy lifted the raccoon mask from his face and threw it to the floor. "Daddy?" he said sweetly.

"What?"

"I think I hate you a little right now."

Drew sighed; he and Alice smiled at each other for a moment. "Don't feel you have to apologize," he told his son, "just because you've humiliated me in front of a perfect stranger."

Alice picked up the raccoon mask and struggled to pull it over her head. "I'd like to tell you my life story," she said from behind the mask, "but I'm supposed to limit myself to small talk."

"You mean like who's going to win the Superbowl?" said Drew. "Forget it. I like to get right to the heart of things. Under the right circumstances I'll tell anyone at all that my wife traded her marriage for the chance to make silver jewelry with some famous craftsperson in Vermont."

"Do you have HBO?" Jeremy asked Alice. "If you have HBO, we could come over and watch *Superman III* at your house."

"Would you believe I don't even *own* a television set?" It was getting steamy under the mask; Alice was sure she could feel perspiration trailing to her chin. She peered through the eyeholes at Drew. She liked it that he needed a haircut, that his jeans were nearly worn out at the knees, and that one of his deck shoes was bandaged with electrical tape at the seams. Men who found themselves unexpectedly alone were no less uneasy than women on their own, Alice thought. Drew looked needy, somehow, and startled, as if he couldn't quite believe the true measure of what he had lost. *I don't want this*, she'd say out loud to no one each morning those first few months after Roger had gone. Riding the bus downtown to her new job, walking the jammed streets at lunchtime, living without him was all she could think of. Like a child thrusting aside a plate of food, or pushing a mother's hand from the back of her neck, she had thought: *I don't want this.*

Alice watched Jeremy, who had kicked off his shoes and climbed out of the stroller, walking the floor with his father's gloves on his feet, looking like some tiny prehistoric creature awkwardly roaming his terrain.

She ran after Drew as he ran after his son, and she thought then of what she was doing—literally running after a man, something she had never done, or ever imagined herself doing. And then she and Jeremy were sprawled on the floor, Alice stroking the suede fingers of the glove on the little boy's foot over and over again as Drew stood above them, smiling.

"Sikhs," Victor is saying now, and it comes out in a hiss. "With or without that ten-foot-high turban on his head, Roger was always kind of a wacko. Even when you two were in high school and he came to graduation in that Superman cape, even then I knew something wasn't quite right."

"You've never said a bad word about Roger before," Alice reminds him. "I thought you *liked* him. Or at least you said you did."

"My mistake," Victor says. "I must have been concentrating on being polite. You have disastrous taste in men, honey, and believe me, that's putting it mildly. In fact, I get a sick headache every time I think of you and Drew fading off into the sunset together." He lifts Alice's head from his lap and swivels around so he can stare directly into her face. His eyes are the most mournful Alice has ever seen. "What kind of man makes it his life's work to manufacture linings for the collars of suit jackets?" he says.

"A pretty successful businessman, for your information,"

Alice says. She sees Jeremy again in the supermarket, hears him saying "I think I hate you a little right now," envying the ease with which he pronounces the words.

After a long silence, she says, "The funeral was a disgrace. Unforgivable. I'm surprised the rabbi was even willing to say those things."

Victor shrugs. "It was terrifying to turn against her like that in front of all those people," he says. "But once I got past that, I was flying. I didn't even feel those kicks that were coming at me, all those dirty looks everyone was shooting in my direction. I was flying above those tombstones, let me tell you." There are tears in his eyes; Alice turns away.

She gets up and takes a handful of pussy willows from a vase that stands on a small pile of magazines on top of a stereo speaker. She holds the branches delicately at her waist and returns to where her father is sitting. "Walk me down the aisle," she says. Her father leans forward, then sinks back into his seat. Alice brushes the velvety catkins against his face. *Be happy for me*, she wants to say. *Or pretend to be happy.* It's all she wants from him.

Victor stands and takes her arm. "I'm not making any promises about showing up on the big day," he says. "Not unless you can come up with an acceptable groom in the next few weeks."

"Stately and dignified," Alice says, as they move in small, measured steps from the couch to the piano, no more than twenty feet.

"If I can't talk you out of it," Victor says, "maybe I can convince *him*. Play up all your faults, make you singularly unattractive."

Alice switches on the radio, fools around with the tuning knob until she finds a station that boasts of playing nothing but love songs.

"The first dance is ours," Victor tells her. He steers her

gently around the room as John Lennon sings "Across the Universe."

"There's something we have to talk about," Alice says when the song comes to an end. She checks her father's face, which she has always found sweet-looking despite the sharp chin and small, crooked nose. It is still a face that warms her, reassures her in a roomful of strangers. "Drew has a toothache," she announces.

"Mr. Wonderful has a toothache?"

"He didn't want me to mention it," Alice says, "but he hasn't been to a dentist in years."

"A dentophobe?" Victor says. "I'm thrilled! Think of the possibilities: I can get him into my chair, buzz the drill right up next to his ear, threaten him with holes in every last tooth until he agrees to do the decent thing and—"

"What's that?"

"Ditch the bride, of course."

Alice pulls away from him.

"Oh, come on, don't look so frightened. You know I wouldn't act in anything other than a highly professional manner."

Alice grabs her father's shoulders. She tries to shake him, as if he were a small child who would yield easily to the weight of her displeasure. But her father stands firm. He looks down at her hands and laughs.

"I'm warning you," Alice says.

"Maybe you'd like a groom with a dazzling smile—a groom with a diamond chip in his front tooth."

Alice disappears into the bedroom without a word. It hits her then, stepping out of her gown, that she could skip the wedding entirely, cancel the caterer, head for a justice of the peace in some quaint and quiet town not too far up the Hudson. After the ceremony, the strangers who'd be her witnesses would wish her well, then politely turn back to their own lives. A wedding among strangers—she likes the sound of it.

"Call my receptionist in the morning for an appointment," her father says a few minutes later when Alice returns to the living room in her bathrobe. "It's probably a wisdom tooth. People often have trouble with them during times of stress: exam time, divorce time, just before a wedding ..."

"Maybe. We'll see." Like her father, she's not making any promises.

"Maybe? How can you be so casual about a tooth in the mouth of the man you love?"

Alice laughs out loud. "What an accusation," she says.

Outraged, Victor's face pinkens; a vein near his eye flickers for a moment or two. "Shame on you," her father says.

Outside the building where Victor has his office, Alice and Drew see a man holding a sign lettered on cardboard that says, "Please give $ for caterak surgury for Dusty"—a soiled-looking German shepherd, one of whose eyes is clouded over with a milky-blue film.

Drew pitches some coins into the guy's open cigar box. "Best wishes for a speedy recovery," he says.

The man is sitting cross-legged on a plaid blanket next to the dog, reading the *Daily News*. "Want to buy some weed?" he asks in a bored voice.

"Not even a thank-you," Alice whispers. "Do you believe it?"

Drew sighs. "I can't go through with this. The drill, the bright light shining in my eyes, making them tear, all those sharp instruments lined up so neatly on a tray, somebody else's hands poking around in my mouth. I can't breathe just thinking about it."

Jeremy is riding Drew's shoulders, high above the Saturday afternoon crowds on Eighty-Sixth Street. The three of them enter the small, dim lobby of Victor's building.

"On the other hand," Drew says, "maybe your father will feel differently about me once he's treated me as a patient."

Alice takes his frozen hand and squeezes it. In the first few weeks she'd known Drew, she had easily recognized him as someone she would never let go of, a man she would follow to Tucson if she had to. The morning after their first date—a candlelit Kentucky Fried Chicken dinner eaten within earshot of the television while Drew's son stood spellbound in front of it watching reruns of *Diff'rent Strokes*—Alice had gone out and bought a small TV set for her apartment, as casually as if it had been a box of Jeremy's favorite cereal. She was not one for extravagant gestures, not someone who went out of her way to please people, but with Drew and Jeremy she grew expansive, sympathetic, indulgent. It was the kind of courtship she had missed the first time around—the relief and gratitude of two adults who had stumbled upon each other at just the right moment. The passion between them bloomed in spite of Jeremy, who often seemed to be at the heart of their affair, always, invariably, needing something: a change of clothes, a bath, a meal, a lap to settle into, a pair of shoulders to ride. He talked incessantly and was astonishingly self-absorbed, and fortunately for Alice, he wasn't able to see through to her faults. She was the one person in the world he allowed to brush his hair, to change the Masters of the Universe sheets on his bed, to clip tiny silvery crescents from his fingernails. Sometimes, lying in bed on Saturday mornings with Drew next to her and Jeremy at their feet mesmerized by a succession of cartoon figures battering each other, Alice thought of Roger and their lost marriage and it seemed that Roger in his high white turban had become a cartoon figure himself, someone she needn't have taken seriously. The betrayal and confusion he had caused were now faint in her memory; all those months of barely getting by seemed only a momentary ache.

"Are you nervous?" she asks Drew. They are backed against a cool marble wall, both of them ignoring the framed directory that lists Victor's name in white plastic letters.

Drew squints at her with one eye. "My tooth is killing me, and the thought of your father coming at me with sharp instruments turns my stomach; in fact, even the thought of your father unarmed and relatively friendly turns my stomach."

Jeremy raises himself on the tips of his toes and smiles at Alice as he makes a grab with both hands for her breasts.

"Excuse me, what the hell are you doing?" Alice seizes Jeremy by the wrists and pushes him away.

"Checking your bosoms," Jeremy says, looking insulted.

"Well, I for one have to say that I feel terrific," Alice reports. "As if I've taken my life in for a tune-up..." She stops, embarrassed. Talking this way was unseemly, like boasting about all the money you had in the bank. If Drew didn't feel the same contentment, the same satisfaction that had filled her like a perfect meal, then what? As soon as they met, she had latched on to him with a vehemence that amazed her: dialing his number throughout the day, mostly for the sound of his pleased voice, inviting him over for dinner night after night, then spending nearly a hundred dollars on a television set so that his son would want to visit her. Humiliated, tears come to her eyes now. She does not want to need him more than he needs her—that would be intolerable.

"I want a chocolate milkshake," Jeremy says. "One scoop of chocolate, one jar of chocolate syrup, all mixed up in the blender for about three days and three nights."

Alice covers her eyes; tears slide slowly past her palms. She wants to weep against Drew's warm, hard chest, but she will not approach him.

"Come over here, you," Drew says, moving toward her and pressing her close to him.

"Actually, what I really want is some pineapple juice," says Jeremy. "In my special cup that I think somebody named Alice gave me."

"The pain," Drew growls suddenly. "The pain." He lets go of Alice and darts across the lobby into an open elevator, and then he is gone.

Drew returns from Victor's office with one less wisdom tooth and carrying a transparent, amber-colored toothbrush that has "Dr. Vic's Magic Toothbrush" printed along the back and front. One of his cheeks is still puffy with Novocain, and he appears to be a little high, giddy with some private pleasure. He can't stop talking about Victor. "I haven't felt this great in years," he tells Alice at her kitchen table. "What a guy!" He smiles, lowers his eyes, notices Jeremy lying under the table napping. "Hello there," says Drew, shaking a foot at his son, then, "He's indeed a beautiful person."

"My father's one of the beautiful people?"

"You're not listening to me," Drew complains. "The man has magic fingers." He puts his head down on a woven place-mat on the table. "And I'm the happiest guy in the world."

"Magic fingers, magic toothbrush," Alice says. "All in a day's work."

"First he gave me Valium and then we talked about life. He has the softest voice in the world, did you know that?" Drew says dreamily.

"He took psychology courses at the New School."

Drew lifts his head from the table. "I'm flying," he sings. "Look at me, way up high…" His head flops down again.

Alice thinks of her father at the funeral, soaring above the tombstones. "You and he, both," she says.

"Goddamn," says Drew. "You know, I think he was pretty impressed with me. He told me I was a wonderful patient, that my teeth were basically in excellent shape, and that it was a pleasure to have worked on me. He did mention, however, that the thought of the two of us getting married gave him acid indigestion." Drew reaches into his mouth and extracts a piece of blood-soaked cotton from deep inside his upper jaw. A bright smear like badly applied lipstick shines above a corner of his mouth; Alice bends forward to wipe it away. She doesn't like to admit that she's even the slightest bit wounded by what Victor thinks of her future with Drew. She struggles to remember what it was like to have a father who was easy to please. Through all the years of her growing up, and beyond that, past her marriage to Roger, he had always been sweetly attentive to her, patient and reluctant to find fault. It is difficult to accept that her father has become unpredictable, someone to be wary of. If she had battled with him all her life, she wouldn't be feeling as bewildered and vulnerable as she does now. It occurs to her that perhaps her father had loved her so unconditionally because he had wanted to steer them away from the rocky path he had traveled with his mother. Now that she was gone, nothing looked the same to him: So suddenly Alice has disastrous taste in men. But what does he think he's going to do about it? *Think of the possibilities*, she remembers her father saying, and hears the buzz of an imaginary dentist's drill in the distance. And then she is laughing, because her stoop-shouldered father, small and slender, his hands graceful and elegant, has never been a threat to anyone. Certainly not to the happiness she's charted for herself—in her mind, a bright arc of endless stars connected across a clear night sky.

She reaches above Drew's head for the phone on the wall, dials her father's office number. Victor answers the phone himself. "Dr. Rosenthal," he says.

"You don't inspire fear in me and that's all there is to it," Alice says, still laughing.

"Who is this? Would you like to schedule an appointment?" her father says.

"The only thing we have to fear," Drew calls out in the background, "is fear itself. Who said that?"

"Franklin Roosevelt."

"Franklin Roosevelt?" says Victor. He pauses. "Alice, is that you?"

Alice nods her head "yes," and hangs up.

Three weeks later, on a Sunday afternoon as bright as the day her grandmother was buried, Alice and Drew dress for their wedding. With Jeremy, they have driven up from the city to New Rochelle, where they will be married on the freshly mown half-acre lawn behind the colonial-style house that belongs to Drew's best friend. Moments before the ceremony is scheduled to begin, Victor arrives, wearing a pale linen suit. "Car trouble," he explains. His face shines with perspiration. He shakes Jeremy's hand, nods at Drew, smiles in Alice's direction. He and Alice have not spoken since the day Drew's wisdom tooth was extracted.

"So what brings *you* to town?" Alice says. The four of them are hidden from the guests, crowded into the small laundry room off the kitchen, next to an aqua-colored washing machine and matching dryer. In the dryer spins a down vest and a tennis shoe; Alice concentrates on the thump of shoe against metal. From the backyard, the sound of a string quartet playing Mozart can be heard.

"You're my daughter," Victor says. "And that's all the explaining I'm going to do. But don't forget the three L's—live, love, laugh. One of my patients had the words made up for me in fourteen-karat gold and hung them on a chain I was supposed to wear around my neck."

"Lucky you," Alice says.

"Too embarrassing to wear on a necklace, but not the worst advice you could get on your wedding day," Victor says. Then the screen door swings open and the caterer, a middle-aged

man in a tuxedo, bursts in. Among other things, he is responsible for organizing the ceremony, for getting everyone down
the aisle in proper order.

"Bride?" he says.

Alice raises her hand.

"Groom? Ring boy? Father of the bride?" The caterer
glares at Victor. "Why aren't you in a tux like your son-in-
law?"

"Car trouble," says Victor.

"Great," says the caterer. "Splendid."

"It's a miracle I'm here at all," Victor says.

The caterer rolls his eyes. "It's two-fifteen," he says. "Are we
ready to begin?"

Jeremy, in gray satin shorts, a round-collared white blouse,
and a bow tie, studies the plastic watch shaped like a turtle
that is strapped to his wrist. "It's two o'clock," he announces.
"Did you hug your child today?"

The caterer disappears out the door, taking Drew and Jeremy with him. Soon the string quartet switches to Wagner.

"They're playing our song," Alice says. She takes her father's
arm and guides him out the door, along the white-papered
trail that carpets the grass and leads them past the rows of
wedding guests seated quietly on folding chairs. More than
halfway down the aisle, just before they reach the wedding
canopy, Victor abruptly hangs back.

"Pretend you're my patient," he whispers to Alice. "Pretend you're in my chair and listening to the wisest man in the
world."

Alice sighs, and kicks him in the shin, gently this time, not
wanting to hurt him, but not knowing what else to do.

There are very few relatives at the wedding; nearly all of the
fifty guests are friends of Alice and Drew's, and Alice floats
among them effortlessly, collecting kisses on both cheeks until

they are bright with lipstick. Toward the end of the afternoon she has had too many drinks and knows it; what she would like to do most of all is collapse on the lawn and watch the wedding whirl silently around her.

Jeremy streaks by in his underwear and for a moment Alice imagines that he, too, is slightly drunk. "Come back here," she says, and when he approaches her, she grabs him and rests the side of her face across the top of his head. His hair is matted together and smells like pineapple juice. "Delicious," Alice says. "But where are your clothes, buddy?"

"Gone," says Jeremy. His undershirt and jockey shorts are patterned with tiny superheroes; beneath the shirt Alice can feel the fragile wings of his shoulder blades. "Don't ever leave me," she hears herself say and then Drew is at her side.

"Your father left without saying goodbye," he tells her. "What do you think?"

"Was he limping?"

"Excuse me," a husky voice interrupts.

Alice and Drew turn to see a tall, gray-haired woman dressed in a long wool coat and earmuffs, carrying, in one hand, a plastic bag that says Foodtown, and in the other, a paper shopping bag from Lord & Taylor. Both of the bags are stuffed to the top; the sleeve of a purple sweater hangs over the side of the Foodtown bag.

Alice grips Drew's hand in panic. Her heart is banging away in her chest, but she doesn't know why.

"Attention, shoppers!" the gray-haired woman shouts, and in an instant she seems to have everyone's attention. She puts down her bags one at a time and tosses her coat to the ground, along with her earmuffs and her gray hair. Underneath the wig, her hair is bright blond and soft-looking. She is young and pretty and is now unbuttoning her blouse and getting out of her skirt as a small cassette player at her feet plays music from *The Stripper*. Most of the wedding guests have wandered over to watch, and the men, at least, are laughing and cheering her on. She takes off a white satin half-slip and drapes it over Drew's surprised face.

"Way to go, Drew!" someone calls out.

The stripper is all in black—black lace bra, bikini underpants, black fishnet stockings held in place by a garter belt—but is surprisingly untidy. There's a hole in her fishnets and her underwear is ill-fitting; several dark curls of pubic hair rise above the rim of her bikini bottoms. From one of her shopping bags she removes a ball of tissue paper and unwraps an enormous fortune cookie. Splitting it open, she reads indifferently, "Congratulations to the happy couple from Victor."

There are some hoots of disapproval, but these few voices are overpowered by the men who are applauding and stamping their feet in the grass. A couple of Drew's friends seize the half-slip from his head, and fling it into the air higher and higher until finally it catches on the branch of a lean, curved poplar tree and is abandoned.

Alice cannot look at her husband; she keeps her eyes on the stripper, who, she is startled to realize, looks mournful and pallid. The stripper is heading toward her now, her shoulders held back stiffly. Her skin is smooth and pale everywhere. In a trance, Alice reaches out to touch her, her fingertips coming to rest against the soft white column of her neck.

"You don't have to remember any of this," the stripper murmurs. "Just the best parts of things, if you want to."

In the poplar tree, the satin slip flutters for a moment, then drifts soundlessly into the grass.

Pleasure Palace (2001)

It took me a while to realize it, but the quality of the construction job in my fabulous new bathroom began to deteriorate as soon as the contractor broke up with his lover, who happened to be my hairdresser. Stuart had been doing my hair ever since Jordan and I moved to Long Island, and he was the one who set me up with Ron when he heard that I was in the market for a contractor. I'd been putting off the construction for months, though originally Jordan and I had planned on a starting date of July first. On April thirteenth, Jordan died of a cerebral hemorrhage that had left him brain-dead, lingering in a coma for six days. The hemorrhage was caused by the cancer that had tormented him for a year and a half, but it came as a complete surprise to everyone, including the squad of doctors on the case. The truth was that, from the start, none of them had been particularly optimistic, but I never did tell Jordan, thinking the knowledge wouldn't have been the least bit helpful to him.

He was thirty-four years old when he died; we'd been married for twelve years and had been in love for even longer than that, since high school.

The last time I saw him conscious, only hours before he disappeared into the coma, he was sitting up in his hospital bed enjoying smoked turkey and Dijon mustard on a croissant. Crumbs littered the bedclothes, and if we'd been home, I would have gone after them with the Dustbuster. But since he was in the hospital (recuperating from a low white count that resulted from his chemo treatments), I just let them stay where they'd fallen.

Jordan was looking pretty good: his bald head was wrapped in a dark blue-and-white bandanna, and the little gold earring in his left ear (I'd pierced it myself with a cork and a sewing needle) gleamed beautifully. He looked like a person who led an exciting life—a rock star or a pirate, maybe. (In fact, he was a lecturer in the Art History Department of a local college and would have been an assistant professor if only he'd finished his dissertation.) After the second cycle of chemo, he lost every bit of his thick, unruly dirty-blond hair. It fell out in handfuls in the shower over a period of about two weeks, and one day there was nothing left. Jordan was depressed, but not too depressed, because he'd been told it would all grow back—maybe even thicker and more beautiful than before, maybe even a different color, but in any event, it *would* grow back. At least that's what they told him. What they didn't know, of course, was that he wouldn't live long enough for any of it.

That last night, as he sat up in bed with his smoked turkey sandwich, his fingers occasionally went to his temples, which he rubbed in an absent way.

"Headache?" I said after the third or fourth time I saw him do this.

"Umm."

"Want to ask the nurse for some Tylenol?"

"Nope. I can live with it."

We gossiped for several minutes about some friends of ours and the problems they were having with their severely dyslexic son, and then the talk turned to the new bathroom. It was going to be a pleasure palace—large as a generous-sized master bedroom, with a skylight, a Jacuzzi, a new toilet that flushed silently, track lighting, a small bookcase loaded with favorite paperbacks. All the fixtures were going to be black and the floor an imported black-and-white tile that cost a small fortune. The new bathroom would transform our home from a three-bedroom to a two-bedroom, and everyone said that just wasn't good business sense. What if we decided to sell in a couple of years? Who'd want to buy a two-bedroom house?

What if, what if, what if? I said.

We're not going anywhere, Jordan said. Not in two years, or twenty. We're just going to hang around forever enjoying our pleasure palace.

"I want heat lamps in the dressing area outside the shower," he told me that last night. "I hate standing there shivering in a towel."

"Me too," I said.

His fingers flew to his temples again and again and I went out and got one of the nurses. Jordan swallowed down the two Tylenol caplets and lay back against the pillows. I sat by the bed in a salmon-colored plastic chair, holding his warm hand. As soon as he fell asleep, I left, though often, during his countless hospital stays, I'd remain awhile longer, sometimes breaking down and weeping with frustration, self-pity, hopelessness, studying the beloved planes of his face. That night, though, I walked away from him without having done any of that, dropping a kiss on his cheekbone and hurrying out, as if I had something better to do than watch over him. I did, in fact, have a headache of my own, which was probably why I wasn't particularly troubled by his.

In the elevator, a husky little kid about five or six, and his mother—the only other passengers on board—gave me the once-over. The kid was holding a black plastic box about the size of a small camera, ornamented with a row of neon-green plastic buttons. He pressed one of them and there was the electronic sound of a phone ringing.

"Answer the phone," he said to me. When I didn't respond, he said, "Answer it!"

"Hello," I said. "Wrong number."

The kid smiled and pressed another button. The sound of bombs dropping filled the elevator, and my headache worsened. Then the phone rang again and the kid said, "It's for you."

"She has a headache and can't come to the phone right now," I said. I stared at his mother, a weary-looking, overweight woman in a lavender sweatsuit and matching basketball sneakers. I wondered if it was her husband she'd been visiting and if, like me, she routinely wept every night before going to sleep.

"Really," I said. "I really do have a headache."

"Turn it off, Michael Isaac Markowitz," the boy's mother said. "*Now*."

"You suck," he said amiably enough, and I understood it might have been me he was talking to.

When Jordan had been in a coma for three days, the sweetest of the handful of doctors assigned to his case took me aside in an empty waiting room and told me that my husband could be taken off the respirator and allowed to die peacefully just as soon as he passed a couple of tests.

"The EEG shows a bit of residual brain activity," he said, his voice whispery. "But that's normal after a massive brain hemorrhage like this one. As far as I'm concerned, he's brain-dead, but we've got to have a completely flat EEG on two consecutive readings before we can let him go. *If* you want to let him go, of course."

"I do," I said, because I knew that was what Jordan wanted. He was already gone anyway—every time I went into his room to hold his swollen, waxy-looking fingers, to watch the slow rise and fall of his chest, to murmur into his deaf ears, I could see that he'd left me for good.

"But of course I have to talk with his mother first," I said. "Simply out of courtesy. You know."

"Absolutely," said the doctor. We both looked down at our shoes, as if they were objects of great fascination, and then I began to weep, but very quietly. The doctor, who was about my age, opened his arms to me, and I leaned into them without hesitation. He had a good thick head of dark-brown hair, and more than anything I wanted to thread my fingers through it, to savor the feel of a man who wasn't dying. Slowly my hands rose up from his shoulders, but I caught myself in time.

"God, I'm going to hate being single," I heard myself say as I drew back from him. It seemed astonishing that I was capable of saying such a thing and yet there was the doctor nodding his head in agreement and sympathy.

"Your husband was an extremely cool guy," he said. "Very intelligent and funny and..." His voice lost energy and trailed off. He looked away from me at a stack of outdated news magazines arranged haphazardly on an end table, at squashed soda cans, and Styrofoam coffee cups marked with lipstick stains left behind by somebody's distracted family.

"And *what*?"

"And life is shitty."

"Thank you," I said, because it was, at that moment, utterly gratifying to hear the simple mean truth.

The bathroom now has two entrances: one leading from my bedroom, the other out in the hallway. I walk unannounced from the bedroom and find the contractor staring up at the skylight, at the snow that is drifting down so lightly upon it. The room reeks of a recently smoked joint, and a portable tape player is blasting the lyrics "I sell sex and can-dy." Stepping over a ladder resting on its side, I turn down the music and frown in Ron's direction.

"What's up, Ron?" I say.

"Oh, stuff and junk," he tells me. He's tall and pale and a little too skinny; he's wearing cream-colored overalls and a black cap with "Beastie Boys" emblazoned across the visor. "It's snowing," he says in amazement.

"I wish you wouldn't smoke pot on the job. It just strikes me as kind of irresponsible."

"Well, we all need to mellow out now and then, you know?" Ron says lamely.

I take his hand and lead him to the drop cloth spread out in the center of the room. "Let's sit down and talk."

"We *are* talking."

"Sit," I say, and give him a little push. "I had my hair permed a couple of weeks ago and while I was there I—"

"Oh yeah? It looks good. Makes you look kind of relaxed and freaky."

"And while I was there," I continue, "I heard from Stuart that the two of you had decided to go your separate ways."

Ron's head droops, and with his fingertips he draws swirling shapes on the drop cloth, one after the other. "You heard wrong—*he* decided, not me. He met some lawyer at a Smashing Pumpkins concert in the city, and now it turns out he wants to marry her."

"He *what?*"

"I know," Ron says. "It's fucking incredible, isn't it. And who could believe in these dangerous times that a woman would even take a chance with someone like him. But he was married once before, years ago. He even has a kid who's a teenager now and living with his mother somewhere on the West Coast."

I can feel Stuart's capable fingers neatly rolling my hair onto thin plastic rods, can hear the confident, satisfying click of the scissors as he thins my bangs into something feathery. He came to Jordan's funeral in a beautiful dark suit, his hair moussed back proudly. When he kissed me, I inhaled the scents of his cologne and mousse and face moisturizer, and nearly swooned.

It's beyond belief to me that there could be a wife in his past and one in his future.

"I'm so sorry," I tell Ron. But really I'm not; frankly, I don't give a shit one way or the other. Because my grief is purer, sharper, more deeply felt. After all, *I'm* the widow here; the love of *my* life has been transformed into ash and chips of bone while Ron's heartthrob is alive and kicking and heading back to the altar for another shot at it. Call me crazy, but the sympathy vote goes straight to me. And furthermore, I win by a landslide. *So cry me a river, Ron, baby*, I tell him silently.

Sighing, he lights a cigarette with trembly hands. "I'm the enemy," he says. "He's the guilty one, dumping me without even an apology, but I'm the enemy for making him feel guilty. He told me he won't forgive me for that, and that now he isn't sure he ever loved me at all."

"No way."

Ron lets out a thin trail of white smoke and begins to cough; tears leak from his eyes. "We were so happy together. You can't imagine how happy we were."

Wanna bet? The loss of my nearly perfect jewel of a marriage pierces me cruelly now. I've lost too much—love, friendship, romance, passion, sex. The sight of Jordan's long narrow almost-pretty feet hanging over the edge of the bed in early morning. The feel of his mouth against the side of my neck. The sound of his voice over the phone. The sloppy heap of his pajamas and bath towel waiting outside the shower door. It seems no credit to me, but merely a fluke that I've survived these losses. Just a few days ago, going through the top drawer of Jordan's dresser, determined to throw out everything that was still left, I found myself holding his contact lenses in my palm. Weightless, nearly invisible, entirely worthless. Tenderly, I replaced them in their plastic case, as if they were heirlooms.

Raising my head now, I look around in my pleasure palace, at the graceful black sink and matching toilet, at the deepset Jacuzzi, its chrome hardware dazzling, at the well-placed window that overlooks my snow-covered lawn. Cartons of tile stand in disorder against one wall, and Ron's tools litter the floor. I get up to examine the shelving he made for towels and supplies of soap and shampoo. The boards are unevenly cut and haven't been planed to a smooth finish. The track lighting has been installed carelessly, at a peculiar angle. And the door that leads out into the hallway, I notice, falls about an inch and a half too short of the floor.

"What's going on, Ron?" I say, as if it's all a mystery to me.

"What?"

"Your work was so professional at the beginning," I tell him. "But it's clear your heart's not in it anymore."

"Look, I'm doing the best I can," he says irritably.

"You're coasting," I say. "Just getting by."

"Just getting by," he agrees, surprising me. "I wake up in the morning and I think, 'I can't *do* this.' I can barely brush my teeth. I stand there in front of the mirror with the toothbrush in my hand and I can hear Stuart telling me in a stranger's voice that it's possible that in the three years we were together he never loved me at all. And just like that he's gone from my life and I'm nowhere. I'm not even in this room with you," Ron informs me. "I don't know *where* the hell I am."

I'm so angry now, I want to shake Ron until he goes limp. *Do you realize who you're talking to, you miserable little self-pitying sad sack?* I want to tell him. *Go cry on someone else's shoulder, buddy.* But then it hits me that maybe by a wild stretch of the imagination I'm the lucky one here, that although there's an excruciating absence of love in my life, a deep hollow I'm almost always aware of, at least I know for sure that Jordan was mine until that very last moment before he slipped away in his hospital bed littered with sandwich crumbs.

Keeping watch at Jordan's bedside an hour or so before they took him off the respirator, his mother and I could only make small talk. When we ran out of that, we fell into a miserable silence.

I fixed my gaze on Natalie as she touched her brightly powdered cheek against Jordan's ashy one. Sixtyish, her hair dyed white-blond, she was overdressed for the occasion in a pink silk suit and pearls, which she fingered incessantly. Her lashes were mascaraed, and her mouth was polished with lipstick that matched her suit. For whose benefit, I wondered. Hers? Mine? Her comatose son's?

Natalie let go of her pearls and went after a thread on her skirt.

"I bet that suit spends half its life in the dry cleaners," I said. I jammed my hands into the back pockets of my jeans and came up with two sticks of gum. "Would you like a piece?" I offered.

"What's that, wintergreen?" said Natalie suspiciously. "I hate wintergreen."

"It's Winter*fresh*," I said. "It has nothing to do with wintergreen."

"That's what *you* think."

"Well, at least it's not spearmint."

"Actually, I like spearmint," said Natalie. "But every time I chew gum I get a headache, so what's the point?"

I slipped the gum back into my pocket.

Sighing, Natalie put out a manicured hand. "You might as well give me a piece anyway. I'll get rid of it as soon as I feel a headache coming on."

"Well, you can never be too careful," I said.

We chewed our Winterfresh discreetly. "Jordan's in Acapulco," my mother-in-law announced after a moment, already loony with grief, her voice oddly animated, enthusiastic, even.

"Pardon me?"

"Oh, he's not here. He's in Acapulco, lying on the beach with the sun in his eyes."

"Acapulco," I said. "Of course." Leading her away from the bed, I laced my arms around her soft fleshy back and felt her face tip clumsily against my shoulder. "Acapulco," I murmured. Jordan and I had been there several times over the years, enjoying the sharp blue water beautifully surrounded by mountains, the ferocious sun that appeared without fail every morning, the wild, bumpy rides in speedboats, the unhurried trips in glass-bottomed ones, the wet, pebbly sand under our feet at the water's edge. It was true that we'd taken pleasure in those things. That our life together had been filled with many pleasures.

"Don't you just feel a hundred percent better knowing he's in Acapulco?" Natalie persisted. "Don't you?"

I couldn't bring myself to tell her what she wanted to hear. Jordan was Natalie's only son, her only child, in fact; her husband was long gone. The loss she was about to endure might very well prove too much for her, I thought, sending her over the edge and into some hellish place that I didn't even want to contemplate. She and I had recently become pretty good buddies in the way that soldiers in a foxhole together might, but I was unnerved at the prospect of the two of us clinging fast to each other in the weeks and months to come; I could see us fixed in a weepy embrace forever, our lives stagnant as the air in a parked car on a sweltering afternoon. What I felt there in the hospital room just before Jordan's death was an extraordinary, overpowering selfishness. And so when the nurse squeaked into the room in her Nikes to tell us she was ready to start the procedure, I backed away from Natalie and headed for the door.

"Where are you going?" she said, sounding terrified.

"I can't stay here," I told her. "It's like I'd be witnessing an execution."

I could hear Natalie sucking in her breath at the word "execution"; perhaps she understood exactly what I meant. But a moment later she said, "That's crazy. How can you even think of leaving him alone?"

Marla, our favorite of all the nurses, years younger than I was and very pregnant with her first child, squeezed my shoulder. "Some family members prefer it that way," she told Natalie. "But I'm sorry, you can't stay in the room while I'm... working in here."

Impulsively, I reached out a hand and placed it on Marla's hard, taut stomach. I felt a couple of good swift kicks and Marla's smile upon me. For years Jordan and I had been ambivalent about having children; when at last we decided to go ahead and give it a try, we learned that I had all sorts of problems that would have required surgery and more surgery, and so we'd agreed to forget it. Now, of course, I wished I'd been braver, wiser, more resolute. If we'd had children, there would have been something left for Natalie to hold on to, as well.

Examining her stricken face, I apologized out loud for having failed in the grandchildren department.

"Oh, Lizzy," she said, and I caught her in my arms as she fell hard against me.

"Take a ride with me," I told her. "We'll drive down to the water and..." And what? I was going to make my escape, but the truth was, I had no plans at all.

"I couldn't," Natalie said. "I have to stay here till it's over. But you go. I'll see you back at the house, I guess."

"Would you like me to call and let you know the time of death?" Marla asked me. "It may take a few hours. Or less. Everyone's different."

I've got a better idea. Would you like to trade lives with me? You give me your husband and your baby and I'll give you nada. Zip. Zippo. Zilch. Deal?

Marla looks horrified.

Can't say that I blame her.

I kissed Jordan on the mouth, my lips unintentionally brushing against the plastic tubing of the respirator that snaked from his mouth and behind his shoulder. "Who knows if I can live without you," I murmured. "Or even if I want to give it a try." My hands lingered along the bones of his skull that lay under the bandanna; lifting my fingertips from him for the very last time seemed the most terrible thing I had ever had to bear. There was a crushing pain in my chest and it occurred to me that I was having a heart attack and would die right there on the floor beside his bed. This seemed a good thing, maybe even something I had willed. But then there I was walking from the room, down a long, waxed, linoleum aisle, past nurses at their stations monitoring the vital signs of the living and the dying and sipping from cans of Diet Coke and joking around with their lovers and husbands on the phone.

Driving home in a trance, I stopped instinctively at red lights, accelerating when they turned green, but seeing and hearing nothing. The pain in my chest subsided and I realized the obvious, that it was only that my heart had turned to glass and shattered soundlessly against the solid wall of my grief.

I walked up two flights of steps to the attic, which we'd redone as a den of sorts before Jordan got sick. The hardwood floor was pickled white and there was a pair of chrome and leather Breuer chairs positioned across the room from a top-of-the-line CD player and a large-screen TV. A triangular window overlooked the Long Island Sound below, and I stood by it and watched the sun set, watched as spectacular bands of crimson and deep blue marked the sky. A cluster of anchored boats remained visible as a full glittery moon and a luminous spray of stars appeared. The phone rang on a little table behind me, instantly raising goosebumps all along the path from my wrists to my shoulders. I should have been prepared, but of course I wasn't. Something bitter rose in my throat and I began to choke on it, coughing uncontrollably as the phone went on ringing. After a while the answering machine in my bedroom picked up and I imagined the sound of Marla's voice carefully announcing the precise moment at which Jordan had taken leave of this earth.

There were friends I could call, and my sister in New Orleans, my father in Fort Lauderdale. And of course there was Natalie, who would be putting in an appearance at any moment, a woman deprived of absolutely everything, including hope. But I preferred to be here alone in the darkness of my attic.

"Will you get a grip, please," I advise Ron now. My voice rises unpleasantly. "Tell your sob story somewhere else. How about a chat room on the Internet?"

Ron looks at me in astonishment. "You of all people," he scolds. "You—"

"That's right," I say, and then I clam up, saving my breath. But he already knows the worst of it, that I'm running on empty; there's nothing left for anyone but me.

"Listen, I swear to God, I don't know which end is up anymore," Ron confesses.

"Go home," I tell him. "Come back to work when you're feeling up to it and not a minute sooner."

In the evening, after a hot, leisurely bath, I gaze out through my skylight. Loony as my mother-in-law, I watch the sky for signs that Jordan has, at last, arrived at some distant place, perhaps settling himself comfortably on a star as small as the earth, or one infinitely larger, as great as the earth's orbit.

LOVERS (1983)

In a pancake house in Gainesville, Florida, Valerie and her mother are silently dividing up a copy of *The New York Times*. Generously, Valerie offers her mother the best section, the one with all the cultural news—the only news Marilyn cares about. In the three days that they have been on the road together, Valerie hasn't had many generous impulses. She wishes she were better company. Apologies and some sort of explanation are in order, but then she would have to open up her marriage to her mother, something she has never done. Her mother, though, is eager to share every small detail of her own current romance. Valerie's father has been gone a year, and recently Marilyn has begun seeing a man whom she met at a concert at Carnegie Hall. Joseph is Hungarian; during the revolution, he somehow managed to get to Israel, and then to New York, where he found work as a diamond cutter. According to Marilyn, he is a man of great kindness and sensitivity. Like someone in love for the first time, she cannot stop talking about him, cannot stop herself from repeating the same details a hundred times over. Her eyes shine with unexpected happiness, even at seven-thirty in the morning, in a pancake house with dusty windows and sticky floors.

A middle-aged waitress approaches their table. In her short-sleeved white pants suit and white shoes, she looks like a dental technician.

"I can't make up my mind," Marilyn says, smiling at her. "What do you recommend?"

"French toast, eggs, I don't know. It's up to you."

Very quietly, Valerie orders an ice-cream soda.

Marilyn looks to the waitress for sympathy.

"Ketchup and French toast, Cheerios soaking in a bowl of Diet Pepsi. I've seen it all," the waitress says. "If this young lady wants ice cream for breakfast, that's just fine with me."

"Thanks," Valerie says, and grabs the best section of the paper back from her mother. "Would it be possible to have us out of here in ten minutes?"

Marilyn explains to the waitress that they are from New York, where people are always in a hurry, even if they don't have anywhere special to go. In fact, the two of them are on their way down to Hollywood, where Valerie's grandfather lives in a mouse-sized house by himself. "He's extremely independent," Marilyn says, "but lately in the middle of the night he's been waking up with sharp pains in his chest, and no matter how many times the doctors in the emergency room tell him it's only indigestion, he doesn't believe them. They tell him not to eat just before going to bed, to eat a light dinner in the early evening and then nothing more until breakfast."

"Got it," says the waitress.

"Every now and then," Marilyn says, "a doctor will surprise you and say something that actually makes sense. I was married to one for a thousand years, and I have to tell you that most of the things he said had to be taken with a grain of salt."

This is the perfect moment for Valerie to excuse herself from the table and make a phone call home. The phones are directly outside the rest rooms, and it's a struggle to hear the operator's instructions. Nick doesn't answer. After twenty-one rings, Valerie hangs up, deciding he's in the shower or on the subway headed for work. But immediately this strikes her as too uncomplicated, too unsatisfying. (The farther she travels from Nick, the more fully her pessimism blooms.) She decides he's gone to see his ex-wife, with whom he says he still feels a tenuous connection. His ex-wife is small and pretty, but not very perceptive. "I don't understand how we can be breaking up when we've just picked out new stuff for the bedroom," she'd told Nick when he said that their marriage was over. They'd ordered several thousand dollars' worth of furniture—an antique armoire, a brass headboard, a chaise longue—and Nick left her anyway, even though he had to admit the bedroom would look terrific.

He and Valerie have been married for almost two years. Valerie works as a loan officer in a bank, and Nick teaches anatomy to first-year medical students. Nick is exceptionally confident, the kind of person who can make Valerie feel uneasy by the arch of his eyebrows, the slightest trace of mockery in his voice. She's vulnerable in his presence, never knowing when he's going to challenge her or prove her wrong—something he rarely attempted before their marriage. Usually it's a simple thing, like keeping the Cornish hens in the oven too long, or choosing wallpaper that clashes with the print of their shower curtain. She makes mistakes like these nearly every day. Even more painful are the times when Nick speaks to her as if she were a child who hadn't done her homework carefully. Where did you see *that*, he'd ask after hearing her say that in some cities in Poland waiting lists for apartments are eighteen years long, or that the average doctor dies at the age of fifty-six. He'd insist that she hadn't read the newspaper article as thoroughly as she should have or had not thought things through properly. (Working as she does in the bank, she knows all about weighing the facts, she wants to say, but it seems too obvious to mention.) That's the scientist in Nick, she tells herself; accuracy and precision are what he's after. But often she has to remind him that school is over for the day, that in any case she's not one of his students, and that he sounds like an asshole when he talks to her like that. And then he apologizes and says he hadn't meant it that way at all. She can't help feeling, though, that their life together is becoming an endless round of accusations and reluctant apologies.

This seems intolerable to her. She has always been a romantic, always believed in love, long-term and sustaining, something that would see her through a lifetime. But when she told this to a shrink she went to see once or twice when things got difficult with Nick, Dr. Schall looked at her mournfully and said, "You and a cast of millions. What else is new?"

Surprisingly, Nick, too, considers himself a romantic: He's saved the ticket stubs from all the movies they've seen together, and the matchbooks from every restaurant they've eaten in, collecting and storing them like treasures in the inlaid-rosewood box that Valerie gave him for his birthday. (Is there a similar collection documenting his first marriage, she wonders.) On her thirtieth birthday this year, he locked himself away in the kitchen for hours, emerging at midnight with a braided loaf of sourdough bread, each braid dyed a different, brilliant color. He took snapshots of a slice of it carefully arranged on a white linen napkin: evidence of the lengths he had gone to please her.

Now and then, Nick meets his ex-wife for lunch—just to see how she's getting along, he claims. He is very casual about these meetings. He sometimes forgets to mention them to Valerie for several days. "Seeing her means more to you than it does to me," he said to Valerie in a soothing voice the night before she left for Florida. She shook her head, reassured of nothing. "What you need," he went on quietly, "is someone without any past at all, a goddamn blank piece of paper." No, she wanted to say; what she needed was someone easier, softer, more patient. When she left the next morning, they kissed for a long while. Finally, she had to pull away. "It's only a couple of weeks," she said, smiling. "I'll be back before you know it." But it hadn't felt like the truth to her; she'd blushed as soon as the words were spoken.

Sitting opposite her mother now, Valerie watches Marilyn write out a postcard to Joseph with a chartreuse pen. "Can I read this to you?" Marilyn asks, and she begins reading before Valerie has a chance to answer. "What do you think? Is it too much to say that I miss him terribly? I said something to that effect in yesterday's card, too. This is just a rough draft anyway." Marilyn reaches into a suede handbag and shows Valerie the pile of postcards she's taken from the motel they stayed in the night before. "These are some other versions—some are a little more restrained than others, if you know what I mean," she says.

Valerie sips at her ice-cream soda, which is warm and slightly bitter.

"What a terrible face on you," Marilyn says. "Am I supposed to take that face personally or are you just mad at the world?"

Valerie gazes out into the parking lot, where a broad-shouldered woman is dragging a small, weeping child from the front of a van. The van has a heart-shaped rear window on one side and a tear-shaped one on the other. "We should have made more of an effort to get airline reservations," Valerie says. "It's crazy to be taking the car this distance."

Shuffling through her stack of postcards, Marilyn says, "Too bad Grandpa couldn't have chosen a better time to fly into a panic. This time of year, everyone in the world wants to go to Florida. He sounded so pitiful on the phone last week, after he'd gotten back from the hospital. Whenever I think about that conversation, I'm convinced this trip was absolutely unavoidable." She picks out a postcard, holds it up to the fluorescent lighting overhead, and smiles. "Now here's one any man would be delighted to find in his mailbox."

"Let me see," Valerie says.

"No," her mother says. "Not this one. This one's strictly personal and confidential." She raises her arm higher and waves the postcard in the air. Valerie is out of her seat, standing on her toes, the backs of her knees painfully stretched, when her mother's arm swoops down suddenly and she tears the postcard into tiny pieces that drift to the floor. "You never listen to anything I say about Joseph," Marilyn says. "You tap your foot, stare at the ceiling, anything to avoid paying attention. When are you going to tell me what I'm doing wrong?" When Valerie remains silent, her mother says, "You'll have to excuse me if my happiness comes at an inconvenient time for you."

"It's not anything you're doing wrong," Valerie says at last. "It's only me."

"You," her mother murmurs. "Every day in the car, I look at you for hints of something—anything. But you're only listening to the rock and roll on the radio, pretending there's no one in the seat next to you, that you're traveling all these hours and all these miles alone."

Valerie's grandfather, Willy, lives in a house of peach-colored stucco, set on a tiny lawn of yellowish grass. The rooms are furnished with aluminum-and-plastic beach furniture, and there's a fine, powdery dust everywhere, even across the TV screen. Assessing the hours of housecleaning before her, Marilyn perks up immediately.

"You can't believe what the bathroom looks like," she confides to Valerie. "You just want to run right out the minute you get in there."

"Sad," says Valerie, who assumes her grandfather is losing his eyesight.

"Sad?" Marilyn is in the utility room off the kitchen, looking for a broom. "Your grandfather was never much of a housekeeper, if you really want to know. He always liked everything neat—magazines in a nice even pile, beds made with perfect hospital corners—but he never went in much for sweeping and dusting."

"True to form," Willy says, joining Valerie at the kitchen table. "She's in my house five minutes and already she's passing judgment."

"Why should I be surprised that a man who doesn't believe in sweeping wouldn't have a broom?" Marilyn says. "How about a sponge?"

Valerie touches her grandfather's smooth, narrow wrist. "Tell me how you've been. Have you been eating?" she asks. At the end of last summer, Willy's brother, Norman, who had shared the house with him, struck up a conversation with a woman on a bench in a shopping mall. A few weeks later, he married her. Willy refused to attend the wedding, and hasn't spoken to Norman since. According to Willy, his new sister-in-law isn't a "high-quality individual." He can't understand how Norman could have married a woman who has dyed red hair and wears perfume so strong it lingers in the house for hours after she's gone.

"I eat, I sleep; I'm surviving," Willy says.

"You miss the company, I bet."

"Never," Willy says. "I've got plenty of company. In fact, I'm surprised my pals haven't been over yet today."

Marilyn is squatting on the floor, sponging down the linoleum with Mr. Clean. Through an open window, a neighbor's television can be heard perfectly.

"So how's your new boyfriend?" Willy says, frowning at the top of Marilyn's curly gray head. "Is he going to marry you?"

"What? When did I ever say one word about marriage? Not that I don't fantasize about it occasionally." Marilyn has eased her way under the table and is crouched there, moving a sponge dreamily across the speckled linoleum.

"That's my foot, in case you're interested," says Valerie.

"Marriage," Willy says mournfully. "It comes when you least expect it. You walk over to the mall intending to do a little shopping, and there it is, waiting for you right outside Drug World." From his seat, he kicks a cabinet door closed with one foot. "That weasel. She was sitting there reading *Crime and Punishment*, trying to pass herself off as an intellectual. 'Tolstoy,' my brother says, and smiles at her with those big white false teeth of his."

"Dostoyevski," Marilyn calls from under the table.

"Yeah, well, the weasel was too lovesick to correct him. In two seconds, she and Norman were across the mall at someplace called Sweet Dreams, enjoying an ice-cream cone. And there I was, sitting on that bench like a big dope, waiting for the two of them to come back. I read twenty pages of *Crime and Punishment* before I realized they'd forgotten all about me."

"It must have been awful," Valerie says, and puts her arms around her grandfather's neck.

"So I stole the weasel's book. I took it home with me and read every last page. Then I mailed it back. They were already married by then, living in that dark little apartment of hers that you have to travel across a catwalk to get into. Sometimes," Willy says, his voice a whisper, "I imagine them in the wind and the rain, crossing the catwalk, huddled against each other."

"Kind of romantic, if you think about it," Marilyn says, and crawls out from under the table. Her face is flushed and sweaty, her pinkish eye shadow smudged over the bridge of her nose. "The wind and the rain, the two of them—"

"Soaking wet," Willy says. "Soaked to the bone. Their clothes have to be dry-cleaned. It costs them a fortune."

Valerie laughs and shakes her head. Her grandfather is unforgiving and unyielding in ways she almost admires. Forty-five years ago, he divorced his wife after she admitted she had a habit of being unfaithful to him. He never remarried and raised their three children on his own. Not a happy life, or an easy one, but simply the best he could manage. Valerie is thinking of Nick and wondering why she had to fall for someone who makes her feel so unsure of herself, so helpless. Over the years, friends have confided in her, come to her for advice, and gone away satisfied. She has always seen through other people's lives with a clarity that eludes her when she examines her own. Eyes open, she imagines Nick's soft, boyish hands kneading dough, remembers the velvety dust of flour that settled across his dark brow, the look of pleasure about his eyes and mouth as he sliced into the neon colors of her birthday bread.

She tells her grandfather that she'd like to use the phone.

"Not today," Willy says. "I haven't had a dial tone all day. Someone from the phone company was supposed to come by this afternoon, but don't hold your breath."

"I should call Joseph," Marilyn says. "Or maybe I shouldn't."

The doorbell rings—a startling electronic buzz. "Come in, come in," Willy yells, and a young Indian woman in a sari and a little boy walk through the side door into the kitchen, a Teddy bear between them, each of them holding one of its paws. Willy smiles as he introduces the visitors. "This is Vijay, my newest granddaughter, and this is Neeraj, my one and only great-grandson."

"Your *what*?" Marilyn says. She's standing on a wrought-iron chair with a feather duster in her hand, swiping at cobwebs in a corner of the ceiling.

"I have no one in America to talk to except Grandpa," says Vijay. "No one." She's a very pretty woman, with a diamond chip decorating the curve of one nostril. Her bare feet are pretty, too; dark, slender feet, the nails polished bright red.

"Grandpa," Neeraj says. There's a thin silver bracelet around each of his wrists. He's wearing a T-shirt with Sesame Street characters on it; across the front is printed "Lunch Is My Favorite Subject."

"My Florida family," Willy says, looking pleased with himself. "And this is my New York family."

"Aren't you lucky," Marilyn says.

"Vijay and Neeraj are Hindu," Willy says. "They're very religious people. Vijay's husband is a psychologist."

"No, no," Vijay says. "Psychiatrist."

"Whatever. They moved in next door a few months ago, just before Norman went off with the weasel."

"The weasel has orange hair like a carrot," Vijay says, as if this were a line she has memorized. Then she laughs and covers her mouth with her hand. Valerie shoots her a sympathetic look. She wants to make up for Marilyn's coldness, to signal to Vijay that her mother's disapproval should not be taken to heart. Willy likes to collect honorary families that he can rave about long-distance to Marilyn; mostly, Valerie thinks, because he knows just how much it hurts her to hear it. Marilyn, who is the only daughter among his three children, is the one who worries most about him. But she has never been able to please him; face-to-face or long-distance, the air between them bristles with discontent. Once, she told Valerie, "If he were a lover whose attention I was dying for, I'd flirt like crazy, say something provocative, spray perfume all over my hair—anything to get noticed. But of course he's only my father." She shrugged her shoulders and gave Valerie a sad half-smile. And yet here was her mother battling cobwebs as if they mattered, as if there were always the possibility that something she did or said might turn out to be the right thing after all.

Valerie gazes straight into Willy's bleached-looking blue eyes. Who is Willy that he can afford to turn down love when it is offered him? He appears to be nothing more than a fragile old man, small and thin as a boy. Valerie would like to shake him hard and see the confusion in his startled face.

She climbs up next to her mother on the chair and takes the duster from her hand. "Stop trying so hard," Valerie whispers.

Tears shimmer in her mother's eyes. "What could be easier?" Marilyn says.

Willy has taken Neeraj onto his lap, and is stroking the little boy's cheek with two fingers. "Sweet boy," he says. "But why can't you ever wear shoes? Your feet will get callused like an old man's."

Giggling, Vijay says, "Sometimes I take your advice, sometimes not."

Willy says, "I told you to keep your car in the garage—begged you, practically. I knew they would steal it." To Valerie and her mother he explains, "It was brand-new, a shined-up Volkswagen something or other. The one week she had it, Vijay and I drove to some new malls and every day to the beach. We sat in the sand on a bedspread with Neeraj and watched the seagulls. I don't mind telling you the beach usually makes me feel lonely, but this particular week was perfect—day after day of unclouded skies and water the color of turquoise stones."

"Perfect," Vijay says, her head bowed. Everyone is silent, contemplating the word. "My husband is never home," Vijay says, and then in a loud voice, "It's not a life. Who can live this life? I want him to be sorry, to apologize—something."

"There are some people," Willy says, "who can't apologize for anything. Can't or won't or don't know how."

"Are you talking to *me*?" Marilyn asks. "Was that an apology drifting in my direction?"

"That was probably just a statement about people in general. And what would I be apologizing for, anyway?" Willy says. He kisses the side of Neeraj's neck, and Neeraj starts to slide off his lap. Willy pulls him back at first, then, sighing, lets him go.

There's a rustling at the back of the house, behind the screened-in porch, where everyone is slouched in lawn chairs, watching the end of the eleven o'clock news. Valerie stands up and presses her face against the screen. A figure dressed in light-colored clothes waves to her.

"Is that Valerie?" the figure asks. "Don't you recognize me?"

Willy comes up next to the screen beside her. "Ah," he says. "The bridegroom returns."

"May I come in?" Norman says.

"What for?"

"I tried calling, but your phone was out of order."

"And?" Willy says. "Go on."

"It's kind of nippy out here. I forgot to bring a jacket. Aren't you going to let me in?"

"I like having this screen between us," Willy says. "It's as if you're in some kind of prison and I'm here on the outside. But of course we can always pass messages back and forth."

Norman knocks on the screen with his fist. "She kicked me out, Willy. I have no place to sleep tonight."

"The weasel?" Willy says. "The phony-baloney intellectual who swept you off your feet right in the middle of the mall?"

Marilyn jumps up and grabs Willy's arm. "Will you stop torturing him, please?"

"Hi, Marilyn," Norman says. "Nice to see you again, even under circumstances as unpleasant as these."

Valerie, at a signal from her mother, darts into the kitchen. "The door's unlocked now," she calls to Norman, and leans out into the darkness. It's cool outside, just as Norman said, but also very humid. At her feet, a slug drags itself along the concrete stoop, then disappears into the glistening ragged grass of Willy's yard. There's a light on in Vijay's kitchen, next door, and laughter from her television set drifts over the unpainted picket fence that separates the two houses. If Valerie were home now, she and Nick would be sitting side by side in bed, books on their laps, their bare feet occasionally touching. She would slip down along the mattress, rest her head on

Nick's chest, and press her ear against his heart, listening for secrets. Funny that you could live with someone for months, even years, and still be astonished at what he was really thinking. Like Nick's first wife, when she found out she'd mistaken a roomful of new furniture for proof that the love between them was secure. And Nick himself, who has no idea that what continues to draw Valerie to him is the faint, ordinary perfume of his hair, his smooth, long-fingered hands, and the slope of his shoulders when he's tired. If she were never to see him again, those are the things that would haunt her the most.

"Valerie, my savior," she hears Norman say. He throws his arm across her shoulders and together they walk into the house. Norman is all in white, very dapper, with a full head of hair and a thin, elegantly groomed mustache. He carries a paper sack that says "Nathan's Famous" on it. "For you," he says, offering her the bag. "For you, who gave me sanctuary." Then he winks at her, just to let her know he's only half serious.

Valerie opens the bag and empties the contents onto the table: two ears of corn, two eggrolls, and two slices of partially eaten pizza wrapped in grease-stained wax paper.

"A romantic dinner for two, as you can see," Norman says. "Unfortunately, the romance has gone from my marriage."

Marilyn and Willy have joined them in the kitchen, where they study the food on the table with their hands behind their backs.

"Jesus," says Willy. "You're breaking my heart."

"You just ignore your baby brother," Marilyn tells Norman. "He's exceptionally cranky today."

"What do *you* know? You don't know anything about it," Willy says.

"I'm here to pick up the pieces of my shattered life," says Norman. He picks up an eggroll and holds it at arm's length. He frowns, as if he were examining it for flaws, then drops it back onto the table.

"So she's through with you," Willy says. "Big deal. People discard each other every day of the week."

"That may be," Norman says, "but this is something new—a marriage down the drain because of a sharp little noise. Did you know my teeth click when I eat? We were in Nathan's, having dinner, when all of a sudden she looked at me in an unfriendly way and said, 'I'm going to scream; my patience is gone. I can't live with that noise anymore. I can't live with *you* anymore.'"

"Life is full of surprises, even at this late date," Norman says. Pressing two fingers against each temple, he closes his eyes. It's as if he were listening for ghosts, or reading minds, attempting miracles of one sort or another. They all watch him, waiting to hear what he's discovered. "Love," he says finally. And then, the next moment, "Damn it all to hell."

Valerie and her mother are preparing for bed in what used to be Norman's room; Willy and Norman are in the master bedroom, across the hall. Marilyn is already in her bed, wiggling around under the sheet as Valerie undresses and shuts off the lamp on the night table between them.

"Joseph," Marilyn says, and sighs out loud. "I feel so privileged sometimes." Valerie has to smile.

"Sweetheart?" her mother says.

"Me? I'm here."

"When I first met him, that night at Carnegie Hall, we ducked into a coffee shop—just to escape the rain, really. He told me all about his life, how hard it had been to start over, to leave Budapest and eventually end up in New York, and how afraid he'd been. He trusted me, for God knows what reason. It was wonderful to be regarded that way, to be the kind of person someone would tell his whole life to."

Valerie is on her stomach, her head tucked into the curve of her arm. Her mother's quiet, careful voice is putting her to sleep, as if she were a child again, listening to some beloved, comforting story about imaginary people.

"Sometimes it's easier to talk in the dark," her mother says.

This is the last thing Valerie hears before falling asleep. In her grandfather's house, in a narrow, unfamiliar bed, she dreams pleasantly of Nick. Arms linked, they're floating above a city street, drifting like balloons high above the pavement; people smile up at them. "Lovers," a man says knowingly. Nick is a calmer, sweeter version of himself, the way Valerie remembers him during the early months of their marriage. In the dream, even his voice is softer; it's a voice she could listen to forever, even though his words are indistinct and impossible to follow as she and Nick descend slowly to earth.

"Valerie," someone is saying close to her ear. "I need your help."

"So you want to know when he stopped making me happy," Valerie says to herself, or maybe aloud; she can't tell which.

"Are you awake?" her mother says. The light from the lamp on the night table is unbearably bright.

"Why are we up so early?" Valerie asks.

"Those two nuts heated up the eggrolls and the rest of that junk."

"For breakfast?"

"I'm talking about a midnight snack. They sneaked out of bed, ate everything in sight, and went back to sleep. Now Grandpa insists he's dying."

"And you want me to drive him to the hospital."

Marilyn tips her head back and yawns. She straightens her shoulders. "He's not going anywhere. All he needs is some Pepto-Bismol and he'll be all set."

"That's what you say to a man who thinks he's dying?"

On the other side of the hall, Willy moans. Valerie hurries into her grandfather's room, her mother behind her. Norman greets them from a lawn chair, dressed only in his white pants.

"I was too hungry to sleep," he explains, "and Willy was kind enough to keep me company."

Willy is in bed, flat on his back, his eyes closed. "It's all true," he says. "Even at the moment you know your life is lost, there's time to travel through it again." Abruptly, he sits up very straight. "There I am! I'm in knickers and argyle socks on the stoop in front of the tenement we lived in on Lexington Avenue and One Hundred and Seventeenth Street. It was a lovely neighborhood. Anyway, there I am, shooting the breeze with my buddies—"

"It was never what anyone would call lovely," Norman says. "Shame on you. I thought dying men told the truth."

Willy massages his chest, then moves his hand toward his middle. "Get out of my room," he says. "Get out of my house. Go home to your wife."

Rising slowly from his chair, Norman says, "Take the medication Marilyn has for you. Don't be so stubborn."

Marilyn approaches her father and sits at the edge of his bed. In her palm are two pink, cellophane-wrapped Pepto-Bismol tablets. "You don't even need water," she says. "You just put them in your mouth and chew them up."

"Get off my deathbed, please."

Marilyn is already off the bed. "I'm going back to sleep. Wake me up if you need me."

"I need you *now*. Don't leave me," Willy says.

"There's always me," Valerie says. "I'm not going anywhere." Her hand closes around the little cellophane package her mother passes to her on her way out the door.

Valerie sits on the webbed green-and-yellow chair at the foot of her grandfather's bed and rubs her eyes.

"Come closer," Willy says.

She's at his side, slipping the Pepto-Bismol into his mouth. "Chew," she says, and Willy obeys.

Gradually the room lightens; a garbage truck groans outside, a telephone rings in a neighbor's house. From a straw mat
on the floor, Valerie keeps watch as her grandfather sleeps,
propped up against the carved wooden headboard that had
been a wedding gift from Norman nearly sixty years ago. Then
suddenly Willy's eyes open wide. He pulls the sheet over his
head until he has disappeared beneath it, a motionless figure
shrouded in white, a child's idea of a ghost.

"In truth," he says, "the weasel, Doris Feldmann, was very
beautiful. Tall and thin, graceful even in the way she sat, the
way she held a book in her hands. I sat down next to her on
the bench almost as soon as I saw her, but my tongue felt fuzzy
in my mouth, and I couldn't say a word. Nothing. And even if
I could have, what would have happened? Sooner or later, she
would have noticed that my teeth click as bad as Norman's."

Valerie nods her head, but she's no longer listening. She
and Nick are at a crowded party in a loft in SoHo, about to
meet for the first time. Nick is stretched out on the floor,
reading a magazine, oblivious of everyone above him. Valerie
hasn't noticed him yet, and at first, when he cries out in pain,
she does nothing at all. She's standing on his fingers, crushing
them! he yells up from the floor. Together, they rush to the
kitchen, and neither of them says a word as Nick holds his
hand under a stream of cold water. When finally he pulls away
from the faucet, Valerie bends forward and kisses this stranger's hand without hesitation, utterly amazed, only a moment
later, at what she has done.

Passenger (2001)

"Basically, I guess you *could* say I have the worst nails in the whole universe," Lacey admits, and this is no exaggeration—her fingernails are tiny chewed-up colorless slivers, painful to look at. Maxine, her mother, has already paid out ten dollars in cash to Lacey on two separate occasions—one dollar per grown-out fingernail. But a week or two later the nails were back to their customary miserable state, and Maxine was back on Lacey's case, nagging at her to get her fingers out of her mouth.

"So stop biting them," Maxine says now.

"The day you stop smoking is the day I stop biting," says Lacey, who is twelve. They are stuck in rush-hour traffic in her mother's cab, and she is staring, fascinated, at the trio of life-sized bronze statues roped together in an open truck alongside them. The figures are nude males, their muscles finely delineated, their yellowish-brown skin gleaming. As the truck inches out in front of the cab, Lacey gets a good look at the statues' extraordinary muscled behinds, the sight of which makes her snort with laughter. "Nice butts!" she says. "How many real-live people do you know who look like that?"

Maxine slams in the cigarette lighter with her palm and unrolls her window halfway. "Would you mind not using that word, please. Frankly, I find it very offensive."

"*Smoking* is offensive," Lacey says. "You're a drug addict, you know that? You're addicted to nicotine the way a crack addict is addicted to crack. And if you get lung cancer and die, there'll be no one to take care of me. I'll be an orphan!" she wails, so loudly and theatrically that her mother reaches over and slaps at her thigh, but only halfheartedly.

Lacey's father, in fact, is alive and well and lives in Los Angeles with his new wife, whose name is Swan, though it had once been Cynthia; they have a six-month-old baby boy named Dakota. (A phony-baloney name if I ever heard one, Maxine had said when he was born. Sometimes she refers to him as Montana, sometimes Idaho or Indiana.) Lacey had spent the summer with them and had arrived back in New York on Labor Day, only two weeks ago. She'd helped Swan take care of the baby, and brought her Diet Cokes whenever Swan asked for them, which was mostly as they sat around the pool in the backyard each afternoon, sunning themselves and trying to come up with something to say to each other. While in California, it became absolutely clear to Lacey that her mother was superior to her replacement in every way; at the very least, she was simply a much nicer person, someone who would pick herself up and get *you* a Coke, along with a glass, a handful of ice cubes, and a paper napkin meticulously folded into the shape of an arrowhead. And so all summer long Lacey was dying to ask her father why he'd moved away and married Swan. When, at last, she felt bold enough to actually pop the question, her father had looked at her in surprise, as if the answer should have been obvious to her.

"I was lonely," he said. "Even when your mother and I were in the same room together, I was lonely. And so was she. We weren't...connecting anymore. I don't know how else to explain it—it's just the way things were."

Lacey hadn't been sure what to make of this. "But when you and Swan are in the same room, you're connecting?" Thinking of plugs and wires and electrical outlets, she almost laughed.

"Oh God, yes," her father said, so enthusiastically that Lacey had to look away. It didn't help that he'd cultivated an unnaturally dark tan and had started dressing in pink polo shirts, baggy white pants, and thin-soled black suede shoes that looked like ladies' slippers with silly gold crests across the front. *Get out of those dorky clothes*, she wanted to say. *Lose that wife and that tan and come back to New York.*

Every day in California, Lacey had marveled at Swan's laziness. Her stepmother stayed in bed in the morning until after eleven, letting the housekeeper, Bernadette, take Dakota from his crib, change him, and feed him his first bottle of the day. Swan never made her bed, or cleaned up her bathroom after a shower. She wouldn't have lasted a day living with Maxine, who had rules about putting things back where you found them and never leaving the apartment until the beds were made and the kitchen sink empty of dishes. She was very strict about these things but surprisingly easygoing in other ways. She allowed Lacey to stay up forever, even on school nights, and for breakfast would fix her a bowl of vanilla ice cream sprinkled with a spoonful of instant coffee, which Lacey was crazy about.

"Your poor mother," Swan had said to Lacey one time toward the end of the summer. The two of them were drinking their Cokes poolside while the baby slept in his stroller in the shade of a grapefruit tree. Swan had waist-length hair twisted into a braid and was wearing shorts and the top from one of her bathing suits, clothing that revealed a lot of flab Lacey would have preferred not to see. According to Lacey's father, Swan was a terrific athlete who could easily bike twenty miles in an afternoon, a world traveler who had once gone alone on a three-month trip to explore Thailand, Malaysia, and Singapore. This was years before Dakota's birth, Lacey knew, years before Swan had become lazy and boring and addicted to diet soda.

"We're not poor," said Lacey, who had no idea what Swan was talking about. "We have a piano and a million CDs and a microwave."

Swan laughed when she heard this. "I didn't mean *that* kind of poor," she said. "Though of course she's got money troubles, I guess. I meant that it can't be easy for her, living in a small apartment, raising a kid pretty much on her own, not having a guy around, holding down two jobs, driving a cab all night. You know."

"All night?' " said Lacey, outraged. "What are you talking about? We're home by seven, usually. I wouldn't exactly call that 'all night,' would you? And her teaching job is part-time, too." Three mornings a week, Maxine taught English as a Second Language at Hunter College, a job she enjoyed far more than chauffeuring strangers around town all day. She'd been hoping, Lacey knew, for the chance to teach full-time, but so far there'd been no offers.

Trailing her hand in the pool's lukewarm water, Swan said, "It's not a life *I'd* want to be living, let's put it that way."

Lacey gazed out beyond the chain-link fence surrounding the yard, out into the canyon, which was wilderness, really, just a lot of bushes and dirt and unseen coyotes that howled at night and sometimes tore apart cats and dogs who'd foolishly wandered from home. Above, the sky was enormous, something entirely blue and silent. Three thousand miles away, her mother was cruising the streets for fares, looking at a sky so cluttered with immense buildings that sometimes there was nothing left of it but a narrow corridor of blue or white that was hardly worth an upward glance. In all the world there was no one Lacey loved more than her mother, who, as she'd imagined her then, was just a tiny figure behind the wheel heading into gridlock, her feet in their ankle-high black boots, tapping the brake and the accelerator impatiently, itching to get a move on.

"My mother," Lacy reported triumphantly, just before she left Swan's side and disappeared into the deep end of the pool, "thinks you're one lazy bitch." Surfacing a few moments later, she shook her hair from her eyes and flipped herself over onto her back. She drifted slowly toward the shallow end, hoping she looked thoroughly relaxed, grateful that Swan couldn't hear her labored breathing, the noisy thudding of her heart. After a while, her fingertips looked wrinkled and bleached, and a sudden breeze brought goosebumps to her arms. She stood in three feet of water, leaning back on her elbows against the ledge of the pool, a skinny little canal where stray leaves and dead mosquitoes floated aimlessly. What could she say to Swan, who had gotten to her feet and was lifting the baby from his stroller and coming toward her, offering a clean white towel like a truce.

"Are you planning on staying in there all day or *what*?" Swan said. "Don't be a jerk, Lace."

"Are you going to tell my father what I said?"

Swan raised Dakota over her head, wiggling him from side to side until he laughed joyously. "You're twelve years old," she said, her voice impassive. "Do you think I take seriously anything a twelve-year-old says to me? And besides, what do I care what your mother thinks of me? She's nothing much in my life, just a name that shows up in my checkbook once a month."

Fearless, her throat choked with anger, Lacey's voice emerged husky and deep. "You're nothing in her life, either. What do you think, we sit around talking about you all day? Don't you think we have better things to do?"

"I'm sure you do," said Swan mildly. She lowered the baby to her chest, nudged his head gently against her shoulder. "Want to get dressed and come to the Farmer's Market with me? I've got a lot of stuff to buy for dinner."

Lacey had only nodded. She felt diminished, as tiny and powerless as Dakota. She ached for her mother, to be sitting at her mother's side in the cab, the two of them laughing it up at the moronic name her father and Swan had chosen for their baby. *Montana?* She could hear her mother saying. *Indiana?*

"Never hit me ever again," she tells her mother now, and rubs the leg that has been slapped so indifferently there's not a mark on it.

"Just don't bug me about my smoking, okay?"

"Fine."

Her mother stops for a fare, a woman and a guy, both of them with long dyed-blond hair. The woman is all in black. On her feet are clunky-looking shining black oxfords, like policemen wear. Her companion has a safety pin fastened high up on the rim of his ear. They're going to lower Broadway, near Astor Place, the guy says, and slams the door.

"Why would I say I'm a witch if I wasn't?" the woman says plaintively. "If I tell you I can predict the future, you'd be really stupid not to believe me."

"So I'm stupid," says the guy. "Sue me."

Swiveling around in her seat for a better look, Lacey says, "*I* believe you." She has broken one of her mother's cardinal rules: no talking to passengers unless they talk to you first. (Let them have their privacy, she's told Lacey a dozen times. It's common courtesy, that's all.) But sometimes Lacey just can't help herself and has to open her big mouth.

"Thanks," says the witch. "I appreciate that."

"Don't you have any math homework to do?" Maxine says. "What happened to all those fractions you were supposed to be converting to percents?"

"Homework!" says the guy. "Far out. I myself haven't thought of homework since the late eighties."

"Did it hurt when you put that safety pin through your ear?" Lacey asks.

"No way. My girlfriend sprayed Freon on it and yours truly didn't feel a thing."

"Ex-girlfriend," says the witch. "And Freon's what they put in your refrigerator, dummy."

Lacey is beginning to feel a little dizzy facing the back seat; reluctantly, she turns herself forward. "Can you see into my future?" she says.

"I need something that belongs to you, something like a fingernail clipping would be good," the witch says.

"Ha!" says Maxine, and thumps the steering wheel. "You see how a nasty habit like biting your nails can interfere with your life?"

"How about an earring?" the witch suggests.

Lacey hands over the silver teardrop that hangs from her ear. She knows she is going to hear something truly awesome, a prediction that will keep her going for weeks, maybe even months. She might even write a poem about it, which she has to hand in for an English assignment due at the end of the week.

An index finger finds its way into her mouth and she chews on it vigorously, waiting for the witch to come through for her. "Please please please," she whispers.

"You are," the witch announces with her eyes closed, "a woman of great passion. But the men in your life have always been a disappointment to you. Except one, a man you will meet sometime around your fortieth birthday. This is the man who will turn your life around, who will set you on fire, as it were."

Maxine hits the brakes suddenly; the cab behind her taps her rear bumper, then blasts its horn. "That's me!" Maxine says. "And that's my earring you've got in your hand."

"Cool," says Lacey.

The witch's friend lets out a long leisurely whistle. "I'm blown away," he says. "But maybe it's strictly a co-inky-dink."

"No way! My mother and grandmother were witches, too. I told you, Howard, it's a gift that's passed down from generation to generation." The witch asks Maxine to let her off at the next corner. "I need to clear my head," she explains. "A nice long walk downtown is indicated, I think."

"What about *me*?" Lacey says. "I'm the one you were supposed to be working on."

"Sorry about that, sweetie," the witch says. "Maybe you should stay out of your mom's jewelry box in the future, you know?"

"Damn," Lacey says, and watches as the witch and her friend disappear down Broadway, their hands shoved into the back pockets of each other's jeans.

"There'll be other witches," her mother says. "Don't feel too badly."

They have come to a red light now; through the open window of the cab, Lacey hears the theme song from *The Brady Bunch* being played on a violin. The musician is someone in a Wolfman mask, tapping his sneaker to the music as he stands under the awning of a video store. "What a nerd," Lacey says, and rolls up her window. She looks at her mother's hands resting on the steering wheel, at her nicely tapered fingers, her sleek, polished nails. Except for the nails, they could be Lacey's hands. Her mother's profile is hers, too, dominated by a strong nose that loses its character whenever her mother turns so that she can be seen full-face. Her mother is, in fact, strikingly pretty. She claims to have been born under a lucky star, a claim Lacey sometimes finds a little hard to swallow. If she had really been born under a lucky star, Lacey bets, the two of them would be living in Los Angeles, lounging around their pool whenever they felt like it, waiting for her father to arrive home from work and open his arms to them, so welcoming and eager that they would fly instantly into his embrace. "What a loser," she says, thinking of Swan, a woman so unbelievably dumb that she is actually filled with pity for Lacey and her mother and their life together.

"Which loser is that?" Maxine says.

"Swan feels sorry for you because you drive a cab," Lacey reports.

"God, do I hate hearing that!" her mother says. "I hope you set her straight, at least."

"I told her she was a lazy bitch. Actually, I told her *you* said she was a lazy bitch."

Her mother laughs. "I can live with that," she says. "Hope she wasn't too upset."

"She wasn't."

"Well, that's good," says her mother, but she sounds disappointed. After a moment she says, "Not at all?"

"No, not really," Lacey says. "That's the way people are in California, I guess."

Her mother is silent for a long while. It is dusk now, and a fine drizzly rain is falling; with a sigh, she hunches up over the steering wheel. "You know," she says at last, "I'm thirty-seven years old and it doesn't feel like I've got my act together yet. But of course in three years or so," she says, turning to look at Lacey, rolling her eyes extravagantly, "I'll be meeting the man of my dreams, so I guess it's just a matter of hanging in there, isn't it."

"You were born under a lucky star," Lacey reminds her.

"That's old news, Kewpie doll."

Lacey backs herself against the door, draws up her knees, and rests her head on them desolately. Maybe it's the rain and the diminishing light that have gotten to her, maybe just the news that her mother has no faith in the witch's prophecy. "In L.A.," she says, "it never rained. Not once, the whole entire summer."

"Amazing," her mother says. "Kind of like paradise, huh?"

"We'd be happy there," says Lacey. She can see herself and her mother in her father's cool bright house, spreading their possessions throughout the endless closets, the two of them wandering from room to room just for fun, chasing each other up and down the winding staircase, collecting lemons and grapefruits from the trees in the backyard, falling asleep at night to the sound of howling coyotes. Swan and Dakota would be living in a house of their own, on some other planet. Her father, a tall guy with thinning blond hair, dressed in his New York clothes—black jeans and a faded denim shirt with pearly snaps—would be content in the company of his real family, connected to Lacey and her mother by a love so obvious that even strangers could see it in their faces. All of this comes to her now as clear as can be, vivid as a series of photographs snapped in just the right light, at just the right moment. She wants to show them to her mother, hear her murmur of approval, see the slow spread of her smile.

"What's so great about Swan, anyway?" she asks. "I just don't get it."

"You don't have to," her mother says. "And neither do I. We just have to get our checks in the mail every month."

Staring through the window, Lacey keeps a lookout for the witch, an ordinary figure in black striding along in policemen's shoes. She's dying to hear a forecast of her own life. Along with her mother's hands and profile, she's bound to inherit other things, as well—excellent driving skills and bad luck in the romance department, maybe. She remembers her mother's date a few months ago with one of her students, a sweet Pakistani guy named Hamza who spoke in a confusing sing-song and looked around their cluttered living room unsmilingly. He'd brought a half-dozen Milky Ways for Lacey in a paper bag, and white carnations for her mother. Returning home from her date with Hamza, her mother had undressed immediately and then sat around in her underwear listening to James Taylor albums from the 1970s, a sure sign that she was in her "depressed mode," as she called it. "Remind me never to go out with one of my students ever again," she told

Lacey. After Hamza came Timmy Wang, Osman Babacan, and Masato Kakuda. One day, Lacey realized, amazed, that she had memorized the lyrics to every song on the first couple of James Taylor albums. Her mother laughed when she heard this, but it wasn't funny.

Her father had found Swan right away, even before the divorce was final; Dakota was already six months old and her mother still hadn't met anyone she was willing to see more than once. It was hard to figure out why this was so or why her mother's happiness (or unhappiness) seemed to be linked to this. Lacey herself could be made happy by any number of things—an order of spare ribs from Chef Ho's, a social studies test that was postponed at the last minute, an invitation from her best friend, Heather, to spend the weekend at her country house in Woodstock. These things, of course, could not do the trick for her mother, who, though generally cheerful and energetic in the daytime, went into her depressed mode at night—more and more, recently, this seemed to be true.

Probably, Lacey thinks now, if you'd always thought you'd been born under a lucky star and then began to suspect that maybe you hadn't been after all, you couldn't help but feel disappointed.

"Want something to eat?" her mother asks her, offering a slightly overripe banana from the glove compartment. "And take those fingers out of your mouth, please."

"I can't," Lacey says. "I'm all stressed out."

"What?" Her mother laughs, a little uneasily. "What are you talking about?"

"There are a ton of pressures in my life," Lacey announces. "I think we should move to California."

"I see," says Maxine in a wobbly voice. "You want to live with your father, is that what you're telling me?"

Confused, Lacey begins to whimper. "We *deserve* to live there. In a big house with a heated pool and a housekeeper to pick our clothes up off the floor. Tell me why we don't deserve that." She thinks of all the hours she has spent riding around with her mother. Some days, after school, she goes home with friends, and once a week she has a piano lesson at the Y, but it seems to her that she spends half her life in this cab, observing the silent electronic accounting of the meter, listening to the exasperated sound of horns clamoring, her mother's exasperated voice telling her to quit biting her nails.

Her mother has double-parked and turned off the motor. She puts her arms around Lacey. Her hair smells of cigarette smoke as it brushes softly against Lacey's jaw. "Screw California," her mother murmurs. "Screw your father and what's-her-face." Lacey waits for the rest, but her mother has fallen silent, her eyes closed, tears leaking discreetly from their corners.

"Screw California," Lacey repeats dutifully, but that's as far as she's willing to go. If her mother wants to dis her father, that's *her* business.

Eventually, a man in a business suit and red snakeskin boots swings open the door and climbs into the back seat. "I need to get to Carnegie Hill," he says. "Ninety-third and Madison."

Maxine looks at him as if he has asked the impossible, to be driven across the ocean, perhaps. "What?" she says. Then, "Can't you see I'm off duty?"

"I see that you've been crying," the man says without much interest. "But I don't see that you're off duty. The sign on top of the cab says you're *on* duty. And if you're on duty, then you have to take me where I want to go. It's the law," he says reasonably. "You know that as well as I do."

"I'm off duty," Maxine says, and flicks the switch that illuminates the sign outside the cab.

"You know what *I* think?" the man says. "I think you just don't feel like going to Carnegie Hill right now. And that's against the law, as I've already pointed out to you."

"Take him," Lacey says. She draws away from her mother and turns to smile at the man. "Don't worry about it, she'll take you."

"It's raining," the man says. And then adds, as if looking for sympathy, "It's murder trying to get a cab in the rain." He rests his attaché case on his knees and snaps it open as the cab pulls out into traffic.

Lacey can tell that her mother is furious with her; she can see it in her rigid posture and the resolute way her hands have seized the steering wheel. In the back seat, the man is shuffling through some papers and whistling blithely.

"You're driving me crazy," Maxine says, but it's unclear to Lacey whom she means.

"Me?" Lacey says, and listens for a response. Now she begins to sing along with the man's whistling: *Ohhh, it's enough to be on your way.* If the witch is right, and there's always the possibility that she might be, Lacey thinks, they've got a three-year wait for the guy who's going to set her mother's life on fire. Or is it that he's going to set her mother on fire, which is something else entirely. Either way, it sounds both dangerous and thrilling, and Lacey wants to be along for the ride, seated up front, so close to the flames that they singe the fine, nearly invisible hairs on her delicate-boned, satiny arms, shaped precisely like her mother's.

PERSONAL CORRESPONDENCE (2001)

H is friends, refusing to listen, had thrown him a fortieth birthday party even though he'd begged them not to, begged like mad to be left alone with his VCR, a couple of early Woody Allen movies, and some chocolate hazelnut spread that he ate straight out of the jar with a spoon—his idea of heaven. Instead, in the end, Marc allowed himself to be dragged out of the city to an indoor tennis club in the suburbs, where he and a baker's dozen of his closest friends played for a couple of hours and shared a birthday cake sculpted in the shape of a Corvette. The word had gone out that he'd recently bought himself a Discman, and so most of his gifts were CDs, current music by groups whose names set his teeth on edge: Toad the Wet Sprocket, Phish, Smash Mouth, Limp Bizkit. "We decided it was time for you to move on," one of his roommates from college explained. "I mean, how many years can you keep listening to the same old Dylan albums, over and over again?" No mention was made that night of Marc's ex-wife, Carole, who had moved on, nearly six months ago, to a new life in Atlanta with her lover, an endocrinologist she'd met at a medical convention. Leaving behind Marc and their seven-year-old daughter, Sophie, Carole had hopped on a 727 with her beloved Dr. X (as Marc called him), promising to come back for Sophie when the time was right. "Over my dead body," Marc told Sophie, causing his daughter to sob softly, even after he explained to her that "over my dead body" simply meant "never." The shrink she'd seen for three sessions reported encouraging news: for a seven-year-old, Sophie was managing remarkably well. "She climbs into my bed every night at two-thirty," Marc complained ruefully over the phone. "Got any suggestions?" The shrink had just one: "Give her another week or so and then start locking your door. She'll get the message." The bill for this brutal bit of advice arrived in the mail only a day later and was for a hundred and seventy-five dollars. *Over my dead body*, Marc thought, and filed it away in an overstuffed drawer where he'd never find it.

Now, several weeks after his tennis party, he waited uneasily behind his locked door for the rap of his daughter's small fist. It was only 2:12; he was expecting her in exactly eighteen minutes. Propped up on one elbow reading *Rolling Stone*, he saw, out of the corner of his eye, the shameful layer of dust that coated the laminated top of his dresser. He'd been meaning, for days now, to get out the can of Endust from under the kitchen sink and take care of it, but somehow, inexplicably, he just hadn't managed it. There were, he knew, stiff dots of toothpaste spattering the bathroom mirror, long loose hairs wrapped around the drain in the shower, piles of unopened mail on the counter in the kitchen. And thirteen thank-you notes to be written for his birthday gifts. There were *some* things, at least, that he was still able to handle: he showed up at work faithfully day after day, shopped for meals on the way home, cooked relatively nutritious dinners for Sophie every night (well, almost every night—once or twice a week, he scooted across Lexington Avenue for pizza or an order of roast pork fried rice and two egg rolls), ran the shower for Sophie until the water was just the right temperature, played limitless rounds of gin with her, read to her for fifteen minutes while she lingered over her bowl of Triple Caramel Explosion ice cream, then slipped away just as she fell asleep. Sometimes he nodded off himself as he lay beside her, awakening in time for the late news and a movie he might have rented. Occasionally, while his daughter slept, he took the elevator to the basement of his apartment building and threw a load of laundry into the washing machine, hurrying back in case Sophie awoke crying for him. In the laundry room was a bulletin board cluttered with notices that had been tacked up by tenants and people in the neighborhood: index cards announcing a secondhand baby stroller or a laptop for sale, Xeroxed sheets from housekeepers and babysitters looking for work, business cards left by piano teachers, French teachers (Learn in your own home from a native Parisian!), and bridge instructors. And from time to time, scraps of paper with threatening messages regarding laundry thieves: "TO THE FUCKER WHO STOLE MY RALPH LAUREN NIGHTGOWN FROM THE DRYER—BEWARE—GOD WILL GET PERVERTS LIKE YOU!!!" Remembering this, Marc laughed out loud, and then suddenly stiffened, watching as the stainless steel doorknob rotated quietly, tentatively, then more rapidly, rattling frantically now.

"Go back to bed, sweetie," he said in a monotone.

The rattling continued. "I can't sleep," said Sophie.

"How about some Tylenol PM?"

"What?"

"This is unacceptable," said Marc. "You're too old for this."

"My eyes won't stay closed. I tell them to, but they won't listen."

"Take your hand off the doorknob, Sophie."

"If you let me in, I'll only stay until I'm ready to fall asleep and then you can bring me back to my own bed, okay?"

"Not happening, kiddo. Get back in your room."

A few moments passed in silence as Sophie considered this. "I love you," she said coyly. "I really really really love you."

"Me too," said Marc. "But in this household everyone sleeps in his or her own bed."

"Mommy doesn't."

"Mommy is no longer a member of this household," Marc said, and got up to open the door.

In the morning, he found Sophie lying diagonally across the bed, the tip of her index finger resting in her belly button. He stroked her fine, tangled hair, traced the outline of her small perfect ear. Opening one eye, she smiled at him.

"Get back where you belong," he said. "Scram."

"Buy me a kitten and I'll sleep in my own bed for the rest of my life."

"Promises promises," Marc said.

At noon he lunched with a client who told him how terrible he looked.

"Define 'terrible,'" Marc said. He leaned forward and his tie grazed a little tin cup of cocktail sauce.

The client, a best-selling author of a trio of self-help books, was thinking of writing her next book about either survivors of incest or preschoolers on Ritalin. She shook her head at Marc. "Your color's ghastly and there are these big pouches under your eyes," she said disapprovingly. "And you're certainly not your usual buoyant self." She was dressed in a flame-red suit without a blouse underneath and Marc allowed himself a good long look at her cleavage from time to time.

"I don't seem buoyant?" he said. "Well, maybe I need a nap."

"Two hundred units of Vitamin E wouldn't hurt, either," said Kristine. "Did you know it prolongs the life of your red blood cells? Four hundred units a day would really perk you up." Stretching toward him, she lifted his tie out of the cocktail sauce.

"You have, what, two kids?" Marc said.

"I've got three," said Kristine. "Three very special boys, though the four-year-old's a big pain in the ass. He's sweet and adorable, but his energy level's way up there, which is why we've got him on Ritalin, if you know what I mean."

"Any of them ever try to come into your bed in the middle of the night?"

"Is the sky blue?" said Kristine. "Do birds have wings? Did you read chapter four of my last book?"

"Yes, and yes, and, I'm ashamed to say, I can't remember a thing about it."

"Well, every child in the world wants to sleep in his parents' bed. And you've got to let them know that's a major no-no. You've got to nip it in the bud before things get out of hand."

"And I won't forget about those four hundred units of Vitamin C," Marc said.

"E," said Kristine. "C's for warding off colds."

Marc nodded. He slid his credit card from his wallet and signaled to the waiter. He took another leisurely look at Kristine's cleavage.

"So," Kristine said, "Ritalin or incest, what do you think?"

Someone had posted, on the laundry room bulletin board, a notice that was unlike anything he'd seen there before. It was printed on mint-green paper and said:

> Too busy to deal with your personal correspondence?
> Columbia grad student with excellent writing skills can
> make your life easier. I can send weekly letters to your
> widowed mother in Florida, birthday cards, anniversary
> cards, thank-you notes, etc. Reasonable rates.
> Leave message and I'll get back to you.
>
> HoneyRose 722-3636

"HoneyRose," Marc said aloud, and it sounded like the name of a stripper, or maybe even a hooker. Certainly not a Columbia grad student with excellent writing skills. He'd forgotten to bring down a laundry bag and his arms were loaded with toasty, neatly folded towels and sheets. It was time for the eleven o'clock news. Upstairs on the eighteenth floor, his daughter was sound asleep, her arms wrapped around the preternaturally gentle, very expensive Himalayan kitten he'd bought from a breeder in Manalapan, New Jersey. "Honey-Rose," he said again, and memorized her number, at least for the short term. In the elevator he wondered if it was too late to call this alleged graduate student. His birthday had come and gone almost two months ago and the thank-you notes were still nothing more than a hazy, guilt-provoking thought that plagued him once in a while. His widowed mother in Boca Raton had always been big on such niceties. (*Someone gives you a gift, you need to write a few lines to show your gratitude. If you don't, you're just being plum rude.* How many times during his childhood had he heard *that* from her?) She was currently in the habit of sending him sweet little notes, usually twice a week, which he couldn't be bothered answering. He felt bad about it, but not bad enough. He was a single parent, for Christ's sake; a phone call to Boca Raton every couple of weeks was the best he could manage.

Maybe this HoneyRose, with her promise to make his life easier, was on to something here.

Upstairs, he checked on his sleeping child, shoved the towels and sheets into the linen closet, and called HoneyRose. Her machine said she was unable to come to the phone, and he left a halting message that made him sound, if not exactly stupid, then ill at ease and inarticulate. Ill at ease about what? He had no idea, really.

After the news, he watched Jay Leno for a while. His guest was Carly Simon, who looked, Marc thought admiringly, pretty damn good for someone over fifty. He dozed off listening to her talk about her ex-husband. When the phone rang, his mouth was dry and there was a damp spot on his shirt sleeve where he'd drooled. "Hello?" he said drowsily, and sank back into his seat on the living-room couch.

"This is HoneyRose. So what can I do for you?"

She didn't sound like a stripper; she sounded businesslike and a little impatient. He didn't know what he was supposed to say to her. Was this like a job interview? If so, he was the one doing the interviewing, wasn't he? "I've never done this sort of thing before," he said, as if she really were a stripper or even a hooker, as if there were something vaguely illegal going on here. At his feet, Jazzmine the kitten meowed piteously; it was more like a whimper and so poignant that Marc reached down to pull her into his lap, saying, "What do you want, darling?"

"What do I want?" said HoneyRose. "I want to know if you're serious about hiring me. Because if you're not, you can't call me 'darling,' okay?"

"Actually, I was talking to the cat, but I do want to hire you. Or at least I think I do."

"Okay, look, what I can be is kind of like your social secretary, okay?"

"I have no social life to speak of," Marc confided. "I'm a single parent and I don't get out much. But I do have a load of thank-you notes that I can't bring myself to write." He paused. "You probably think I'm incredibly lazy, don't you?" he said apologetically.

"I never pass judgment on my clients," said HoneyRose. "How many of these notes do you need?"

"Thirteen."

"Well, let's see, how about...a hundred and thirty dollars for the whole deal? And I don't take checks or credit cards."

"No problem." That he was willing to blow more than a hundred bucks to dispense with some thank-you notes surely didn't speak well of him. *You lazy bastard*, he thought. "Did I mention my widowed mother down in Boca Raton?" he heard himself say.

"That's another one of my areas of specialization," said HoneyRose. "I know just how to deal with those old ladies.

Too bad, I could have helped you pick out a Mother's Day present last month. I charge twenty-five dollars an hour to act as your shopping consultant."

"Sounds reasonable to *me*," said Marc. He could feel himself growing lazier and lazier as the conversation progressed, the will and energy to take care of anything at all draining swiftly from him. Even the thought of rising from the couch and going into the bathroom to wash his face and brush his teeth before bed seemed wearying. And showering and shaving tomorrow morning—forget it. Ever since Carole had flown the coop, he'd been scrambling urgently to keep the gears of his daily life properly meshed, and sometimes—big surprise—the effort exhausted him. It *was* a big surprise. As it turned out, he'd underestimated what it would take to keep a seven-year-old happy. A couple of mornings ago, after he'd braided his daughter's hair to the best of his limited ability, Sophie looked in the mirror, frowned, and told him it was pigtails she wanted after all.

"With scrunchies at the top *and* the bottom," she said, like a diner in a restaurant decisively adding mushrooms and onions to her order.

"I don't *do* pigtails," he told her.

"You do," Sophie insisted. "It's easy. You make a part in the back, a *straight* part, and then you do the rest."

"I'm not good at those things." *Why can't you just do it yourself*, he almost said.

"But you have to be," Sophie told him. "You're the only one here, right?"

"Right," he said. He was close to tears, which frightened him. He contemplated calling Carole and ruining her day with a few casually chosen words. How had he fallen in love with a woman willing to abandon her child in greedy, self-indulgent pursuit of her own fucking happiness? He'd underestimated a lot, it seemed, and recalled another one of his mother's incantations: *You wheel with people and you deal with people but you're a fool if you think you can ever really know them.*

Not even your own wife?

Apparently not.

He'd done a crummy job on his daughter's pigtails and could tell he wasn't going to get any better at it.

"So when do you want me to come over?" HoneyRose was saying.

The sooner the better.

He vacuumed and dusted in honor of her arrival, and print-ed out a list of names and addresses of everyone who'd been at this fortieth birthday, along with the gifts they'd given.He put Sophie and Jazzmine to bed together, and shaved for the second time that day. He swept the coffee table clean of mag-azines and newspapers and videotapes, and put out a bowl of low-fat vegetable chips. His khakis were pristine, the cuffs of his denim shirt neatly rolled past his wrists.

HoneyRose was, he realized, the first woman to set foot in his apartment since his wife had vanished from the scene.

"Hey," she said. "How are ya?" She dropped her briefcase to shake his hand.

"It's nice to meet you," he said.

Well, it was and it wasn't. She was slender, with a slight-ly sharp nose and pretty, hazel eyes. Her black jeans were very tight and her cropped T-shirt revealed an impressively flat stomach. The blazer that went over the T-shirt had a pin about the size of a half-dollar stabbed through the lapel; a Star of David was printed on it. Marc squinted at it, as if he were near-sighted, which he wasn't. "Oy vay, I'm gay!" the pin proclaimed in bright yellow, and it was like a kick in the teeth. He hadn't had sex in six months, a fact that was on his mind more than he'd like to admit. Without sex, you had no life to speak of, not really. Or at least the life you had was a sadly incomplete one. There was no getting around it; he lusted after this girl with her exposed stomach ornamented with a gold ring that gleamed so compellingly in his living room. Never mind that he hadn't a prayer of getting his hands in her nearly pitch-black hair that was swept away from her face with two tortoise-shell combs, or that his mouth would never come anywhere near her breasts with their nipples that had hardened in the breeze of his air-conditioner. Of course, if she'd been straight, he still might have lost out on everything, but surely there would have been a chance of winning her over one night while she worked composing clever, heartfelt expressions of his gratitude to his friends. Or so he imagined.

"Would you like some chips?" he asked indifferently as she sat herself down on his couch.

"They're pretty weird-looking," she said. "What are they?"

"Oh, yucca, taro, parsnip, all kinds of stuff that's probably good for you."

"I generally don't like stuff that's good for me."

"No?"

"I'm a drinker and a smoker," she confessed, "and I sleep about four and a half hours a night. But that's all going to come to an end soon enough." She took off her blazer and squashed it into her lap, then crossed her legs. He watched her every move with great interest; he just couldn't help himself.

"Really?" he said.

"Absolutely. My girlfriend and I are planning on having a baby as soon as we can, and since I'm the one who's better suited for this pregnancy, I'm obviously going to have to turn over a new leaf. But let's get back to the thank-you notes." Unbuckling her briefcase, she took out a large manila envelope and opened the flap. "I brought some samples of my work. Everything will have to be on the computer, of course, since I can't possibly duplicate your handwriting, but don't worry, it's all going to be very personal."

"Why are you the one who's better suited for the pregnancy?" Marc said recklessly. "If you don't mind my asking."

HoneyRose shrugged. "Well, I'm twenty-nine and Lily's forty-one, does that answer your question?"

"What about graduate school?"

"One more semester and I'll have my master's."

"Raising a child is an enormous effort," he said. "It ain't easy, trust me."

"Thanks for the warning," HoneyRose said.

"And what about your parents?"

"Excuse me?"

"What do they think about all this?"

"I wouldn't know," HoneyRose said brusquely. "We don't speak. I mean, we haven't spoken in a long, long while."

"I'm sorry," said Marc. "As a parent myself, I was just wondering, that's all."

HoneyRose smiled at him. "You're a very nosy person," she said. "But I don't mind, I'm nosy as well."

Was she? She hadn't, after all, asked him a single question about himself. "Well, my life's an open book," he said. "What do you want to know?"

"What style would you like to have the notes written in? Gracious? Affectionate? Funny?"

"All of the above," Marc said.

"Okay. I'll have them here for you in a week so you can sign them. Either I can mail them to you or I can come back and we can go over them together, just to make sure you're happy with them, but I get paid no matter what. Oh, and your mom in Boca Raton? What are your, uh, needs regarding her?"

To tell the truth, he'd forgotten all about her. "Could you write to her twice a week?" he said. "Something short—four or five sentences ought to do it."

"And what would be the subject?" HoneyRose had a legal pad in her lap now and a pen in hand.

"Nothing," Marc said. "That's the beauty of it—you can write about absolutely nothing, just like she does. It's the idea of it, the idea of getting mail from me that's the important part here."

"Exactly what kind of nothing are we talking about?" HoneyRose asked. "The weather? What you had for dinner last night? The movie you went to last week?"

"Rented," said Marc. "The movie I *rented*. I never go out to the movies, it's just too much of a hassle to get a babysitter. And anyway, who would I go with? All my friends are married or remarried and I'm not the kind to be a third wheel, if you get the picture."

HoneyRose was writing furiously on her legal pad now. "You have a child, right? I need to know his or her name, of course, and age. What grade is he or she in school?"

Taking the legal pad from her, and the pen from between her fingers, he filled in the details. He tried to read the notes she had written, but surprisingly, her handwriting was a god-awful mess and he could barely make out a single word. "What does *this* say?" he asked, pointing to what appeared to be two words separated by an ampersand.

"That?" HoneyRose said. "That's my own personal shorthand."

"So what does it say?"

"It doesn't matter," she said, retrieving the pad and pen and putting them back in her briefcase. There were silver rings on three fingers of each hand, and her child-sized nails, not much bigger than Sophie's, were polished a silvery pink. Her hands moved swiftly to zip and buckle the briefcase shut.

"What does it say?" Marc persisted. He guessed it wasn't anything of much consequence, but he needed to know anyway.

"Subject presents symptoms of lethargy and depression," HoneyRose murmured, keeping her head down.

"SUBJECT? What is this, a psychology experiment?" Marc said, outraged. "What kind of grad student are you, anyway?"

"Don't get pissed off at me," HoneyRose said. She put her small hand on his knee. "Please."

"Some social secretary!" Marc said. "And your handwriting is abominable."

"Look," said HoneyRose. Her hand was still resting on his knee. "I *am* getting my degree in psychology, I'll cop to that. But I really am in the letter-writing business. And my interest in people makes me all the better suited for it, don't you think?"

"What I think," said Marc, "is that I'm capable of writing my own damn thank-you notes. Despite my lethargy and depression, that is." He stared coldly at the button on her lapel; he was on to her now. "You're not even gay, are you?" he said. "That's part of your experiment, isn't it? Just to see how people react."

"Oh, I'm gay all right," said HoneyRose. "And there's no experiment, believe me. I was just jotting down some clinical observations, that's all. Force of habit," she said. "Can't you forgive me?"

"And why would I want to do that?"

"Because fundamentally you're a nice guy, and because I need your business. And I'm a terrific letter-writer. Your mom's going to be delighted with you, trust me." She was already at the door when she proposed, "How about I do this all on spec? I'll come back next week, and if you're not happy with my work, you don't have to pay me."

"All right all right," he said, and she smiled at him.

"By the way," she said casually as she opened the door to let herself out, "Lily and I are in the market for a donor, so if you know of anyone, gimme a buzz."

"Donor?"

Sperm donor," said HoneyRose, and shut the door behind her.

Now that Sophie was content in her own bed, it was the cat who insisted on resting her head against Marc's pillow night after night after she left Sophie. Jazzmine had pale blue eyes, a wedge-shaped head, and chronic, though minor, respiratory problems. She kept Marc up with her wheezing and snorting, and no matter how many times he shoved her to the foot of the bed, she returned to his pillow, purring so blissfully that he didn't have the heart to lock her out. At the office he occasionally dozed over the manuscripts that cluttered his desk, and drank endless cans of Pepsi in an effort to stay alert. He tried, too, to avoid thinking about HoneyRose, to avoid fantasizing about proving himself to be the sperm donor of her dreams. It was a crazy idea, really, but in his moments of greatest optimism, he had to admit he had a lot to offer—he was smart and decent-looking and in perfect health, and there was no history of cancer or heart disease or diabetes in his family. And, of course, though this probably wasn't a point in his favor and might, in fact, instantly disqualify him, he was dying to sleep with HoneyRose. He would never let her know this, he decided, but would, instead, present himself as someone possessing a diploma from an Ivy League institution, stellar SAT scores, and twenty/twenty vision. Never mind that his wife had wearied of him and traded him in for an upscale model with an MD to his name; this, too, Marc would keep to himself.

When his client Kristine called to say she'd decided to do a book on pregnancy after forty, he made no attempt to talk her out of it even though he was sure there must have been dozens of books on the subject. A best-selling author was, after all, a best-selling author.

"This will be from my own personal perspective," she told

him. "I myself was forty-one when my youngest was born and I came through with flying colors."

"Got any thoughts on sperm donors?" he said nonchalantly.

"Well, that's fine for people in desperate circumstances, I suppose, though not for a normal, healthy person with a normal, healthy husband for a partner...Maybe I ought to include a chapter on it," Kristine mused, "for all those women out there in desperate circumstances. Thanks for the suggestion, cutie. And speaking of which, have you been taking your Vitamin E?"

"Religiously," Marc lied. "Type up a proposal and an outline and email it to me, okay?" After he hung up, he rested his head on a three hundred and fifty-page epic poem and napped for a while.

On his way home from work, on the crowded shuttle between Times Square and Grand Central, he found himself seated across from a young guy wearing a soiled three-piece white suit and a dingy-looking stovepipe hat. "Sod-om and Go-mor-rah," the man sang tunelessly, again and again. And then, at last, he cut to the chase, and boomed, "GOD CREATED ADAM AND EVE, *NOT* ADAM AND STEVE! AND WOE TO THOSE WHO DO NOT HEED!"

"Shut up, you asshole, you're giving me a headache," a man in paint-spattered workboots and overalls growled.

"Me too," said Marc. A growl was what he'd had in mind, but the two little words came out in a whisper, and he hung his head, like HoneyRose when she'd diagnosed him with a psychoneurotic disorder or two.

Well, he had news for her: he was healthy as a horse. His depression had lifted, and he was, like the lunatic across the aisle, a man on a mission.

They went over the thank-you notes together at his dining-room table. The perfume HoneyRose wore smelled delicious and expensive, like some extravagant dessert he couldn't wait for a taste of. Her mouth was glossed the same silvery pink as her nails and he imagined himself getting a taste of that, too. The thank-you's were printed on heavy, cream-colored paper that had been folded meticulously into note-sized cards. She'd done excellent work; each note was, as promised, humorous and affectionate, each slightly different from the one before it.

"And here's a note for your mom," HoneyRose said. "It touches all the bases—the weather, which I described as 'summer-like,' the Italian dinner you cooked for a couple of friends, the—"

"What friends?" Marc interrupted. "I never cook for friends."

"Well, you do *now*," HoneyRose told him. "I used some of the names from the thank-you notes. Logan and Wayne, I think."

"Very resourceful."

"Yup. You fixed them home-made lobster ravioli, made fresh with your new pasta machine."

"And what pasta machine might that be?"

"I don't know, I'm trying to give you a slightly more interesting life here, all right? Don't you want to know what you guys had for dessert?"

"What?"

"Tiramisù, home-made, obviously."

"Have I taken a cooking class recently?"

"At the Y," HoneyRose said. "It'll do your mother's heart good to know you're keeping busy."

"I guess I'm impressed with the new me," Marc said hesitantly. This was rather like cheating, wasn't it, and probably he ought to put a stop to it. *Stick to the facts*, he should have told HoneyRose, *you know, the dry, unembellished truth.* So his mother thought he was out there making an effort; where was the harm in that, really? "Very impressed," he repeated, this time a little more enthusiastically.

"Thanks," said HoneyRose. "I told you I'd do a good job." She went through her purse and handed him several books of postage stamps. "So that's a hundred and thirty-nine dollars, plus ten, plus twenty for the stamps."

"Fine," he said, but made no move to get his wallet. He stared at the clingy V-necked shirt HoneyRose was wearing. "Any luck finding a sperm donor?"

"Not yet," she said, "but we're working on it."

"I was thinking," he heard someone say, and then his mouth went dry. His palms and the hollows under his arms suddenly felt damp. Oh, for a beta blocker or two, he thought. He rubbed his gluey palms together in disgust.

"You were thinking what?"

"Actually, regarding the sperm donor search, I was thinking about me."

"You?" She looked at him with amusement and, perhaps, the slightest distaste. "You?"

"What's wrong with me?"

"No offense, but for one thing, you're not tall enough."

"I'm six feet even," he said defensively.

"No way!"

"Five eleven and a half, I swear."

"In that case, I'd have to say your posture could be better."

She was right about that; he immediately sat up straighter in his seat, throwing back his shoulders hopefully.

"And for another thing," HoneyRose continued, "we were looking for someone with blue or green eyes."

Now he was truly incensed. "Oh, give me a break," he said. "How shallow is that? What kind of values do you people have?"

"Excuse me?"

"Look, here I am, a Phi Beta Kappa, summa cum laude

graduate of an Ivy League school, a guy in terrific health, willing to do you and your girlfriend a big favor, no strings attached, and you're ready to disqualify me because of the color of my irises? If that isn't the very definition of superficial, I don't know what is."

"Well...all right, what were your SAT's like?" HoneyRose said, reconsidering, and he was back in the running again.

"Combined scores of 1530," he said proudly, though more than two decades had passed since anyone, including himself, had given a shit about them. "And that was without a prep course of any kind," he added.

"And what Ivy League school are we talking about here?"

"University of Pennsylvania."

"Penn?" HoneyRose said, and that not entirely benign look of amusement crossed her face again. "Well, it's an Ivy League school, but just barely. I mean, no offense, but what kind of cachet could it possibly have when people are always confusing it with Penn State?"

She was insufferable; he saw that now, and almost wanted to smack her, at the very least wanted her insufferable presence gone from his sight this instant. The V-necked shirt she'd chosen to wear for this business meeting of theirs showed, at the bottom of the V, a bit of black lace from her bra, and he couldn't help but envision his finger slipping gently under it, just to feel the warm, delicate flesh so close to her beating heart. "I was Phi Beta Kappa," he said meekly.

"Yeah, so you said. Can you prove it? Don't they give you a little gold key or something?"

He couldn't tell her the truth, which was that his mother wore it around her neck on a gold chain, along with a charm which said "#1 Grandma" and which had been given to her by Carole after Sophie was born. "Prove it?" he said, and then he was leaning toward her, his eyes half-closed now as his mouth met hers. It seemed an act both foolhardy and brash, even a little perverse, but what did he have to lose? Her lips tasted pepperminty and made his tingle, and he understood that she was returning his kiss, not tenderly but urgently, the lovely warmth of her tongue generously filling his mouth.

"Well, that proves *something*," she said, drawing back from him and wiping her mouth daintily with one finger. "Though I have no idea what."

"I can provide letters of recommendation as needed," he said.

"We're interviewing a couple of other candidates," HoneyRose told him. She touched his mouth with the fingertip that had just touched her own. "Or at least Lily thinks we are."

"Lily," he said darkly, and sighed.

"I'm so confused, I feel as if my head is going to explode," said HoneyRose.

His mother called to thank him for his notes just as he and Sophie were sitting down to dinner. "Two in one week," she said jubilantly. "Imagine that." And then, sounding suspicious, "What's gotten into you all of a sudden?"

"Nothing," Marc said. He spooned some chicken casserole onto his daughter's plate and poured her a glass of soda.

"I'm not hungry," Sophie announced.

"It's dinnertime. You *have* to be hungry," Marc said, and told his mother to hold on.

"Well, I'm not," Sophie insisted. "But if you let me watch TV, maybe I *will* be."

"Not a chance," said Marc. In the background, Yo-Yo Ma played a haunting, melancholy Bach sonata. "Dinnertime is classical music time, you know that," he said firmly.

"That chicken is so gross," said Sophie. "It's a yucky color, and it smells like throw-up, kind of."

She had a point there. "It's the cream of mushroom soup, I

think," Marc said. "I followed the recipe exactly, and this is how it turned out."

"Talk to me, sweetie," his mother urged. "If you don't, I'm going to fall asleep with the phone in my hand."

Though they'd had pizza the night before, Marc slipped a frozen Pizza for One into the toaster oven. He let Sophie turn on the TV even though it violated one of the household's cardinal rules. Clearly he wasn't much of a father tonight; if anything, he was a cartoon of a father, a buffoonish figure easily manipulated by any child at all with half a brain in her head. Well, sometimes you just couldn't do any better than that.

"Sweetie?" his mother said in her most plaintive voice.

"Sorry," he said. "I'm listening."

"Well, don't be angry at me, but I thought I saw your father again today. He was one of the EMT workers who came to get poor Mrs. Lasky who lives on my floor. She's ninety-six and lives with her seventy-five-year-old daughter and has everything in the world wrong with her, but she's all right, it was nothing life-threatening. But I took one look at that EMT worker and for a moment his face became Daddy's and I'll tell you, I almost fainted. Sometimes, you know, I think I'm losing my mind. Do *you* think I'm losing it? If it's Alzheimer's, I'd rather shoot myself right now," his mother said.

"You're not losing your mind," Marc reassured her, as he had twice before when she'd imagined she'd seen his father—once when a repairman came to fix her dishwasher, and once when her podiatrist walked into the treatment room where she'd been waiting for him and began to cut her toenails for her.

"Well, if I'm not losing my mind, then what is it?"

"You miss him," Marc said, "that's all." It was canned laughter flowing from the TV that set his nerves on edge and he yelled at Sophie to lower the volume.

"Missing someone that much can't be good for a person,"

his mother said. "Which is why I was so delighted to hear about this new girlfriend of yours."

"What?" He flew to the TV and put it on "mute." "Get into your pajamas!" he hissed at Sophie, who looked at him as if he were deranged.

"I didn't have my dinner yet. And I'm watching *Friends* without the sound on," she complained.

"Go!"

"Not that three dates makes her your girlfriend exactly," his mother was saying, "but it's a step in the right direction, don't you think? I'm thrilled for you, pussy cat, even as my heart aches for yours truly."

"You've got to get out more, go places with your friends, join one of those reading groups where they discuss a different book every week or every month or whatever," Marc said, desperate to end the conversation and call HoneyRose, who had already, in her second letter, gone too far. What chutzpah! Really! He'd have to establish some guidelines, set limits on this life she was so keen on inventing for him. Otherwise, next thing he knew, he'd have a new wife and a brood of stepchildren to contend with. And he wasn't even officially divorced yet.

"Well," his mother said, "at least one of us is headed in the right direction."

"A positive attitude, that's what *you* need," Marc advised. He was flipping through his tiny leather address book frantically, searching for HoneyRose's number. He'd put his life in her hands and he didn't even know her last name, he realized.

He found her on the inside of the front cover of the address book, next to the numbers for Sophie's pediatrician and the Chinese restaurant where he got his roast pork fried rice once a week.

"I wish you all the best," his mother said, "and please send my regards to this new lady friend of yours, this Joanna."

"Joanna," he said grimly. "I'll be sure and do that."

Dialing HoneyRose's number a moment later, all he got was her answering machine. His blood was boiling but he managed to keep his voice clipped and controlled as he left his message: "Please be advised that Joanna and I are not now nor have we ever been, a couple." Was that enough? "And you and I need to talk," he added. "ASAP."

Sophie had returned and positioned herself an inch or two from the TV set; she was reading the actors' lips, Marc realized. Her nightgown was on back to front and she sucked absently on the tip of her braid. Marc snuck up behind her and carted her back from the TV, but first he turned the sound on.

"I'm sorry I yelled at you," he said. "You're a wonderful little girl and I shouldn't have yelled like that." Sophie sniffled a few times and he wondered if she'd been off crying in her room while he was on the phone. "Oh, sweetheart," he said guiltily.

She sniffled again. "The pizza's burning," she said. "Maybe it's on fire."

He was watching *Inspector Morse* on PBS when, a little after midnight, HoneyRose returned his call. Morse was a man after Marc's own heart—he was smart, cranky, and almost never wrong about anything. He probably wouldn't have made a particularly good husband or friend, but you had to admire the guy, Marc thought. He would, no doubt, have made a top-notch sperm donor, with his clear blue eyes, splendid bearing, and his degree from Oxford. Knowing HoneyRose, she might have dismissed him simply because he fell several inches short of six feet, Marc thought irritably, and then had to remind himself that Morse was, after all, a fictional character, and that it didn't matter *what* HoneyRose's opinion of him was.

"What's up with that message you left me?" she said. "If

you're going to criticize the work I'm doing, we might as well call it quits right now."

"You stepped over the line," said Marc. "I don't *want* an imaginary girlfriend, if that's all right with you."

"I'm adding texture to your life, okay? We don't want your mother thinking you're circling the drain, do we? Like she doesn't have enough to worry about."

Stung, Marc said, "Is that what you think of me, that my life is going down the tubes?"

"Relax," said HoneyRose. "Calm down and listen to me, will you. I actually have good news. It turns out Lily wants to meet you."

"Sweet!" he said. He'd forgotten all about Inspector Morse, who, detesting the sight of blood, had turned his head away as a corpse was being removed from the crime scene. "Hold it a sec," said Marc, and went to feed a tape into the VCR. It occurred to him that he'd been watching all too much TV since Carole had left him, but perhaps that was to be expected. What else was he going to do? Enroll in a cooking class at the Y with a bunch of desperate singles openly on the prowl? But HoneyRose was right; his life *did* need more texture.

"So let's make a date," she said.

"Joanna's back in the game," he said. "I've reconsidered."

"Smart move," HoneyRose said. "Good for you!"

"So are we all going to go out for a drink or something?" he asked her. "Minus Joanna, of course."

"Here's the thing." HoneyRose paused, just long enough for Marc's heart to sink in anticipation of what had to be bad news. "Lily wants to see you in your...natural habitat. And she'd like to meet Sophie as well."

"Sophie? No way. We're leaving her out of this, if you don't mind. And what's this about my natural habitat? What am I, an animal in the wild?"

"Look, I'm going to be straight with you," said Honey-Rose. "Basically, I've decided you're my first choice, but there are still a couple of other candidates Lily's sort of hot on. And the competition's pretty impressive, that's all I'm saying."

Instantly, he envisioned a line-up of doctors, lawyers, and Yale professors, all of them blue-eyed, well over six feet tall, and clever enough to charm the pants off HoneyRose *and* her girl-friend. How could he possibly compete with these guys, these fucking übermenschen of his imagination? He let out a long, deep sigh of helplessness. He remembered the warmth of Hon-eyRose's tongue so unexpectedly filling his mouth; there would be more of that little piece of heaven but only if he won Lily's vote. He sighed again, this time with utter resignation. "Fine, she can meet Sophie, but only for five minutes," he conceded.

"She's not an ogre or anything," HoneyRose said. "She's the love of my life, for God's sake."

There it was: a sick headache that got him right between his unexceptional brown eyes. It descended with a cruel swift-ness and intensity, and just before the room began its slow spin, he disconnected HoneyRose without apology.

Leaving nothing to chance, he hired a housekeeper to turn the apartment upside down and shake out all the dust, straight-en up his closets (in the unlikely event that Lily happened to peek inside), and wash the kitchen and bathroom floors, something he hardly ever remembered to do. He went for a haircut, not at the barber's, but at a trendy place on Second Avenue called Hair, Thair, and Everywhair, a salon where the stylists were dressed in what looked like black surgical scrubs and the guy who worked on him kept trying to convince him that a couple of artfully placed streaks of color were just what he needed. The haircut and shampoo set him back eighty-five bucks, and he cursed Lily silently but fiercely as he plunked down his Mastercard.

He told Sophie that a couple of new friends of his were stopping by and that, as a special treat, he would rent her a movie.

"On a school night?" she said, astonished. "That's breaking the rules."

"Sometimes rules are meant to be broken," he said, but didn't elaborate.

"Can we break some other rules tonight?" Sophie asked, getting into the spirit of things.

"Nope, just that one."

"Well, I'd still like to sleep in your bed with you. Even though I have Jazzmine, I'm still a little bit lonely."

Join the club, he wanted to say as she rested her head against his shoulder.

"I think I'm going to make a list of all the rules I hate the most," Sophie said.

"Do you need paper?" he offered. "Pencils?"

Sophie pursed her sweet, rosy lips disapprovingly. "You should be nicer to me," she recommended. "I'm the only child you have."

So this was the love of her life, this little blond shrimp with her short, gelled hair slicked back so severely, showcasing those ears busily lined with a dozen of the tiniest silver hoops. She couldn't have been more than five feet; beside her, half a foot taller, HoneyRose loomed like a giant in shorts and a T-shirt. The shrimp herself was wearing a black pants suit and a closed, unfriendly expression; clearly this was no social call. She was here on official business, like some caseworker who'd been assigned to evaluate his fitness as a father. (One false move and poor Sophie could wind up a ward of the state.) When she finally smiled at him, it was a smile that showed no teeth, no warmth, no sign that she knew damn well this was excruciating for at least one of them.

"Come on in," Marc said, resisting the impulse to yank HoneyRose inside and then slam the door shut as rudely as possible in Lily's cold white face. She was already looking him over appraisingly; what was he, after all, but a male of the species capable of providing stud service? He'd brought this on himself, of course, but what had he been *thinking*? Only of HoneyRose's hardened nipples grazing his bare chest, his hands cupping the sharp blades of her hips, their bodies so gracefully entwined it was obvious they were meant for this.

And now he was going to blow it all by saying exactly what was on his mind. "You know," he began, and ushered them into the living room, where the two women seated themselves on the love seat, nearly on top of one another, their thighs and elbows touching. "You know, I've never felt so uncomfortable in my own home before."

"That's terrible," said HoneyRose sympathetically. "This is not a big deal, I'm telling you."

"Not a big deal?" Lily said. "Are you kidding? What could be a bigger deal than this, honey."

"Is that Honey with an uppercase 'H,' short for Honey-Rose?" Marc asked. "Or just an ordinary term of endearment?"

"I told you he was funny," said HoneyRose.

"Yeah, hilarious," said Lily. "Who plays the piano?" she asked Marc, gesturing toward the black walnut Yamaha that fit perfectly under the dining-room window.

"That would be me," he admitted, feeling as if he'd just confessed to a crime.

"Well, could you play for us? I'd love to hear something."

What was this, an audition for Juilliard? He hadn't played in many months, not since his marriage had gone belly-up. And he'd forgotten to tell the housekeeper to dust the keys, he realized. He blew at them, scattering tiny gray puffs in the air, and played, resentfully at first, the opening of "Rhapsody in Blue." Though the book was in front of him and he flipped the pages at the right moments, he was playing by heart, doing a pretty good job of it, his fingers moving deftly along the keyboard, body and soul overtaken by the music as Lily and even HoneyRose became ghosts whose presence he could no longer feel. And then, in the middle of a page, he simply came to a stop, exhausted. He slumped at the keyboard, carelessly displaying his bad posture.

"Wow," said HoneyRose reverently.

"Thanks for the concert," said Lily. "I'd like to meet your little girl now, if that's okay."

"Second bedroom on the left," said Marc, pointing. "Just give me a minute."

"And I'd like a drink of water," HoneyRose said. She followed Marc into the kitchen as Lily went down the hallway toward Sophie's room. He poured her a glass of filtered water from a pitcher, but after a sip she set it aside on the counter. "I'm blown away," she said. "Totally."

He shrugged. "I took lessons for years and years," he said. "I used to play all the time, and then..." His voice trailed off. "Never mind."

"Tell me."

His hands were hidden in the back pockets of his khakis; she reached for one of them, drawing it out and turning it over gently, running her fingertip across his open palm, as if she might discover something there. It seemed an intimate gesture, full of promise.

"Come with me," he said.

"What?"

"It won't take long."

He closed the door quietly behind them; in the elevator they stood next to one another shyly.

"Why do I feel like we're on some kind of weird date and you won't tell me where you're taking me?" HoneyRose said.

"Not that I'm complaining."

"There's something I want you to see," said Marc.

When they got to the basement, he led her by the hand into the laundry room, which was deserted and sweltering. A washing machine on spin cycle trembled convulsively, as if it might self-destruct at any moment, and a couple of dryers, their portholes steamed over, revolved noisily. At the back of the long, linoleum-lined room hung the cork board where HoneyRose's mint-green notice was still pinned. "ARE YOU FOR REAL?" someone had scrawled across it in black Magic Marker.

"*Are* you?" Marc said. He had her by the shoulders now, but lightly, tentatively; she was free to bolt at any moment. It was always a mistake to ask too much of someone; even a simple question could be a burden, he knew. Unaccountably, he'd stumbled and fallen for her, but he wasn't saying a word. Let her watch for it in his eyes, let her feel it in his skin that sizzled now under her surprisingly cool, wandering hands.

The washing machine stopped its wild shuddering, the dryers at last fell silent. "*Are* you?" Marc said again, light-headed in all that heat, listening hard for whatever she might offer him—a murmur of assent, of longing, or, perhaps, something else entirely.

Housecleaning (2000)

The young husband-and-wife team that the cleaning service has sent over arrives ten minutes early, which pleases me no end.

"There's nothing like starting off on the right foot," I tell them buoyantly, and hold the door open as they drag in an industrial-strength vacuum and a shopping cart full of cleaning supplies. The man, who introduces himself as Dell, is startlingly tall—halfway between six and seven feet, I'd guess—and has a cigarette tucked behind each ear. His wife, Starlet, a tiny figure in a zippered teal-blue jumpsuit, has her hair just like Mary Martin's in *Peter Pan*. I eye her worriedly, already convinced that Starlet is too small and delicate for the heavy workload in store for them.

"And who's this?" I ask. Hanging back behind the threshold of the doorway is a little girl; as the child stands there gazing downward at the rubber welcome mat, I admire her dress, which has a large black-and-white likeness of a winking cat across the front, one eye ornamented with a rhinestone. The child is wearing black leggings that end a little past her knee and beat-up-looking sneakers with Velcro closures.

"That's Princess," Dell says. "Just stick her in front of the TV and you won't hear a word out of her."

"I'm hungry and I have to go to the bathroom," says Princess, but remains in the doorway. She flicks away the thin dark bangs that are hanging in her eyes and takes a single step forward.

"You know," I say to Dell, "I've got mattresses that need

to be turned, heavy couches that have to be pulled away from the wall...there's actually quite a lot for you to do. Do you really think your wife's strong enough for that kind of work?"

"Not to worry," says Starlet, and places her hand briefly on my shoulder. "We're the best in the business. We're a great team."

At fifty dollars an hour you ought to be, I almost say, but do not. (Having lived through the Depression, I can still remember when you stopped in the street to pick up a penny because it was worth the effort.)

"Fine," I say now. "My husband's being discharged from the hospital tomorrow and what I'd really like is to have everything spotless. If you can manage it."

"Heart attack?" Starlet says.

"What? No, he's asthmatic. He had a very severe attack. It scared the hell out of me," I say. "He—"

"The master bedroom's that way?" Dell asks. "We'll set up in there first."

I nod, waving him past. My husband, Sidney, stopped breathing halfway through the eleven o'clock news last week, and if not for a neighbor in our condo who knew CPR, I would have lost Sidney right there in our den, just as the weather forecaster in his smart-looking blue blazer was poised in front of his map predicting three straight days of rain for the Miami–Fort Lauderdale area. Marvin Greenspan, the neighbor who resuscitated Sidney and summoned the paramedics, happens to be a courtly, handsome man with not a hair on his head. Twice-divorced and a champion tennis player (at least on the local senior citizen circuit), he's much admired by the numerous widows in the building. He drove me to the hospital in Fort Lauderdale the night Sidney was carried off in the ambulance; later, the two of us went for coffee in the hospital cafeteria. Holding my shaky hands between his own steady ones, he listened patiently as I talked a nervous blue streak, outlining my worries one by one, thanking him extravagantly, then returning to my long list of fears before setting out to thank him again. (What a frazzled wreck I'd been that night, all wilted and dry-mouthed and unable to keep silent for even a moment.) I remind myself now to pick up some small gift for Marvin, an expression of gratitude for bringing Sidney back to life.

"You do have a TV set, don't you?" Starlet is saying. "Princess is just a lost soul without her TV shows."

"Shouldn't she be in school?" I say.

"Not if I don't wanna," Princess says. "And today I definitely don't wanna."

I don't know what to make of this. "In my day," I tell them, "they used to send the truant officer after you. But of course my day has come and gone."

"Princess is a school-phobic," Starlet explains. "It's like a disease, sort of. Sometimes she wakes up in the morning and pukes, just because she's afraid of going to fourth grade. The school district has a special counselor for her. It's part of her treatment—two hours a week with a very sweet lady-psychologist."

"School-phobic," I say, marveling that they already have a name for it. "What will they think of next?"

"Oh, it's real common these days," says Starlet blithely. She puts on a pair of elbow-length turquoise rubber gloves and rummages through the shopping cart. "There's lots of kids like Princess all over the district," she says, and trails down the hallway, arms loaded with sponges and an assortment of bathroom cleansers.

"Swell." I look at Princess, whose fingernails are rimmed with an accumulation of moss-green dirt. "Would you like to wash your hands?" I say. "And then Mrs. Sugarman will slice up an apple for you. Would you like that?"

"Who's Mrs. Sugarman?" Princess says suspiciously.

"Me."

"Why do you call yourself 'Mrs. Sugarman'?"

I smile at this. "Because a long, long time ago, when I was very young, I married Professor Sidney Sugarman. And that's how I became Mrs. Sugarman."

"I'm hungry for a baloney and cheese sandwich on an onion bagel."

"It's nine o'clock in the morning," I say, as shocked as if Princess had asked for a martini.

"I'm hungry."

"Didn't your mother give you breakfast?"

"Maybe, but I threw it right up," Princess says. "How about if you make me a hamburger? I like it red on the inside and burnt on the outside, okay?"

"I can't give you a hamburger so early in the morning. It wouldn't be right. But what about a bowl of cereal instead?"

Princess looks me straight in the eye. "You're not so nice," she says. "I thought you were, but you're really not."

"Excuse me," I say stiffly. "Right now you're a guest in my home. And in this house we don't insult people, we speak nicely to them, do you understand what I'm saying?"

"This isn't a house," Princess says. "It's an apartment. Why do you call it a house?" She saunters from the foyer into the kitchen, where she heads straight to a half-open cabinet and selects a bag of salt-free pretzels for herself. "We live in an apartment, too. It's Dell's apartment, actually."

"Actually," I say. I follow Princess into the kitchen and shake my head now as the little girl tears open the bag of pretzels with her teeth.

Lowering her voice, hunching down over the cellophane bag, Princess says, "Dell's not really nice, either. Well, sometimes he is, but mostly he isn't. Once, on purpose, he made my mom fall, and she broke two ankles. Wait, that's not right; I mean she broke one and sprained the other one. I had to do a lot of things for her, like make her sandwiches and change the channels on the TV for her because the remote was broken. And she was such a grouch."

I shiver in my air-conditioned kitchen. I imagine Dell thrusting out one of his extraordinarily long legs to trip Starlet, imagine Starlet's shriek of astonishment as she goes flying. "Poor thing," I murmur. "And Dell is your father?" I ask Princess.

"No way! He's like the biggest dork," Princess says.

"Then let's not talk about him." The truth is, I don't want to contemplate whatever dark things might or might not have transpired in somebody else's household; I just want my apartment shining by noon. There's plenty to do today, but I can't remember what's first on my list. It's Princess and her chatter that's thrown me off course. I try to recall my plans, but my mind is a dull stubborn blank. Sidney's homecoming, which I'd been looking forward to all week, suddenly seems like something I'd rather postpone. What if having been brought back from the dead has permanently altered him? In the hospital these past few days, he seemed pretty much his old prickly self, though he'd been a little passive, I'd noticed, a little too eager to have me take charge of things, asking me to brush his teeth and his hair for him, and even to strap his watch around his wrist. Yesterday I'd glimpsed, through the fly-front of his cotton pajamas, something droopy and sad between his legs; for only an instant, I'd been appalled at the sight, but then, recovering, remembering all my affection for him, I'd pulled the blue hospital blanket up under his arms and launched into an entirely irrelevant story about one of our neighbors. The humiliation Sidney surely would have felt if he'd seen, in that instant, what I had seen, was my humiliation, too—wasn't that always the way it was when you loved someone? Observing Sidney in his bed, it came to me that I couldn't imagine Marvin Greenspan lying in a hospital, vulnerable and exposed like that. The half-hour or so we spent together in the deserted cafeteria that night seems to have taken on, for me, a dreamlike quality, and also a bright sheen of romance and possibility. In my mind, I keep returning to it, remembering the feel of his cool hands over mine, his soft, subdued voice gently reassuring me, his head gleaming brilliantly under the cafeteria's fluorescent lights.

At the kitchen table now, I let out a lingering sigh that ends in a little moan of pleasure and longing. I listen to the distant heavy rumble of the vacuum cleaner. "See how hard your mother's working?" I say.

"This is pretty boring," says Princess. "Don't you have any coloring books for me?"

"If you were in school, where you're supposed to be," I say, "you'd be too busy to be bored. You'd be reading and writing, and borrowing and carrying numbers, and probably your teacher would be reading you *Charlotte's Web*."

Princess hisses noisily, puffing out her cheeks. "My teacher," she says, "is an A-hole."

"What?"

"Don't you know what an A-hole is?"

"As a matter of fact, I do," I tell her. "But we don't allow people to talk like that here. If they want to talk like that, they have to step outside into the hallway."

"Do they get to come back in again?"

"I suppose so," I say. "It varies from case to case, I suppose."

"I wanna see my mom," Princess says in a wobbly voice, and runs from the room. I brush some crumbs from the table into my hand and put the bag of pretzels back in the cabinet. I've frightened off Princess, which isn't surprising: the truth is, I've never had a way with young children, not even my own. And my two daughters would be the first to tell anyone who'd listen that I just didn't have the boundless patience that would have made all the difference, that, years ago, would have sweetened the tone of our household. Instead, I lost it, and dug my fingers into their slender wrists, shrieking, *Why can't you just listen to me? I'm not asking you to climb Mount Everest, I'm just asking you to take those filthy feet off the couch. Am I asking the impossible?* I would cry, never breaking their delicate skin but marring it with tiny violet marks shaped like crescents on the underside of their pure white wrists. *No I am not—all I'm asking for is a little consideration!* And now Sidney and I are in Florida and the girls are nowhere in sight, Renée comfortably settled in the suburbs of Seattle, Eileen in San Francisco. Unaccountably, both always seem to have their answering machines switched on, no matter when I happen to phone. ("This is your mother calling from Florida," I say self-consciously at the cool, electronic sound of their respective beeps. "Don't you think your father would love to hear from you more than once while he's in the hospital? Don't you think the familiar sound of your voice would do him a world of good?") It's been ages since we all lived together under one roof; sometimes the thought of our separate, distant lives still makes me a little weepy. The therapist I dragged myself to nearly twenty years ago— when both girls married and moved away within months of each other—had been sympathetic but firm. "You had each of them for what, eighteen years?" Dr. Hirsch asked me. "Well, you have to remember they were really only visitors, just passing through. And take it from me, it can't be any other way, not really."

A fundamental truth, maybe, but one that sometimes strikes me as absolutely heartbreaking.

Silently I make my way into the bedroom now, where I discover Starlet and Princess standing over my dresser, fingering the bottles of perfume I keep lined up in two precise rows on an ornate mirrored tray. "I happen to know this one over here is like forty-two dollars an ounce," Starlet is saying to her daughter. "So you can figure out what a bottle this big must have cost. Wanna try some on your wrist?"

"Excuse me," I interrupt, and I feel a wave of dizziness sweep over me. "My husband gave that to me for an anniversary present," I inform them.

Starlet swings around to face me, the bottle upright in her palm. "That's real sweet," she says, shaking her head, as if in astonishment. "What would it be like to have a husband like that, I wonder."

"Put that down, please," I tell her warily. "I'm sure we'd all be very upset if it broke."

Unscrewing the cap, Starlet tips the bottle against her fingertip. She guides her finger slowly down the side of her neck, then under Princess's nose.

"Yummy," says Princess.

"You had mildew in the shower," Dell announces, suddenly emerging from the bathroom. "Nothing too serious, but I took care of it. Better to nip that kind of thing in the bud, that's my policy." He slides a cigarette from behind one ear and pokes it into the corner of his mouth. "Just taking a three-minute break before I start on the other bedroom."

"My husband's an asthmatic," I say. "The smoke is very bad for him."

"Your husband's not here," Starlet points out. Picking up a comb from the perfume tray, she runs it languorously through her hair, then frowns at herself in the mahogany-framed mirror above the dresser. "This is just the worst haircut, don't you think? They call it a pixie cut but I'd say it makes me look like a little mouse. Maybe if I had some blond highlights put in, I'd look more, you know, glamorous."

"You're not the glamorous type," Dell says matter-of-factly. "Never were and never will be." He taps the ash from his cigarette into his cupped palm, making me wince.

"I'm sure I can find an ashtray somewhere," I say. "Maybe in the kitchen." I picture myself dialing 911 from the phone on the kitchen wall, whispering urgently for a patrol car. *She used my perfume without my permission. And also my comb. And he smoked a cigarette in my bedroom when he knew I didn't want him to.* I can hear the snort of laughter from the operator at the other end: *Don't you know better than to be tying up the line with that kind of silly stuff? Call back when one of them puts a gun to your head, lady.*

"What do you mean, I'm not the glamorous type?" says Starlet, as Dell steps into the bathroom to ditch his cigarette. "I could be if I wanted to. Why do you think my mother named me Starlet? She had high hopes for me, probably still does."

Dell stands framed in the bathroom doorway, a Marlboro lingering behind his left ear. Caressing the cigarette, as if it were something beloved, he says, "Your mother's a big fat fool. The day she moved to Tennessee with that pathetic excuse of a boyfriend was one of the best days of your life, whether you know it or not." He nods in my direction, saying, "This mother of hers is a deluded tub of lard and a nosybody besides, calling every hour of the day and night to give out advice nobody in their right mind would ever listen to."

"A deluded tub of *what*?" Starlet's blue eyes widen; she seizes a bottle of Windex with Vinegar and aims the nozzle at Dell's belt buckle.

"Don't you pull that trigger, Star," Dell says. His hands are on his hips and he is staring down at Starlet grimly. I can see the ten-gallon hat tipped back against his head, the dusty boots with spurs at his ankles, the spurs glittering in the Wyoming sunlight.

"Oh Lord," I murmur.

Hearing this, Princess lets out a squeal and dives under

the bed, the soles of her little white sneakers peeking out from under the bedspread. Starlet squeezes the plastic trigger; a delicate spray of something sour-smelling darkens Dell's faded jeans just under his belt. "You slimeball!" she says in a screechy voice, and then aims the trigger at his heart, soaking his shirt. Swiftly, Dell cracks her on the wrist and the bottle of Windex pitches to the floor.

"That's it! I'm outta here!" he announces. "And I'm taking the vacuum with me!"

"Like I give a flying you-know-what," says Starlet, rubbing her wrist against the side of her face. "Like I need you, right?"

"Like a hole in the head," Dell says, in a falsetto that somehow sounds menacing.

Starlet looks at him, surprised. "That's right," she says. "How did you know?"

Looping the vacuum cleaner cord fiercely around its handle, Dell sighs. "Because you're so fucking predictable, that's why."

"Will you please," Starlet says. "Not in front of Mrs. Sugarbaker."

"Sugarman," I correct her. On my knees now, I flip up the bedspread and speak to Princess. "Are you all right, cutie?" I ask. "Would you like to go see what's on TV?"

"No."

"You can put some of that delicious perfume behind your ears if you'd like."

"Can I take the bottle home with me?"

"Come out and we'll talk about it." I wait a few minutes, listening to the sound of the front door banging shut, and then Starlet's rapid footfalls approaching down the hallway.

"Get yourself out here right now, Princess," Starlet says. "We've got to go and call ourselves a cab." Her eyelashes are wet and gleaming, and she's sniffling into a handful of tissues patterned with pink and blue flowers. "I'm going to count to three. Here goes: *uno. . .dos. . .tres.*"

"I peed in my pants, I think," Princess confesses in a tiny voice. "I tried very hard to hold it in but I couldn't."

"I know," Starlet says. "I know you tried." She blots her eyes with the clump of tissues. "Listen, we'll rinse out your undies and use the hair dryer on them, how's that?" And then, to me, "Got a blow dryer for us?"

"What a terrific idea," I call out from my place on the floor. "Don't you think so, Princess?"

"Oh yeah," says Starlet. "I'm just full of terrific ideas."

"Don't be so hard on yourself," I suggest as Starlet stands up. "I don't know that spraying your boyfriend with Windex was the smartest thing you could have done, but we all have our ways. One time when Professor Sugarman said something very cruel to me, I poured a cup of coffee into his lap. Lucky for both of us it was lukewarm, or he might have ended up in the burn unit at Jackson Memorial." Stricken with shame at having shared this with a stranger, I hear myself gasp. "That was a lie," I tell Starlet. "I would never lose control like that. I was just trying to make you feel better, that's all."

Starlet grabs Princess by her skinny little ankles and pulls her out across the carpet. "Let's have a look," she says, and shoves a hand down her daughter's back. "Damp," she reports. "Not too bad at all, actually. But what I'm real interested in knowing is, what was it your husband said to you that got you so ticked off?"

"I don't even remember," I say, "but even if I did, it wouldn't be right for me to tell you, would it."

"Why not?" says Starlet. She and Princess are back at my dresser, stroking perfume on their wrists. "This is my absolute favorite," she says. " 'Escape,' by Calvin Klein."

"Why not? Because some things should remain private between husband and wife, that's why."

"You mean like sex?" Starlet says. "That's not as private as it used to be, you know. You ever watch any of the talk shows? Some people, and I'm not saying I'm one of them, are perfectly willing to let forty million people in on their little secrets. And sometimes it turns out that I can, like, relate to what they're saying. Like these three ladies whose boyfriends were into tying them to the bedposts with silk scarves and stuff. Not that Dell can afford silk—polyester is more his speed—but the idea is the same."

All at once, the air seems saturated with a mix of sickeningly sweet fragrances; breathing in, I feel confused and light-headed. For a moment I can't place the two small figures in my bedroom. The one all in teal looks elfin, like Peter Pan. I don't want to imagine her tethered to her bed with silk scarves as her lover eagerly lowers himself onto her, overcome with passion. After a long slow cooling off, there is no longer any passion in *my* life; sometimes it seems that it's inexplicably dried up like a parched, neglected flower, turned brittle and then to dust. I find myself wondering what Marvin Greenspan's smooth handsome head would feel like against my flesh, in my hands. He'd saved my husband, breathed life into Sidney's open mouth while I'd looked on fearfully, utterly helpless. The connection between us, between me and this man whose lips had touched my husband's, is something I can feel simmering under my skin; whatever it is, it's miraculous, something to be savored.

"You've got to get rid of this Dell," I hear myself say. "I just know you can do better."

"If he bought me perfume like this, I'd be in heaven," Starlet says. "Fat chance."

"I can see you're not going to listen to me. Neither of my daughters listens to me either," I say. "Well, I'm used to it."

Starlet nods. "I *am* going to clean your house, though. But first thing, you got a full-length mirror?"

"Behind the closet door." I watch as, motionless and unsmiling, Starlet inspects herself in the mirror, then slams the closet door shut.

"I need six-inch heels and a miniskirt," she says glumly. "And a job behind a desk—answering phones, opening the boss's mail, ordering his lunch. You can't be glamorous and be in the housecleaning business, they just don't mix."

"Mom?" says Princess. She's been silent so long that I'd forgotten all about her. "When are we going home?"

"Never!" Starlet says exuberantly, rushing toward her and swooping her up in the air. "We're gonna move into this nice apartment and have Mrs. Sugarbaker cook for us and do our laundry and take such good care of us we'll never wanna leave. How would you like that?" she says, and parks Princess at the edge of the dresser. "Wouldn't that be cool?" I smile faintly. My heart is racing, alert to danger and also, I have to admit, an inexplicable excitement. I imagine myself flipping the most delicate of omelets for Starlet's breakfasts, roasting chickens for her dinners, folding her laundry, leaving foil-wrapped mints on her pillow at night. And I could never explain to Sidney how it happened, how it was that I'd been unable to resist a stranger's neediness.

"I'm teasing you, baby!" Starlet says, but Princess has already burst into tears. "Tell her I was teasing, Mrs. Sugarbaker."

"Of course she was teasing," I say, and wait for my heart to slow. "Don't be a silly goose."

"Why do you keep calling her 'Mrs. Sugarbaker'?" Princess says. She licks the tears that have made their way slowly to the corners of her mouth. "A hundred years ago she married Professor Sidney Sugarman and that's how she became Mrs. Sugarman."

"A hundred years ago. No way," says Starlet.

"It's true," I say, and sigh. "Grover Cleveland was in the White House and life was sweet."

"Who's this Grover Cleveland character?" says Starlet. "Anybody I should know?"

"Never mind," I say, but I'm surprised at how disheartened I feel. It could be that I expect too much of people, wanting my daughters to fly to their father's bedside, my husband to be moved at the sight of my flesh, my cool, elegantly bald neighbor to appear wordlessly at my doorstep simply because he can't stay away. I slide my hand now along the surface of the night table next to Sidney's side of the bed; dust darkens my fingertips, dangerous stuff for a man with asthma. There's probably dust everywhere in the apartment—in the week since he's been in the hospital, I've done very little with my time except try to keep him entertained with a steady stream of talk that exhausts us both. Sweeping the sleeve of my sweatsuit across the table, I send dust into the air, above the three bright rectangles of sunlight that pattern the avocado-colored carpeting and rise halfway up the bedroom wall.

"I gotta call a cab," Starlet is saying, her hand on the telephone. "It's like I can let Dell stew in his own juices for only so long and then it's real bad news."

"Have some coffee before you go," I offer. "Your boyfriend will wait."

"Well, maybe one cup. A little milk, two Sweet'N Lows. And I swear to God," Starlet says, "I'd finish up the work you hired me for if I could. But I know I couldn't do a super job right now—my heart just wouldn't be in it." She seems to be puzzling over something, running a hand through her Peter Pan hairdo then resting it awkwardly on top of her head. "I think maybe I should just quit the business," she says uncertainly. "As of this minute."

"Good for you," I say. "I like to see a young person taking charge of her life." In the kitchen, I boil water for instant coffee and set out two blue-rimmed ceramic mugs on a Lucite tray monogrammed with my initials. I arrange some Oreos on a plate, and napkins and spoons. It's been a while since I've had company, I realize, since any of the neighbors have stopped in to ask how Sidney's doing. Everyone has his own troubles here—cancer, heart disease, Parkinson's. *What a crew*, Sidney had said one afternoon down at the pool, looking around him at all our waxen neighbors sunning themselves on chaise longues. Fresh from a couple of sets of tennis, Marvin Greenspan had been the sole swimmer in the water, making his way vigorously from one end of the pool to the other. Silently, I'd applauded him, watching carefully as he pulled himself from the pool and draped a white towel across his tanned shoulders. Even then, before he figured in my daydreams, he had been someone to take notice of.

At the edge of the glass coffee table in the living room, Starlet and Princess sit mesmerized by the sight of a newly selected contestant on *The Price Is Right*. The woman, tall and scrawny-looking, wearing sunglasses and a racing cap and hoop earrings large enough to put your arm through, is embraced by well-wishers in the audience as she approaches the stage. Asked to bid on a brass crib filled with stuffed animals, she looks back over her shoulder for advice from the audience.

"One thousand dollars!" Starlet urges, ignoring me but taking a cookie from the tray. "Fifteen hundred!" The audience clamors suggestions of its own; the woman crosses herself, then opens her mouth. "Two thousand dollars?" says Starlet. "No way, lady."

"Drink your coffee before it gets cold," I tell her. Beside me, Princess splits open an Oreo and scrapes her front teeth across the bright white cream, leaving behind what looks like trail marks in fresh snow.

The woman in the racing cap raises her arms in triumph; it's her bid that's come closest to the actual retail value of the merchandise. The emcee thrusts the microphone at her, looking on in amusement as she speaks into it breathlessly. "This is the happiest day of my life," she pronounces. "This is it!"

"She doesn't mean it," I say. "It must be that they coach

them before the show and tell them to say things like that, but you just know she doesn't really mean it."

"Of course she does," says Starlet. "And anyway, what do you know about her? What do you know about her life?"

I pretend not to hear. I think uneasily of Dell, cooling his heels, listening for the sound of Starlet's apology, of Sidney waiting in his hospital bed for the start of visiting hours. Not long ago, the morning before the asthma attack that nearly killed him, I emptied a cup of coffee into his lap. We were in the kitchen, lingering over breakfast, sections of *The Miami Herald* spread across the table between us, neither of us speaking. Dreamily I opened my robe to him, shyly guided his hand to my breast. He pulled away so swiftly, so instinctively, it was as if his fingertips had been scorched. *You're embarrassing us both*, he said, his voice whispery, as if I'd disgraced myself in a roomful of people. Seizing the coffee cup, just for something to hold on to, I suddenly let go, casting my arm in Sidney's direction without looking at him. Afterward, I made no offer to help him into dry clothes or to mop up the kitchen tiles where the coffee had spilled in a thin muddy pool. *What's eating you?* Sidney asked me. *Could you give me a hint, at least?* Fleeing, I went downstairs for a swim and then out to a string of malls, searching half-heartedly for something that might appeal to me. At home, my husband waited all day for my apology, is still waiting for it, for all I know.

Starlet is smiling at the TV screen now, at a freeze-frame of the woman who won the brass crib caught in a jubilant pose, arms stretched high over her head, mouth opened wide, utterly enraptured. "Will you look at that!" says Starlet. "Will ya?"

"I'm looking," I say, and see myself somewhere beyond reason and self-control, my ankles and wrists bound in bright silk as my lover's knowing hands drift lightly along the smooth path of my flesh.

BANISHED (2021)

At first he'd expected to be in mourning for the rest of his life; after all, his marriage to Penni had lasted forty-three years, mostly happy, untroubled ones, complete with a set of identical twin granddaughters who proved to be both gifted gymnasts and award-winning junior cheerleaders—on something called the Glam Squad—by the time they celebrated their sixth birthday. Penni had been gone now for almost a year and a half, and late on this summer afternoon, Cliff found himself headed toward the entrance to the subway on Fifty-Ninth Street, when he saw a homeless man squatting beside a revolving door at the front of Bloomingdale's, holding in his lap a handwritten cardboard sign that announced, in Magic Marker,

HOMELESS, HUMILIATED VETERAN

"It's that comma that really gets me," said a woman next to Cliff on the sidewalk, after she deposited a five-dollar bill into the homeless guy's empty Starbucks cup, which he was shaking up and down so you could hear the rattle of the few coins inside it. "Plus, the word 'humiliated.' Retired English teacher that I am, I have to admit the comma between 'homeless' and 'humiliated' kinda breaks my heart," the woman said *sotto voce*.

Cliff said he understood, pulled a handful of singles from his wallet, and stuffed them into the green-and-white paper cup. He was a widower who'd lost his wife, unexpectedly and not very long ago, to a ruptured cerebral aneurysm; surely he knew all about broken hearts, he wanted to tell the woman. She was tall and narrow, dressed in black jeans and what he suspected his daughter, Rachel, would have called, unflatteringly, "comfortable shoes." Though her hair was a mixture of gray and white, it was thick and glossy, and he could tell by her still-youngish face that he was at least a half-dozen years older than she was. He silently admired her slender, elegant thumbs, and though he usually didn't take note of these things, observed that her maroon nail polish matched her lipstick. Penni, he recalled, hadn't believed in manicures, or even lipstick, come to think of it. If asked, he would have said she didn't need any of it; she was lovely just as she was.

As he was about to turn away and continue along to the subway and back to his apartment on the Upper East Side, he heard the woman who found the comma so poignant tell him that her name was Jessica, confiding, a moment later, that, in fact, she was called "Jessa," at least by the people who knew her best.

"Way to go, Jessa!" the homeless guy yelled.

"I'm actually desperate to find birthday presents for my twin granddaughters," Cliff confessed, and then he was asking Jessa if she'd like to join him, wondering, a bit uneasily, if he sounded as if he were inviting her out on a date. "I tried, and failed, just a few minutes ago in Bloomingdale's, to choose something for the twins on my own. I feel like an idiot. Or maybe just a shamefully incompetent grandfather."

Jessa smiled, and he could see her teeth were exceptionally even and white; maybe veneers, he thought, or implants? It occurred to him that perhaps she was married, possibly to a dentist.

"My apologies," he said. He thought about the times his sister and brother-in-law had insisted on fixing him up on what always seemed to be agonizingly awkward blind dates with friends of theirs who were single, never understanding that what he wanted, and was waiting for, was for Penni to simply return from the dead, rising effortlessly from her grave and making her way back to him, dressed not in the plain white shroud she'd been wrapped in before being arranged inside her coffin but, instead, in her skin-tight black leather pants and the almost see-through black silk shirt that was his favorite.

"Apologies for *what*?" Jessa said. Then she offered him a mint from a small tin box from Trader Joe's.

"Let's see...I guess I'm apologizing for assuming you were unattached—that was stupid of me. For all I know, you've been blissfully married for decades." *To a dentist*, he almost added. (Later, on their first *official* date, he would learn that her ex was Dr. Morton Horowitz, board-certified endodontist, and "one of the very best root canal specialists in Manhattan," at least according to a comment posted by a highly satisfied customer on Dr. Horowitz's website.) Cliff selected a mint from the tin box and was disappointed to realize it was peppermint, the taste of which he'd hated since childhood. But he was sixty-seven years old now; wasn't that too old to have to eat things he despised? He was still a fairly cool dude, he thought, cool enough to have gone to Woodstock, never mind the nightmarish traffic along the New York State Thruway he and his buddies were trapped in that weekend in August nearly fifty years ago. Thanks to his father, that summer before college and four years before Cliff entered law school, he had an excruciatingly boring job, working in the mail room at a law firm near Wall Street, earning ninety dollars a week, relatively big bucks for a teenager in the Sixties. And along with a triumvirate of his high school friends, he paid his eighteen dollars and was able to get tickets to Woodstock, where he was privileged to hear Jimi Hendrix, live and in person, in his fringed white shirt and red bandana, playing his extraordinary, harshly dissonant version of "The Star

Spangled Banner" early that Monday morning. Though he and his friends were ensnared in another bad-news traffic jam on their return trip to the suburbs of Long Island—the traffic so insane that they'd witnessed a couple of guys who got out of their cars and were standing on the highway leisurely brushing their teeth and shaving with electric razors—it was unquestionably worth all that hassle just to see Hendrix, who would die not much more than a year afterward, choking on his own vomit while intoxicated. Cliff had become sort of emotional when he heard the news in his college dining hall in New Haven, and he cried real tears, ten years later, when John Lennon was shot on the Upper West Side, not far from the cramped apartment where Cliff and Penni were living at the time with their young daughter.

"I think I'll just put this mint in my pocket and save it for...tomorrow," he mumbled now to Jessa.

"No worries—and by the way, I'm divorced, and frankly, pretty sick of those slim pickin's out there on silversingles, eharmony, or whatever," Jessa said, rolling her eyes.

This was the time to identify himself as a widower; it never got easier, and it always pained him to hear that sharp intake of breath and that *OhI'msosorry* that inevitably followed. The moment passed quickly, and he acknowledged Jessa's sympathy with a subtle, but grateful, nod of his head and a whispery *thank-you.*

She helped him choose a couple of sequined Minnie Mouse sweatshirts and sparkly black leggings for Charlotte and Madison, his gymnast-granddaughters, and when they were finished shopping, suggested a Thai restaurant for an early dinner. It was while they were walking over to First Avenue to the Siam Noodle House that she talked for a couple of minutes about her career as a middle-school teacher in the City's public school system. "In *my* day, we called it 'junior high,' " she said.

"Mine too," he said, smiling.

The coconut soup and salmon pad Thai she ordered for them at the Noodle House were both overly sweet, and the spring rolls were so damp and shiny, Cliff had to ask for more paper napkins so he could blot all the excess oil. But he felt at ease in Jessa's company and was happy enough listening to her talk about her students, many of whom she kept in touch with on Facebook and Instagram, and one of whom had become a grandmother at the astonishing age of thirty-three. Cliff had been a law professor at NYU, specializing in civil procedure and family law. Aside from a celebration he and Penni attended following the City Hall marriage of two of his favorite protégés, since his retirement he'd had limited contact with his former students, which bothered him at first, but no longer did. He just wasn't a Facebook or Instagram kind of guy and felt no need to offer any excuses for it.

When he told Jessa he had not even one social media account, but that he did have a remarkably affectionate cat named Sallie to keep him company, Jessa offered him that vivid smile again; this time he was sure she had a mouthful of veneers, which, he knew, cost an impressive two thousand dollars a pop.

"Sally was my mother's name!" she said with what sounded like a tiny squeal of joy, and for only an instant her eyes looked moist with tears.

He didn't tell her that unlike her mother's name, his cat's was spelled with an "ie," nor did he tell her Penni's death had hit him so hard that eighteen months down the line, he occasionally still found himself weeping. But the worst was one night last winter, when he was removing a double load of mostly sheets and towels from the dryers in the second-floor laundry room in his apartment building, and discovered a pair of Penni's underwear entangled in a twisted-up T-shirt of his. He'd extracted her panties gently from the shirt, and cradled them in both his palms; they were lavender, with a thin elastic band at the waist imprinted with yellow flowers. When he raised his hands to his face, he could smell the sugary fragrance of the sheets of fabric softener; Tropical Paradise was the name on the box. *My darling, darling girl*, he murmured into his sweet-smelling hands, into Penni's underwear. He remembered her, just a few months before her utterly unforeseen death, standing barefoot in their bedroom, in her panties, lifting one slim arm and then the other to slide on her bra, and asking whether Cliff thought she looked, in her underwear, pretty good for someone in "early old age"—a phrase they'd seen in *The New York Times* and convinced themselves not to be insulted by. And he'd answered, "Do I think you look good? Yes, baby, pretty damn good, absolutely."

Bloomers, he suddenly remembered Penni telling him her mother had called her underwear when Penni was a child; he must have said the word out loud because Jessa was saying, "Sorry, *what?*" and had a quizzical expression on what he now saw to be her sweet but ordinary-looking face.

"Oh, sorry," Cliff said, though he wasn't certain he had to apologize. "Just, you know, talking to myself."

"It happens," said Jessa. "I totally get it. We who live alone are known to do that every now and again." When their dessert arrived, she stretched out one arm across the table and put a spoonful of sticky-rice cake and mango sorbet in front of him. "Open up, please," she said, and slid the dessert into his mouth. She gave him a moment, then asked for his verdict.

"Excellent!" said Cliff. "More, please."

He has waited nine months, patiently and empathetically, he believes, to break the news to Rachel, his daughter, that he has a girlfriend. Rachel lives in a suburb southwest of Boston with her husband and their identical twins. She has always been bossy and energetic, and forced Cliff and Penni to go kayaking in the summer and cross-country skiing in the winter whenever they came up from New York for a visit. When she was in high school, she made them feel as if they had no choice but to obey her commands to read the first two Harry Potter books and to buy movie tickets to see *Beavis and Butt-Head Do America*. She is an only child, one who had been conceived after several miscarriages; maybe, Cliff has sometimes thought, he and Penni spoiled her from day one.

There are, as yet, no plans to disclose to Rachel anything about Jessa's recently broken lease and her move into Cliff's apartment. He worries, now and then, that perhaps he shouldn't be doing this to his daughter, shouldn't be moving his girlfriend into the home that had belonged to Penni and him and to the life they'd shared. But then he reminds himself that Rachel will be turning forty soon—forty! Not fourteen! By somebody's calculation—though not his—she's about to officially become a middle-aged woman; isn't that old enough not to feel betrayed by the simple fact of her father's new live-in girlfriend? So why does he continue to worry?

In truth, he hasn't yet grown accustomed to the sight of the pink bristles of Jessa's toothbrush facing the turquoise of his own planted in the shiny metal holder on top of the bathroom sink, or to the sight of Sallie, his fourteen-year-old cat, looped around Jessa's hip when all three of them arrange themselves in bed together at night. It's a new queen-sized mattress and frame; sleeping with Jessa in the double bed he shared with Penni—the bed where she died—felt like a betrayal of sorts, and so he'd ordered a new one shortly before Jessa moved in. And summoned a pair of maintenance workers in his building to haul the old one out of the apartment as he stood by, trying not to feel undone by its disappearance.

Calling Rachel from his landline in the bedroom while Jessa is in the kitchen unloading the dishwasher, Cliff talks first to whichever granddaughter has answered the phone.

"Hey, sweetie!" he says. "Um, to whom am I speaking?"

"It's me, Grandpa," one of the twins says helpfully.

"Madison, is that you?"

"Wrong!"

Of course. "Okay, Charlotte, so what's new in third grade?"

"Well, my boyfriend Liam is gonna be an actor in *Charlie and the Chocolate Factory* and is gonna be on tour and won't be in school," Charlotte says breathlessly. "I'm, like, so so so upset."

"And I'm so out of it, I didn't even know you had a boy-friend," Cliff says. "Who's this Liam, anyway? Is he handsome? How long have you two been a couple?"

"I don't know, I just know I'm gonna miss him, Grandpa."

Madison has picked up the phone as well; Cliff can hear her breathing noisily into another landline, until finally she says, "Liam's not even Charlotte's boyfriend—she just pretends he is!" Madison sounds deeply affronted.

"*You* don't have *any* boyfriend, Maddy, so just *shuh* up and don't be jealous, okay?" Charlotte says.

"You can't tell me to *shuh* up!"

Settled into a cozy armchair in Cliff's bedroom, Sallie is keeping watch over the ashes of her beloved feline companion, Russell, currently stored in a glazed ceramic urn on the window sill. It's the piece Cliff was working on in his ceramics class at the Y several days before Penni died. He forgot all about it in the aftermath of her death, and when his instructor at the Y reminded him weeks later, all Cliff could think was that he'd started the urn as a long-married man and returned as a widower to add a final coat of glaze. He'd taken the plastic bag of Russell's ashes from the unadorned cardboard box sent by the pet crematorium, and gently deposited it into the copper-red urn, looking around him, an instant later, for Penni, wanting her approval.

It has been more than two years now, but from time to

time he still catches himself expecting to see her in the apartment or next to him in line in Whole Foods; still catches himself listening for her distinct sigh of contentment, or the sound of her amused voice saying, *That's a joke, right, baby?*

"I can SO tell you to *shuh* up," he hears one of the twins repeating several times in a progressively louder voice, until Rachel takes over, ordering the girls to get ready for a quick shower before bedtime.

"Bye, Grandpa!" they shriek in unison.

He listens to Rachel gripe good-naturedly about the twins' endless squabbling over this and that, and then, suddenly chickenhearted, he says, "So here's the thing, honey," and reports only that the plus-one he's bringing to her fortieth birthday party is someone named Jessa; he's going to keep the word "girlfriend" to himself for a while longer, he's just this moment decided.

"Okay, cool," Rachel says, but doesn't ask a single question about that plus-one of his.

He is disappointed—and also a little insulted—by her lack of curiosity, but won't offer any further information on his own.

She tells him all about the party, which will be held at a venue that was formerly a 9,000-square-foot garage: there will be vendors offering steamed Japanese dumplings, pizza, barbecue ribs, pulled pork sandwiches, and of course, plenty of alcohol.

"Sounds awesome," Cliff says. "Can I wear jeans? Or is this a formal affair?"

"You can wear anything you please. And you'll probably wanna bring some ear plugs, because we hired a kickass deejay," Rachel warns. "And, sorry, but Bob Dylan's not on the playlist."

"Damn, no Dylan? But that's my favorite party music! How could you disappoint me like that?" he kids her.

He remembers Rachel at her mother's funeral, standing graveside on the first day of winter and reciting wisdom that had been downloaded from the Poetry Foundation's website onto her iPhone. *After great pain, a formal feeling comes.* The poem, unsurprisingly, induced tears at Penni's grave, but he still wishes he could have seen Rachel reading from an actual book clutched in her hands. Just the sight of her reading Emily Dickinson's words typed on a sheet of copy paper and fluttering in the noisy wind over the newly dug grave would have been of comfort to him. He knows the world will always be in flux, sometimes painfully so, and he has come to accept this, but the very notion of Emily Dickinson being read from a smartphone continues to spark a small flame of outrage in him.

"Love you," he tells his daughter just before hanging up, and though he thinks he hears Rachel echoing his words, he's not entirely sure.

Ankles crossed, her heels resting against the dashboard, Jessa fools with her smartphone, which is connected to the sound system in Cliff's compact Audi sedan. They're en route to Massachusetts the day before the party, and even though her shoes are off and her socks look perfectly clean, he'd like to ask Jessa to please take her feet down from the dashboard of his almost brand-new car. Her socks are patterned with images of neon-colored ampersands, exclamation points, and hash tag signs (which he recently learned from his beloved OED are technically called *octothorpes*); looking at all of these has brought a smile to his face.

"So would this be considered a high-performance car?" she asks him. "Like a BMW?"

He gets a kick out of hearing the words "high-performance" coming from Jessa; cars have been one of his passions since adolescence, though not something Penni ever wanted to hear much about during their long marriage.

"Yup, like a BMW M2," he says happily, ignoring the sight of Jessa's feet on the dashboard and forgetting about the marks her socks might leave on its pale gray leather. Ever since he retired, he spends hours online studying the comparison tests and the glossy photos of his favorite sports cars. And unlike Penni, Jessa doesn't seem to mind a whit. She will sit beside him on the couch in the den, her feet up on the swivel chair she's wheeled over from his desk, reading novels by Henry James and Edith Wharton, their covers ornamented with images of unsmiling women showing off noticeably large broad-brimmed hats.

Using her fingertip, Jessa scrolls through her iPhone until she arrives at "A Whiter Shade of Pale," and hums along with the baroque-sounding organ music.

"You know, Procol Harum was the very first concert I ever went to," Cliff says. "It was at the Anderson Theatre on Second Avenue in the East Village, and I was seventeen. And the very next month I saw the Doors at the Fillmore," he boasts. He instantly remembers the girlfriend who accompanied him—a dark-haired girl with a high-pitched voice who, years later, he was surprised to learn, had become a neonatologist. "Deb Sommers," he says, but is drowned out by the sound of Gary Brooker's melancholy voice. He is thinking of Deb next to him in his British racing green MGB, the two of them parked in front of her house on so many Friday and Saturday nights that last year of high school, Cliff hoping for a chance to slide his hand under her sweater, under the thin turtleneck beneath it, and then—if he was parked beneath the luckiest of stars—under her bra, her flesh warm even on wintry nights. Although he'd never loved Deb Sommers, he did love the feel of her cupped flesh in his palm and remembers, with embarrassment, how he always had to warn himself not to squeeze too hard. If he did, she would slip her tongue from his mouth and complain, *Gently, Cliff, gently!*

"I'm sort of nervous about those gifts I bought for the twins," Jessa is saying. "What if they already have all the coloring books and colored pencils and markers they need in this world? What if they roll their eyes contemptuously and flounce away in a huff?"

"They're eight years old," Cliff says. "I guarantee you they don't know the meaning of the word 'contempt,'" he reassures her, but, in fact, he knows no such thing. "At the very least," he says, "they're going to love that pencil sharpener in the shape of a nose. What eight-year-old wouldn't love to sharpen her pencils in those beautiful plastic nostrils?"

"I should have bought two of those fabulous noses," Jessa says. "I could kick myself."

"Trust me," Cliff says, "it's all fine."

Maybe it is, and maybe it isn't.

Rachel has a master's degree in landscape architecture, but works full-time selling software for commercial mortgages. She's elfin, with hair that's still reddish and wispy, still trailing past her shoulders, just as it did when she was in high school; Cliff can't quite believe forty looks so very young to him.

"Hey Gramps," she says, and welcomes him in the foyer with an enthusiastic smooch on each cheek. When he asks where her husband is, she says Jack is still in Cambridge, in his office at MIT, but will be home in time for all of them to have dinner together.

Fine. His son-in-law is a mensch, he thinks—smart, hard-working, and given to calling Rachel *sweetheart* rather than by her name.

Just as Cliff is about to introduce Jessa, there's the sound of canine nails scrabbling furiously on the living room's polished granite floor. It's Spike, Rachel's Yorkie, and he's got something lodged horizontally across his mouth—a small white plastic tube smeared with red markings—which he drops proudly at her feet.

"Jesus Christ!" Rachel yells, and she and Jessa exchange a look that seems to shift from horror to amusement and then, finally, disgust, all of it meaningless to Cliff.

"What?" he says. "What am I missing here, guys?"

Spike is wagging his tail, apparently expecting a reward of some kind, but what he gets is the word "naughty" repeated again and again, along with, "How many times do I have to tell you to stay out of the garbage, you rotten kid?"

Jessa explains to Cliff, in a whisper, that the plastic tube is a tampon applicator. *A used one*, as it happens.

"Well, he's a cute little pooch nonetheless," Cliff says. *Oh, and by the way, I'm Jessa*, he hears her officially introducing herself to Rachel an instant before the twins come strolling down the stairs, barefoot, in satiny, ankle-length costumes, one granddaughter in pale blue, the other vermilion. After eight years, he thinks sheepishly, he still can't tell them apart, and broods over how likely it is that he ever will. The twins have thick, wavy brown hair that falls into their dark eyes, and chartreuse polish on their tiny nails; they're small for their age, but for a couple of pipsqueaks, they possess surprisingly lusty voices.

"Guess who *I* am, Grandpa!" one of them says.

"Charlotte?"

"No, Silly, I'm Princess Elena of Avalor!"

"And you are...?" Cliff asks the other twin.

"Can't you tell I'm Rapunzel?"

"Frankly, I'm not that into fairy tales," he says apologetically. "But I could really use some kisses from you two."

He gets a couple of juicy ones from each of them and feels no need to wipe them away with his fingertips; he savors the dampness on his cheeks left by those he loves best in this world.

"Hey, girls? Come say hi to Grandpa's friend, Jessa," Rachel says before disappearing into the kitchen, the errant tampon applicator now wrapped in a tissue and headed to another, presumably more secure, garbage pail.

Hand on her hip, the twin dressed as Rapunzel stares at Jessa for a long moment, then advises, "Basically, I really think you should blow-dry your hair."

"*Basically*," the other twin says, "my new Barbie really needs a manicure *and* a blow-dry."

"In that case, I'm not the slightest bit insulted by your suggestion," Jessa says. "And I might even start blow-drying my hair one of these days."

He loves her for this, Cliff almost says aloud; it's the first time he's aware of actually connecting the words *love* and *Jessa* while in her presence.

Rachel returns with a glass bowl of taco chips and a porcelain mug filled with salsa. "I need some napkins, girls," she says, but neither of the twins bothers to look at her. They're on their stomachs on the living-room floor, busy with the art set Jessa has given them, along with coloring books full of trolls and Hatchimals.

"What *are* those?" Cliff says, down on his knees, pointing to outlines of smiling, teddy bear-like creatures with big heads and diminutive bodies.

"Oh, that's an Owlicorn, and this one's a Bearakeet," one of the twins says. Cliff thinks it's Charlotte, because he's pretty sure she's the twin with the huskier voice, but hey, he's probably wrong. If his family lived in New York and he had the privilege of seeing the twins every week, would that make him less of a shamefully incompetent grandfather? An undergrad degree from Yale and a law degree from Harvard, and he can't differentiate between a pair of identical twins who share his DNA. And whom he surely adores. He watches as they take turns sharpening, so industriously, some colored pencils in the nostrils of the plastic nose Jessa gave them, and he wonders what they will do with their lives as adults—perhaps, like their mother, they will study for a master's in landscape architecture but end up in the business world or, like their father, pursue a doctorate in American Studies. And he wonders, too, whether *he,* the retired dude who's presently in early old age but who doesn't feel old at all, will be around to see these grandchildren of his flower into adulthood. He thinks of Penni running vigorously on the treadmill in their den for a half hour every morning in her pajamas, and following that with exactly one hundred and two sit-ups, and always eating wisely, never putting even one cigarette to her lips, but look—*just look*—how her life ended. In their bedroom, on a comforter embellished with a red-robed geisha feeding a pair of koi, only a few feet from the treadmill where Penni had started her day that very last morning—struck down by what she warned Cliff, in an anguished, bewildered voice, was the single worst headache she'd ever experienced.

By the time a trio of EMTs from the Fire Department arrived, she was already gone. *Thank you,* Cliff managed to say in his quietest voice, after one of his neighbors down the hall, a young anesthesiologist, pronounced Penni dead; even in the worst of circumstances, even as he sat shell-shocked and perfectly motionless at Penni's side, Cliff was nothing if not polite.

Later, waiting for the courteous, black-suited employees from the funeral home to show up, murmuring things he can no longer remember, Cliff held one of Penni's damp, ice-cold hands in both of his own, but failed to warm her.

"Dad!" he hears one of the twins shrieking, and here's his son-in-law, over six feet and muscular, his beard thick and threaded with sparks of silver, though you can see that his is the face of a man still young, Cliff thinks.

"Hey, how's it going?" Jack says, and he and Cliff hug

briefly but warmly, as they always have. Feeling Jack's fingers pressing lightly against his back, Cliff remembers the big white bandage enveloping his son-in-law's ring finger after he accidentally gouged it with an X-Acto knife in Cliff's garage in the suburbs the day before Rachel's wedding; Jack had been cutting wood for an oak bookcase he was going to build for the new apartment he and Rachel would be sharing in Cambridge. It was Cliff who had driven him to the ER to get stitched up that morning a decade ago, Cliff who had made him soup that came in an envelope in a cardboard box, throwing in a chopped-up carrot and onion he'd cooked in a saucepan first, serving it to Jack on a wicker tray as he relaxed on the living room couch, his injured hand resting on a small velvet pillow.

He'd been a good father-in-law from the very beginning, of that there is no doubt.

This time it's one of the twins who introduces Jessa, while the other displays the nose-shaped pencil sharpener with a long purple pencil protruding now from one plastic nostril.

"Cool!" Jack says admiringly.

There are Rachel's home-made fish tacos decorated with cilantro and shredded manchego for dinner; afterward, following an impassioned discussion of the president's latest follies both domestic and international, the conversation shifts to the Glam Squad and Madison and Charlotte's devoted coach, Angela, who came to the house bearing pints of ice cream for the twins after their respective tonsillectomies several months ago. Cliff and Jessa watch a video, on Rachel's tablet, of the twins performing in a competition, the exact nature of which he doesn't quite catch; staring at images of his granddaughters on the screen in their shiny pink leotards, black short-shorts, and glittery white eye shadow, he gets lost in some rap music he can't identify playing in the background and the row of tiny, similar-looking girls waiting their turn to perform handsprings and one-handed cartwheels. He and Jessa applaud loudly as Rachel gestures with a fingertip toward one of the twins cartwheeling her way across the floor of a school gym. It's a talent that's alien to him; in childhood he was one of those kids who could barely complete a somersault when ordered to do so by, as he remembers it, some grimly zealous gym teacher sporting a military-style crewcut. Unlike his granddaughters, rolling his body head over heels, end to end, was never one of Cliff's favorite activities. But watching on the tablet's screen as they perform smartly for the Glam Squad, he is especially proud of the twins. And proud, too, of the busy, comfortable life he knows Rachel and Jack have made for themselves and their daughters, here in their black-and-white colonial in this placid, leafy suburb where they've fit so easily, so confidently, these past few years.

He takes nothing for granted—neither the peaceful contentment of his daughter's life, nor any happiness of his own.

The twins have gone to sleep upstairs, each into her own separate bedroom and queen-sized bed—beds, Cliff marvels, as large as the one he and Jessa share in his apartment—while the grown-ups are watching, on a 65-inch curved-screen TV hung against a brick wall in the den, as Stephen Colbert handily ridicules a politician's misspelled Tweets.

"One can only guess at the depth of frustration felt by his seventh-grade English teacher," Jessa says, "and I'm not talking about Colbert's." Her left hand is entwined with Cliff's right, and when she yawns now, she lifts both his and hers to cover her mouth, leaving a silent kiss near his wrist.

"Ready for bed?" he says quietly; he doesn't want to disturb anyone's enjoyment of Colbert's entertaining litany of grievances, large and small, against various politicians. "So I think we're going to hit the sack," Cliff reports, more forcefully this time. His hand still in Jessa's, he pulls her up from the love seat and tells Rachel that the bedroom on the first floor, beyond the kitchen, where he's already wheeled their suitcases, is where they'll be sleeping. *If that's okay with management.* "Not that we have anything against trekking up and down the stairs to the guest bedroom on the second floor. We're just lazy," he teases. "Or as some might say, not as young as we used to be."

Rachel doesn't look amused; in fact, she looks alarmed and Cliff doesn't understand why.

"What, the downstairs bedroom? Nuh-nuh no, perfect for *you*, maybe, but not for the two of you, Dad," she says, then explains that Jessa would be a lot more *comfy* by herself in the guest room upstairs, the one next to the nicest bathroom, the one with the renovated shower. "She'll love the heated towel racks," Rachel says, sounding like a real estate broker, Cliff thinks. "Downstairs for you, upstairs for Jessa," she says. She's looking at him hopefully, but he's not buying. Now she's looking at her husband for confirmation, but Jack's throwing his head back against the couch in laughter as Colbert expertly mocks the commander-in-chief's insistence on pronouncing "premeditation" as "premedication."

"Unbelievable," Jack says, when he's stopped laughing, "that this...this...could possibly—"

"Jack! Pay attention! We're all going upstairs to check out the heated towel racks," Rachel says.

"What?" It's Colbert he's listening to, but clearly Rachel's not giving up.

"*Upstairs*, Jack—you know, where we thought Jessa would sleep?"

"We what? I don't get what you're talking about, sweetheart."

Cliff would be whispering furiously in Jessa's ear now if only he had the opportunity, he thinks, but the two of them have already begun to climb, obediently, the carpeted steps to the second floor, Rachel leading the way, talking over her shoulder about a Carrara marble sink from Tuscany. In what is clearly an effort to impress them further, she shows off the frameless shower door, the mosaic tile flooring, and those famous heated towel racks.

"Lovely," Jessa says politely, and then she and Cliff are on their way downstairs to retrieve her suitcase from the bedroom not far from the kitchen, accompanied by Rachel on this trip as well.

But he's a man in early old age—according to *The New York Times,* anyway—old enough to recognize that he will never grant his daughter what she wants from him, which is the right to insist that he spend the night alone. Guess what, not happening, not when the woman he loves could so easily be within reach. So he's going to do his best to explain to Rachel what should, he thinks, be as transparent as can be: that it's she who has overstepped the well-drawn lines here in her own home. And he would like to remind her of the various men in *her* life who were allowed to stay overnight in *her* bedroom long ago when she was home from college for winter break, spring break, summer break. He will remind her of the guy from Dartmouth who went directly into the Peace Corps after graduation, the guy from Georgetown who dropped out senior year to join some tech company in Silicon Valley, and whose father, astonishingly, invited Rachel to brunch with a friend of his named Al Pacino. Those guys who slipped into bed beside her while Cliff and Penni looked the other way because, hey, they'd come of age in the Sixties, hadn't they, and were hip to the most seductive of life's pleasures.

Listen to me, Rachel, he begins, and he's two minutes into setting her straight, as delicately as he can, when she interrupts him to announce, urgently, and with unmistakable authority, that, you know what, it's time for him and his girlfriend to just leave. *Get out get out get out,* he hears his daughter saying, weepy now, her voice full of the sound of all her disappointment in him, Jack at her side, shrugging one shoulder lamely, offering Cliff a *Sorry, bro,* but nothing more. *Don't you owe my mother* something? she's asking him, *anything at all?* And Cliff thinks of that much-loved wife of his, who should have been here to celebrate their daughter's fortieth birthday, and who would, perhaps, be ashamed of him now, though maybe she would have understood that, for him, there is no choice but to continue moving forward—right this minute, and to the nearest Best Western or Econo Lodge, whichever turns up first on his way home, back to New York with his girlfriend, almost a full day before the party even begins.

Never mind that he and Jessa—who's looking a little old and drained and grief-stricken at this moment as she clings to his hand—will miss out on the party tomorrow now that his daughter has shamed him, and their invitation has been revoked. Never mind the shumai dumplings, the margherita pizza with fresh basil, the whiskey-grilled baby back ribs, the tiramisù birthday cake. Never mind all of that. He hasn't a clue how hard he will have to work to earn his way back into his daughter's life; all he knows is what he will so deeply regret tomorrow, that lost opportunity to get a good long look at the twins at the party, at the promised sight of their faces made up to resemble tigers by a professional face-painter hired to work the room. A young woman who will, Cliff imagines, transform his granddaughters into spectacular creatures with their cheeks painted gold, orange, and bronze; their eyebrows ghostly white; a black muzzle drawn between their nostrils and their chins; and best of all, a pair of fierce, pale fangs outlined in black sitting at the corners of their sweet, child-sized mouths.

But flying back to New York tomorrow morning along the Mass Pike in his tango-red Audi, his heart sinking lower and lower, he won't be able to catch even a momentary glimpse of any of it.

TODAY IS NOT YOUR DAY (2015)

The uniformed EMTs, a pair of forty-something blondes friendly as can be, arrive only six minutes after her fall, before Lauren has felt even the faintest pinch of pain, despite the fact that her kneecap seems to have vanished. Rolling onto her side, staring upward at the coolly modern, glass-and-steel light fixture on the ceiling in the narrow hallway of her apartment, she pretends that everything that has gone wrong today is about to be righted.

Yeah, good luck with that.

At her side, Alex, her onetime fiancé, hovers, his phone in hand. He is big-boned, six feet four inches tall, but still must watch his weight, which he does, vigilantly. He sells security systems to large companies in the US and abroad, and makes more money in a year than Lauren, a caseworker for the homeless in Manhattan, will probably see in five.

So be it, as her mother liked to say.

The EMTs, who are named Courtney and Rayanne, squat beside Lauren, asking how she happened to find herself on the floor, and praising her for having been smart enough not to try to move from where she'd fallen. "Such a dumb thing," Lauren acknowledges, wincing as she offers her quick little synopsis: polished floor, heels on her favorite black leather boots dangerously worn down, she herself racing along the slightly slippery hallway, needing one of her Marlboro Lights before running out to dinner with Alex.

She won't, in fact, be eating dinner of any sort at all until Tuesday. And today is only Sunday, the day, she will soon learn, that her patella shattered into five pieces the moment she hit the floor. And also the day that, just minutes ago, Alex broke the news to her—like a fierce bolt of lightning from the clearest of skies—that he was having second and third thoughts about their recent engagement.

The two of them were standing in their narrow kitchen, facing each other as Lauren leaned her elbows against the counter; she could see the constellation of fingerprints on the stainless steel refrigerator and thought of taking a few steps forward and wiping them off with a paper towel.

Oh, and to be entirely honest, Alex went on, he'd decided that, given those disturbing thoughts of his, it would be best if he *withdrew* (and here he'd coiled his hand into a fist and coughed into it) *from the, um, relationship.*

Withdrew?

People withdrew money from their checking accounts at the ATM, they withdrew from the world, perhaps, but they didn't withdraw from their fiancées. They broke up with them and left them reeling.

But obviously, Alex added, Lauren should feel free to keep the ring, a slightly flawed one-carat diamond that had belonged to his long-deceased great-grandmother, Gussie. And of course he and Lauren could still have one last dinner out together, if that's what she wanted, he told her.

"You're kidding, right?" Lauren said. "Very funny. I mean, hilarious," she continued, smiling in confusion. And her heart began to tick faster than usual.

"*Not* kidding," Alex said. He sighed, jutting his lower lip forward unattractively, though he was, certainly, an attractive guy—square-jawed, straight-nosed, hazel-eyed. "Not kidding, and really, really sorry," he told Lauren. "As sorry as I can be."

"Are you on drugs?" she said. "Have you been talking to Keith again?" Keith was one of his old friends from grad school who liked to drink on the weekends until he passed out. And who also had something of a coke habit. Like Alex, he had an MBA from Harvard, but he was still, in Lauren's opinion, kind of an idiot.

Alex shook his head. "*Definitely* not on drugs. And haven't spoken to Keith in a couple of months."

"So wait, can you please tell me what these second thoughts are?" Lauren managed to say. The inside of her mouth felt sandy, and when she tried to swallow, it was as if her throat had closed up.

"You know," Alex said vaguely.

No, she *didn't* know, but she planned to find out every last mortifying detail. Just as soon as she got her pack of Marlboro Lights from the bedroom the two of them shared.

"Uh-huh, uh-huh, just a simple slip 'n' fall," Rayanne—who seems to be in charge—is saying now. She slides her fingertips into the empty cavity formerly occupied by Lauren's patella, and announces that, with any luck, it may turn out that the knee itself is only dislocated.

"So maybe you'll be lucky today," Alex says, on his own knees now beside Lauren. "Wouldn't it be great if it was just a dislocation?"

"Fuck you," she tells him through clenched teeth, though she's never spoken to him like this in the nearly four years they've been together. "Like you *give* a crap," she says for good measure. The EMTs show no sign of having heard her, though it's impossible that they missed those half-dozen little words. They've probably heard plenty worse, Lauren thinks, and anyway, it's none of their business *what* she says to Alex. Or why.

"Hey, do you guys have scissors I can use?" Rayanne asks. "I need to cut your pants, Lauren, so we can get a better look at this knee of yours."

But these are Lauren's favorite pants, designer jeans plucked from the racks of Second Chance, one of those stores full of formerly pricey, "gently used" merchandise; visiting her neighborhood tailor a few years ago, Lauren had these particular jeans shortened to fit her flawlessly. And there's no way in hell she's going to let this kind, well-meaning EMT destroy them.

"Sorry, but believe it or not, we don't," she says.

"Don't be ridiculous," Alex says. He immediately goes off to get the scissors they keep in the ceramic mug that rests on the kitchen counter.

It's Courtney's brilliantly simple idea that Rayanne cut along the seam so that Lauren can return the pants to the tailor for a quick fix sometime soon; even so, the sight of those all-purpose, blue-handled steel scissors clicking their way up the leg of her beloved jeans upsets Lauren more than it should.

Now she's being lifted onto a stretcher and wheeled to the elevator and through the lobby of the high-rise where she and Alex have lived so happily, so cozily, these past couple of years since they both turned thirty, first Lauren and then Alex, their birthdays only a few months apart.

In the lobby, the doorman and the concierge on duty wave goodbye and wish her a speedy recovery, then turn their attention to the delivery girl from Get Reel Videos, who, unaccountably, has arrived carrying a pizza.

It occurs to Lauren that this one-bedroom condo of Alex's legally belongs only to him, and that, quite possibly, she's in imminent danger of becoming homeless. Not unlike the clients whose lives she works so hard—and often, so fruitlessly—to improve. (Fruitlessly, she's discovered, because not everyone who desperately needs help actually wants it.)

She tries to bar Alex from the ambulance, but he insists he wouldn't dream of leaving her alone (*Oh really?* she thinks), insists on accompanying her on the half-mile trip to the hospital. When, in the ambulance, he takes her hand and pats it, Lauren tells him that he's gone too far. For someone who no longer loves her, she means. "Touch me again, and I'll blow you away," Lauren warns him. And this is when it hits her that today is December 7th, Pearl Harbor Day, commemorating that surprise military attack conducted almost three-quarters of a century ago.

The ER doc is even blonder than the EMTs and smiles inappropriately as she interprets the X-rays for Lauren. "I see right here, and here and here and here and here, the five pieces of your messed-up patella," she says. "I mean messed up *big* time, but one of our surgeons will put it back together nicely for you, okay? You're scheduled for surgery sometime Monday morning, how's that?"

"Sweet!" Lauren says with enthusiasm, because this is what's expected of her. She's still reclining on the stretcher she was carried in on, with a dense pillow beneath her head and her eye makeup a little smeary, and though she's almost always warm, even in winter, she's feeling a chill now, and has to ask Alex to look for an extra blanket. She hopes never to have to ask him for anything ever again; even asking for something as insignificant as a hospital blanket makes her uneasy. If Alex no longer loves her—and evidently he doesn't—she just wants him to disappear from her life as swiftly and as cleanly as possible. At least that's what she's telling herself. Repeatedly, ever since the moment when Alex assumed his new role as her ex.

He finds a thin white cotton blanket for her that looks and feels like a cheap bath towel.

"The nurse says they'll have a room ready for you upstairs in an hour or so," he reports, adjusting the blanket carefully at her waist.

"Go home," Lauren tells him. "If I start to feel lonely, I'll call my father to come and sit with me."

"Your father lives in Westchester. By the time he gets here, you'll be upstairs in your room."

Miraculously, Lauren's wrecked knee is still scarcely painful at all; she told the ER doc and the pair of nurses who've been checking on her that on a scale of one to ten—ten reflecting unbearable agony—her pain registers only an unimpressive two. Well, maybe three.

Everyone remarks on her good fortune; to be honest, one of the nurses confides, they were expecting to hear her shrieking for morphine.

Later, up on the orthopedics ward, a fourth-year med student, age twenty-five, stops by her bed and suggests, somewhat condescendingly, that Lauren is in shock, her mind refusing to accept her injury, this nasty affront to her body.

Oh, she's in shock all right. And hasn't yet been presented with even a scintilla of evidence of what she has or hasn't done to earn Alex's dissatisfaction, disapproval, disdain, you name it. She's been made redundant; isn't that what they call it in England when you've been sacked?

But the knee, at least, is fixable; a couple of hours in the OR on Monday morning, and Lauren will be good to go, the med student assures her. As for the rest of her life (the life which, a scant few hours ago, included Alex and his nicely appointed Upper West Side apartment—which Lauren helped decorate with those carefully chosen steel-framed reproductions of Pollock and Rothko prints, not to mention the industrial carpeting in the living room and the glass-topped dining table and black leather chairs surrounding it)—well, if love and a comfortable place to live in Manhattan are no longer part of the equation, it seems she'll have no choice but to leave them behind and move on, never mind that placing one foot in front of the other and propelling herself up and out aren't in the realm of possibility for her at the moment. *And she doesn't yet know the half of it:* not a thing about the foam-padded, metal-hinged brace that will, post-op, extend from her ankle to her hip, immobilizing her knee for eight interminable weeks. Nor does she have more than an inkling of the morti-fying assistance she'll need, once released from the hospital, in getting to and from the bathroom, into and out of the shower, even into and out of the bed she and Alex have shared for a couple of happy, mostly uneventful years together.

In all honesty, Lauren can't imagine where she might have gone wrong. And if she weren't currently confined to a hospital bed, facing a two-hour surgery and God knows what else on Monday morning, she'd press Alex to tell her right now why their engagement has come undone. And why so uncer-emoniously. But she just doesn't have the stomach for it now. Looking down at the brilliant-cut diamond on her stubby lit-tle ring finger, she contemplates yanking it off and flinging it in Alex's direction. But he's busy channel-surfing on the small flat-screen TV suspended above her bed, and the moment isn't quite right. Seriously, though, what *is* she going to do with the ring, she asks herself. It doesn't belong on her finger; the sight of it there makes her feel pathetic. Not to mention unloved and abandoned. How hard could it be to remove it from her finger and offer it back to Alex? She gives it a shot, but Great-grandma Gussie's ring seems to have a mind of its own and refuses to slide over the second joint of Lauren's finger no matter how vigor-ously she twists it. A squirt of liquid soap would take care of things, but even the thought of that ordinary effort drains her.

"Not much of a selection here," Alex complains. "No HBO, no Showtime, no Cinemax."

"Alex," Lauren says, "go home."

"You want me to leave?" He looks genuinely puzzled. Weekends, to keep in shape, he often rides twenty-five miles a day on his $3000 Schwinn, and Lauren has to admit that standing here now in his navy blue V-necked sweater and olive green corduroys, he looks fit and handsome, so much so that she wants to slug him.

"You better get out of here before I punch you," she advises.

And is startled when he recklessly drops a kiss on her forehead just before he leaves, promising to return tomorrow morning before her surgery, which has been scheduled for eleven a.m.

"Gimme a break and don't bother coming back," Lauren calls after him; she pretends that her roommate, the plumpish, middle-aged woman in the bed next to hers, can't hear her.

Why would she want this man, who has fallen out of love with her, to hold her hand tomorrow just before the surgeon takes a whack at her?

She doesn't start to weep until after Alex leaves and a plate of sickly yellow mac and cheese is delivered to her bedside table on an eggplant-colored tray, along with a mini-bowl of chicken broth, a sealed plastic cup of applesauce, and an individual-sized can of pineapple juice.

Her roommate, who evidently has rejected her hospital gown and is dressed in clothing from home—a lilac sweatsuit and matching terry cloth slippers—asks if Lauren's planning to eat her applesauce.

"What? You can have the whole tray if you want," Lauren tells her.

But her roommate only wants the applesauce, and instructs her to toss it across the room to her. "I'm Serra," she says. "Not Sarah," she explains, and spells out her name for Lauren. She is, she soon volunteers, fifty-one years old with two ruined kidneys and a spot on the transplant waiting list— along with 80,000 other hopefuls—at the United Network for Organ Sharing. Even one good kidney would be a miraculous gift, she explains. Until a kidney is offered, however, she's forced to spend nearly four hours, three days a week, in dialysis. "In my spare time," she says, rolling her eyes, "I work thirty-five hours a week as a legal secretary, a job I can't afford to quit because the medical benefits are so good. I'm running on empty," she admits, and shrugs.

"I'm so sorry," Lauren murmurs.

"But why are *you* crying?" Serra asks. "And maybe I'll take some of your mac and cheese after all. But only if you're sure you don't want it."

"I'm positive," Lauren says, and then, quietly, "My fiancé dumped me today." She has two perfectly good kidneys and is, except for her knee, healthy as a horse, but nonetheless, she can't resist feeling sorry for herself here in her hospital bed, too queasy to contemplate what it might be like to swallow down a small mouthful of glutinous-looking mac and cheese. Even this smallest touch of self-pity is a character flaw, she realizes, and feels so ashamed in the presence of poor, unlucky Serra that she actually blushes. Under her breath, and to make herself feel better, she curses Alex and his unaccountable failure to continue to love her. And then curses *herself* for not offering up one of her kidneys to Serra here and now.

Serra is out of bed and approaching Lauren's mac and cheese, brandishing a salad fork. "Hold on, he dumped you *today*? When you broke your, what, knee? What an asshole!"

This assessment seems accurate enough, though, in all fairness to Alex, Lauren tells her roommate, he did, in truth, dump her several minutes *before* she fell. And has never, that she can recall, shown himself to be anything other than a pretty good guy. (Except, perhaps, when she asked him to accompany her and her father to synagogue services the Friday evening after her mother's death. *The atheist in me just won't allow it*, Alex told her. *Not even to make you happy for an hour.* The two of them had sex in her childhood bedroom that night, while Lauren's bereft father slept in the room across the hall, and Alex did make her happy, though for somewhat less than an hour.)

"He's *not* a good guy, he's an asshole," Serra repeats. "You're lying to yourself, Lauren, whether you know it or not. It's just like with my brother and me. Until I asked him for a kidney, I would have described *him* as a good guy, too. My sister told me not to ask him, told me that he didn't want to offer me the kidney and that I absolutely shouldn't ask. But he's a potential match, so how could I not? I called him up because I was too chicken to ask in person, and when he said, 'Um, sorry, no can do, kiddo,' it hit me that nothing he could say or do in the future would ever repair the damage he did in that one single moment. Nothing! He wouldn't even agree to get tested. He's my brother, but, well, screw *him*." Tucking into Lauren's mac and cheese now, Serra says, "But the thing is, he's got a set of three-year-old twins to take care of, and it was his wife who told him he had to say no. So...maybe I should stop being so angry, right?"

"I don't know what I..." Lauren begins, and then an Indian nurse with a maroon-colored bindi at the center of her brow arrives to check her blood pressure and Serra's; a few minutes later, another nurse appears, checks their IVs, and wishes them both a blessed night, which she pronounces "bless-ed."

"A bless-ed night to you, too," Serra says, but Lauren merely offers an utterly nonsectarian "thank you."

She feels thoroughly embarrassed the instant she awakens from her dismal dream. In it, she was wearing a wedding gown, a none-too-shabby Vera Wang (which, in real life, Lauren had admired in *Modern Bride*), and escorted by her father, made it halfway down the aisle, where Alex met her—dressed, oddly, in jeans and a sweat-drenched T-shirt. Drawing back Lauren's veil, Alex kissed her before the seated rows of smiling guests, then announced, in a booming voice Lauren never knew he possessed, that he felt it best to withdraw. *Withdraw from what? Are you insane?* her father said, echoing the guests, every one of whom looked clueless.

When the orderly comes to transport her to the O.R. at ten forty-five in the morning, Alex still hasn't shown up, though he does call to wish Lauren good luck. He claims to have been caught up in a lengthy conference call with a client in Mumbai, and even though Lauren doesn't believe him and his uninspired excuse, she finds herself grateful for his call.

"Right, thanks," she says. And then, to annoy the atheist in him, adds, "Oh yeah, and don't forget to have a bless-ed day."

So much for her simple, pain-free slip 'n' fall: awakening at precisely six o'clock the morning following her surgery, Lauren knows she needs something truly potent, a narcotic that will do the job and do it right. She squeezes the call button, and waits anxiously, staring as the large circle of a classroom-appropriate clock on the wall across from her bed reports that nearly ten minutes have passed. And she's still no closer to being pain-free than she was when she first pressed the button. On the other side of the room, Serra appears to be sleeping comfortably; even though Lauren knows it's senseless, she envies her. And tries the call button again. Another ten minutes pass, and at last, a nurse appears. But in reality, she's a nurse's aide, and cannot help Lauren, as she is quick to communicate. "Your nurse is on her break," the woman says indifferently, "and I can't do anything for you."

"Please, I'll take *anything*," Lauren says. "Even just plain Tylenol with codeine, anything you have for me." She stretches out her arm and touches the woman's wrist. "Please."

The nurse's aide remains unmoved. She makes no attempt to soothe or sympathize; she just turns her back to Lauren and leaves the room. Lauren is reminded of a T-shirt she saw a guy wearing on the subway last summer:

I CAN ONLY BE NICE TO ONE PERSON A DAY
AND TODAY IS NOT YOUR DAY

At seven o'clock, after she's finally given the Percocet she so richly deserves, she realizes she has to pee. The nurse's aide returns, draws the curtain around the bed, and helps Lauren onto the bedpan, none too delicately.

"I'll be back," she says.

"Please don't leave," Lauren says. "I'll be finished in a minute, I promise."

"You do your business, and I'll do mine," the woman says. And vanishes.

Abandoned, still sitting on the bedpan eighteen minutes later, Lauren is near tears. She can't reach the call button to summon assistance without moving off the plastic basin fitted beneath her, and is stuck, mortifyingly, behind a curtain, unable to do anything but pray that help will be along soon enough. But it isn't, and so she makes what feels like a decision of real importance, and eases herself off the pan on her own, then gingerly lowers it to the floor beside her bed, careful not to swish any fluid over the top and onto the linoleum floor.

"What's this on the floor here?" the next nurse to saunter by asks. "What if I'd stepped into your mess and knocked it over, then what? Can't you be a little more CONSIDERATE?"

Lauren's knee is in pieces, tethered by loops of wire and metal hooks. Her leg continues to ache, no matter what drugs she swallows, and her face hasn't been washed since Sunday, which, she believes, was two days ago. And now she's been criticized for being inconsiderate. "My fiancé just broke up with me," she hears herself say, hoping for a smidgen of sympathy, hoping that there's not even a trace of whininess in her voice. But is there no end to her mortification? If her homeless, paranoid schizophrenic, drug- and alcohol-addicted clients could hear her now, they would laugh in her pained, sweaty face. *No offense, but what the fuck's wrong with you, Miss Lauren? You got to get yourself some dignity, baby!*

The nurse fails to be impressed by what Lauren knows to be her pathetic confession about Alex. "You look like you need a sponge bath," is all the woman offers.

"I do," Lauren agrees. "And a fresh gown, please." She has no desire to study herself in a mirror, knowing that what she will see is the face of someone in need of lipstick, mouthwash, a toothbrush adorned with a half-inch of Crest, Colgate, or Aquafresh, and most important of all, a long, very hot shower—the longer and hotter the better. And after that, a few swipes under each arm with a stick of Soft & Dri. As much as she wants these things, the thought of attending to them, even lifting a toothbrush to her mouth, exhausts her. She who works ten-hour days along the Bowery, engaged in the hard, hard work of coaxing her clients off the street and into shelters and hospitals.

Face it: she's a mess. And one without a significant other. Though here's her father, visiting at lunchtime now, staying long enough to inform her that she looks terrible. *(Gee, thanks, Dad!)* And that the Belgian chocolate he's brought her costs fifty-two dollars a pound. "Can you believe it?" he says. "For chocolate!" When he kisses Lauren goodbye, he says he'll be back tomorrow, and this time might even bring his girlfriend, even though all three of them know that Lauren's never been able to warm to her. (For the usual reasons—Roxanna's hair is a strikingly unnatural shade of orangey-red; she talks way too much and says too little; and most annoying of all, has a sibilant "S" that drives Lauren crazy.)

"Roxanna really wants to come and see you, despite the fact that she's fully aware you don't like her," her father says.

"I do too like her," Lauren says, but without much conviction.

"Honey, you don't," her father insists. "And Roxanna's fine with it. She understands how much you loved Mom. She wouldn't dream of trying to compete with a dead woman."

Lauren's father is a psych professor at Rutgers, but sometimes, she thinks, he seems bent on proving that he's not the sharpest crayon in the box. Or even the second sharpest.

As he talks, she lies silent, wiggling the toes of her bad leg (as the nurses call it, as if the leg itself has been disobedient), and imagining how lovely it would be to stand behind the glass door of the shower at home and let the steamy water run over every inch of her.

(Her surgeon will pop in for a cursory visit later in the afternoon and let her know that there will be no showering for *the next fourteen days,* not until after the many stitches in her incision have been removed—a piece of news that will reduce Lauren to bitter tears. Over a shower, of all things! Because without her daily shower, she just isn't her real self, the one who runs with the homeless and does her best to significantly improve their sad, mean lives.)

"Give my love to Alex," her father says innocently, sailing out the door in his coffee-colored shoes and long tweed coat.

Over my dead body, Lauren thinks, but she smiles and nods politely as her father disappears.

A fresh gown has been deposited at the foot of her bed, but the nurse's aide who left it there has vanished. The next time an actual nurse materializes, Lauren asks for help in getting out of her old gown and into the new one.

"Oh, I don't *do* that sort of thing," the nurse says, as if she's been asked to give advice on where to go to procure the services of the hottest hookers in town. "Do it yourself, it's good for you," she orders. No smile of encouragement accompanies her behest; she's here to check Serra on the other side of the room, and the look she flashes in Lauren's direction strongly suggests that Lauren is nothing more than a particularly distasteful blood-sucking insect.

Bending from the waist, attempting to lean across the bed to grab the gown just out of reach, Lauren shuts her eyes against the pain. It just hurts too much; she'd rather lie here in her gown spotted with rust-colored blood from a leaky IV site than cause herself any further pain. This shames and worries her, as if she might be judged weak or lazy, but come *on*, wasn't it only yesterday that she had surgery? Isn't she entitled to a little help from these folks whose job it is to heal her?

B-I-T-C-H, she spells silently as the nurse leaves the room. And for additional satisfaction, Lauren gives her the finger.

Shortly before dinner, an angel of mercy she hasn't seen before agrees to help. "I'll do whatever I can for you in the next three minutes," the nurse promises cheerfully. "But after those three minutes are up, my break starts. And you know I got to have my caffeine, right?"

In just under three minutes, Lauren gets a new, pristine gown patterned with fleurs-de-lis, though the sponge bath she's dying for has been put on hold indefinitely. This is one of Manhattan's finest hospitals, but here's one patient whose face hasn't been washed in over forty-eight hours and who is still waiting for a fucking toothbrush. She's a little bemused; how is it possible that she's been transformed into someone incapable of walking to the bathroom and washing her face on her own at the sink? Only two days ago, she had a pair of utterly dependable knees that could get her anywhere she wanted to go (even up the eighty-six flights of stairs to the top of the Empire State Building, if necessary). And, oh yeah, also a fiancé who presumably loved her enough to spend the rest of his life in her company.

She looks over at Serra, who, in the presence of her elderly mother, is devouring what appears to be a Big Mac or its Burger King equivalent. Lauren can smell that supersized order of fries from across the room. Her own mother is gone from this world, but in any case, she probably couldn't have been persuaded to bring even the tastiest junk food to Lauren. She was done in by a spot of melanoma that spread, disastrously, just after Lauren moved in with Alex. And she is still sorely missed two years later. Her mother's ideas about food, Lauren recalls, were a little wacky during her childhood: only five M&M's, one of each color, were allowed every night after dinner. And only half a Twinkie, the other half wrapped and put away in the refrigerator, where it remained until the following night when Lauren was permitted to finish it.

If her mother had been luckier, she'd be fifty-eight years old now, still a middle-aged person with, presumably, much to look forward to. And with, presumably, some good advice for Lauren—who could use a little hand-holding as she sits in her hospital bed eyeing the sweetness with which Serra's mother pushes Serra's hair from her face and arranges it behind ears so large and cupped that, well, only a mother could love them.

"Enough, Mommy, leave it, I just wanna eat my dinner, okay?" Serra says in annoyance.

Hearing this big, ungainly, chronically ill fifty-one-year-old refer to her mother as "Mommy" makes Lauren's heart hurt, as her own mother used to say.

Though Alex had apparently been fully prepared to send her packing, he hasn't once, in this first week during which Lauren has been homebound and glued to his bed, mentioned even a word about her departure. Beyond that, he's been so attentive, so utterly deferential, that if Lauren didn't know better, she might almost be convinced he's forgotten his particular griev-ances (still unnamed) and fallen back in love with her. Each morning before leaving for work, he prepares a tray to fit over her lap, arranging a small glass bowl of cat-shaped mini-cook-ies from Trader Joe's for her breakfast, and for her lunch, a Saran-Wrapped peanut butter sandwich, a navel orange, and a Granny Smith apple. All Lauren need do is reach for it at the foot of the bed, a feat of which she's now capable. There's a brand-new mini-fridge at her bedside, stocked with bottled water and cans of Diet Coke. Several times throughout the day, Alex calls to check on her, and when he returns at night after first stopping at the grocery store (formerly *her* responsibility), he prepares dinner for them both (also *her* responsibility), which Lauren eats in bed and which he eats seated on the floor next to her bedside, his plate resting on his knees, a glass of wine nearby. Afterward, he goes off to do the dishes. And, twice this week, a load of laundry (half Lauren's responsibility). All of this uncomplainingly.

Maybe it's guilt that has made him ever more attentive. The hard truth is, she can't survive without him right now, and he knows it.

They both know that if he were to kick her to the curb, Lauren would have no choice—with that ankle-to-hip brace on her leg—but to move in with her father and his exasperating girlfriend, Roxanna. An option that would probably make killing herself an attractive alternative.

Of the numerous humiliating favors Lauren is forced to ask of Alex, one of the most humiliating of all must be requested every night at bedtime. Now that two weeks have passed, and the sutures have been removed from her knee, she's finally permitted to shower every night. But there's a catch.

"Alex!" she calls. She knows he's in the living room watching *Dazed and Confused* on HBO and doesn't want to be disturbed. Can't she at least allow him to enjoy his movie in peace? But she has already undressed (by no means a minor accomplishment) and is waiting, a trifle impatiently, at the side of the bed for Alex to wrap a thirty-dollar waterproof plastic bag around her leg. Because even though the sutures are gone, the brace itself still has to remain dry in the shower.

Sitting in her bikini-cut underwear and favorite black bra, she calls Alex's name one more time, trying not to appear too needy. Though of course she's never been needier in her life.

When he arrives, a couple of minutes later, he ignores Lauren as she takes off her bra and bikini panties (a miserably obvious sign right there that, two weeks after her accident, he's undeniably no longer interested in her—not in *that* way, at least) and goes straight for the water-proof bag he generously charged on his Mastercard at a store called Medi-Supply across town. Its taxicab-yellow plastic is uncomfortably chilly against Lauren's skin, but she keeps that information to herself, not wanting to sound like a complainer. She eases herself timidly, painfully, into the shower, and settles, with difficulty, onto a small plastic bench meant for disabled people like *her*. Alex closes the shower door behind her and waits for her to dismiss him. Lauren wants him to stay and keep an eye on her, but hasn't she asked enough of him? *Thank you*, she mouths from behind the clear glass door of the shower, and then he's off to see the rest of *Dazed and Confused*, the movie conveniently frozen in place by the miraculous technology of their DVR.

The hot water, as it streams across her body, offers Lauren a bit of sensual pleasure, though certainly nothing like sex with Alex used to. Sex with Alex; isn't that the sort of notable pleasure she will never again experience with him? After much prodding, just a few days ago she finally learned—over a homemade dinner of veggie burgers adorned with Brie and mushrooms, and made-from-scratch sweet potato fries—Alex's chief reason for wanting her to take a hike. "Okay, look, the thing is, we're just not soul mates," he announced from his seat, the tiniest sliver of sautéed mushroom clinging to his neatly groomed beard. "To reduce it to a very basic level, I like the Beatles and you pretend to like the Stones."

"What are you *talking* about?" Lauren said. "Of course I'm your soul mate. I love you!" she said indignantly.

He shook his head. "We definitely feel affection for each other, we enjoy each other's company, but at the end of the day, we just don't have that soul mate vibe." What he meant,

Alex explained, is that while he failed to see the virtues of opera, Broadway musicals, and Charles Dickens, Lauren had never been enamored of Thai food, science fiction, or David Mamet.

Well, maybe so. But what did any of this have to do with love?

Lauren hates the expression "at the end of the day." And at that moment, she was pretty sure she hated *him*. "Oh, for God's sake," she said. "Do you really think I could love someone who wasn't my soul mate?" Only minutes before, using a metal walker, its legs tipped with rubber so she wouldn't slip, she'd made her way laboriously down the hallway to the dining room, where Alex helped her into her wheelchair; positioned at just the right angle, it allowed her to sit and eat at the table. Like an ordinary person, not some loser who had to take all her meals in bed. But if, as Alex said, she failed to hold her own in the soul mate department, well, didn't *that* render her a loser?

No matter how vehemently Lauren protested, Alex could not be persuaded. "You saintly social worker types are all the same," he went on. "Thinking that the rest of the world can never rise to the occasion. Well, you know what? I can't spend a lifetime with someone who doesn't fully embrace the person that I am, i.e., a guy who makes a damn good living out there in the business world."

His accusation, after the more than two years they'd spent together, might almost have been funny, Lauren thinks, if only it hadn't been so infuriatingly wrongheaded. Not to mention insulting. Because she's not some snob, not someone who thinks that the measure of a man or woman is necessarily to be found in what they happen to do for a living. The truest measure of a man is deep in his marrow, isn't it? And look what a good soul Alex has proved to be in all the time she's known him; he's the good-hearted guy who marches every year in the

Making Strides Against Breast Cancer Walk in memory of his best friend's mother; he's the uncle who showers his two little nephews with extravagant electronic toys; he's the one person Lauren knows who never allows himself to get entangled in family arguments but will, instead, work as a peacemaker to keep his family intact.

It is this good-hearted peacemaker who so recently informed her—during that dinner of veggie burgers and fries—that as soon as the brace was off her leg and she could get around reasonably well on her own, she would have to find herself someplace else to live. In the meantime, Alex has continued to be helpful and solicitous; really, Lauren couldn't ask for a better home healthcare attendant. And this is how, brokenheartedly, she has come to think of him—as a live-in, impressively conscientious healthcare worker. Someone who will meet all her physical needs except one.

Lauren calls his name now; she's finished in the shower, and needs help stepping out and then onto the bathmat. She can dry herself off, but needs help, as well, getting into her underwear and flannel pajama bottoms. Holding on to the edge of the sink and obediently lifting one foot and then the other so that Alex can get her panties on her, she feels like an overgrown, ungainly child who has failed to keep pace with her peers.

"I'm sorry," she says. "I hate to bother you." In the aftermath of her hot shower, the edges of white wallpaper patterned with black-and-gray confetti curl up slightly around the mirror above the sink. This is the same wallpaper she and Alex spent half a day putting up together when she first moved in with him; afterward, Lauren remembers, he slowly lowered the straps of her overalls and slipped her T-shirt and sports bra over her head, admiring the look of her, topless, reflected in the mirror, her hair drawn back in a small knot, her feet in black flip-flops imprinted with peach-colored seashells.

Making love with him on the bedroom carpet just beyond the bathroom, dressed only in her flip-flops, Lauren listened closely, taking delight in the urgent sound of Alex's breathing in her ear.

She stares now at the chipped, did-it-yourself silvery polish remaining on her toenails. No professional pedicures on that skimpy take-home pay of hers.

Forbidden to put any weight on her bad leg, she's beholden to Alex for the smallest, most commonplace things: Every night he holds her firmly around the waist as she stands on one leg in front of the bathroom mirror and uses both hands to floss her teeth. Without him, she might lose her balance and go crashing to the ceramic-tiled floor.

"Close your eyes," Lauren instructs him now, because it's just too creepy to have Alex watch her floss. "I'm sorry," she repeats.

"Apologize again and I'll blow your fuckin' head off," he says casually, repeating a line they both love from the TV show *Deadwood*. They laugh together for the first time in three very long weeks and it feels like something to savor.

At night, in bed, forced to sleep flat on her back or on her side instead of in the fetal position she's always favored, Lauren gazes at the cottage cheese ceiling overhead, aware of Alex's gentle snoring beside her. How strange it is to be sharing a bed with someone who no longer wants her there. Occasionally, in his sleep, Alex casts an arm around her and unknowingly pulls her close. She snuggles up to him as best she can, her bum leg rigid in its brace. It feels dishonest, somehow, as if she's taking advantage of affection unconsciously offered by this man who, during waking hours, has carefully explained why he wants her out of his bed, out of his apartment, out of his life.

She hasn't yet shared the news with her father or with any of her friends that the wedding is off. As long as she and Alex appear to be a couple, living, as they still do, in the same apartment, why bother to spill the beans? Her father and friends feel sorry enough for her as it is because of her stupid accident; garnering even more sympathy from them would just be too much.

Sometimes, on weekend afternoons, after he returns from biking, Alex takes her out for a spin in her wheelchair, and Lauren waves gaily to the doorman as she whooshes by.

Sometimes she's out on her own, using her walker on a wintry day, forcing herself to make it to the Starbucks on the corner, amazed by the white-haired old ladies in the neighborhood who, in comparison with Lauren and her halting baby steps, seem to move like the wind.

"I'm not going to hurt you," her physical therapist promises, but at first Lauren doesn't believe him. He is a thoughtful, middle-aged Polish guy from Krakow; his eyes are a stunning turquoise, his hair pitch-black and stick-straight. His name is Tomasz and Lauren finds herself wondering if his father, who was a teenager during World War II, threw rocks at his Jewish neighbors before they were rounded up, forced into the Krakow ghetto, and soon enough, hustled off to the gas chamber. (If he could read her mind, would Tomasz ask her to leave his office and make her promise never to come back?)

He treats her with something approaching tenderness; he undoes the Velcro flaps of her brace and lifts her leg from it so gently, it's as if he's unwrapping some treasure, one of those $5 million Fabergé eggs speckled with 3,000 tiny diamonds, perhaps. Frowning, he assesses Lauren's thin, pale leg, her skin peeling sickeningly, and says that when he's finished with her, several months from now, she will be able to bend her knee considerably more than the ninety degrees required to walk up and down even the shortest flight of stairs.

Sounds great, Lauren says. Since she's currently incapable of descending into the subway, taking cabs to work, which used to be a luxury, is now a necessity. And way too expensive for someone whose salary is really just peanuts.

She has excellent health benefits, though, and so is able to visit Tomasz three times a week. As usual, today she sits on an upholstered table in one of the offices Tomasz shares with two other physical therapists. She is dressed for the occasion in gray yoga pants and a Harvard B School T-shirt. Standing alongside her, Tomasz extends her leg and raises it until the sole of her bare foot is resting against his shoulder. He tells Lauren about his aging parents, who still live in Poland and somehow managed to survive first the Nazis and then the Communists.

Over the past couple of weeks, she's found herself confiding in him the way, she imagines, other women confide in their hairdressers. (*She*—the ill-paid social worker—doesn't have a hairdresser per se; her hair can be trimmed every few months in any neighborhood salon by anybody for about twenty-five bucks, tip included, and she's absolutely content with that.) Today she and Tomasz return to the subject of Alex and how the two of them had met online and the swiftness with which he'd invited Lauren to move in with him.

"Ah, love at first sight?" Tomasz says, and lowers her leg to the table.

"Something like that," Lauren says ruefully. "But now it looks like we're over."

"You want me to 'friend' you on Facebook and make this boyfriend of yours jealous?" Tomasz offers.

"That's sweet of you," Lauren says, "but I don't think that's going to help any."

"'Facebook helps you connect and share with the people in your life,'" Tomasz recites, sounding like a commercial. He's been in the US for seven years and is still hoping to improve his already excellent English, the nuances of which he's learned from watching television. He asks Lauren to roll over onto her stomach now, and attaches a four-pound weight to her bad leg. "You are a Jewess, yes?" he says. The tone of his voice is pleasant, conversational; he might just as easily be asking, "You are a vegan, yes?"

Lauren's face burns, but isn't it Tomasz who should be embarrassed? "I'm *what*?" she says. Because isn't it just possible she's misunderstood him?

"You know what they mean by an Ashkenazi Jew, yes? I read an article in the *National Geographic* that says these particular Jews have the highest IQs of any people in the world. They are the smartest and the most accomplished. And since I believe you are a Jewess—yes?—I thought it would be nice for you to hear this. And now I want you to lift your leg slowly, very slowly, ten times, with the weight on it like this. Then rest, and do another ten. I have to check on another patient and soon I will be back."

She's on the honor system here; when Tomasz returns and asks Lauren if she's done her leg-lifts twenty times, she can lie and say that she has, and he'll never know the difference. The reason for lying, Lauren understands, is this: the slower her progress, the longer it will take before Alex deems her fully dump-able, ready to be kicked out of what she still deludedly thinks of as "their" apartment.

See, they don't call those Ashkenazi Jews smarty-pants for nothing.

Lauren's six-week, post-op checkup is not going well. Her surgeon, who is just about her age (Lauren Googled her and knows that her husband is a weekend anchor on MSNBC and quite a hunk), reveals that she is disappointed in Lauren. The doctor wears impressively high heels, and one of those tiny phones smartly in her ear, and she walks with the hint of a swagger. As is befitting for a very busy surgeon inhabiting the world of sports medicine.

Alex, looking every inch like Lauren's significant other, smashes his knuckles together and furrows his brow. "You promised us the brace would be off in six weeks," he says. He sounds plaintive.

"I warned you guys at the beginning—your physical therapist needs to *hurt* you, Lauren," Dr. Gilchrist says. "But I can tell by your not-great progress that he's a wuss."

Sitting upright on the examining table, Lauren swings her good leg and looks down at the floor. "Tomasz is a sweetie," she reports.

"Well, he sounds nice but not like someone who's going to whip you into shape so that you'll be back to commuting to work on the subway every day," Dr. Gilchrist says. "You and your PT guy need a wake-up call."

"So the brace isn't coming off?" Alex says. His hands are in the front pockets of his jeans now, and he's taken a step back from Lauren and the examining table.

"Not at the moment, no. And that's because your progress, Ms. Bachman, is worthy of a B, B minus, when you should, in fact, have been striving for an A plus."

Lauren's always been such a diligent student, but now, of course, she's a deliberate failure. And who knows how many more weeks with Alex that crappy grade may have earned her!

"Lemme show you something," Dr. Gilchrist says. She takes Lauren's bad knee and bends it for her, viciously, as Lauren yelps in pain. On a scale of one to ten, Dr. Gilchrist's manhandling rates a ten. "*That's* the kind of progress we're interested in," she says. She pats Lauren on the shoulder. "Try harder," she advises.

Lauren's heart is thumping mightily; her knee is killing her. She'd like to get Dr. Gilchrist on the table, take a hard-faced ball-peen hammer to *her* left knee and see how the doc likes it. If it's tough love Dr. Gilchrist is advocating, why not show her exactly what she's referring to? Lauren thinks.

During the cab ride home, she and Alex silently retreat to their separate corners in the vinyl back seat patched in several places with white duct tape. And then, while stuck in rush hour traffic on upper Broadway, Lauren watches as Alex's arm suddenly extends toward her and his left hand seizes her right. They haven't held hands in she can't remember how long—at the very least, six weeks—and she foolishly allows this small, familiar gesture to inspire the tiniest whiff of hope to take root in her big dumb heart.

The shower seat, along with the thirty-dollar plastic bag that was formerly necessary to waterproof her leg, are sitting in the foyer, soon to be offered up for adoption in the laundry room of Alex's building, where tenants and owners leave all manner of things for anyone who might be able to make use of them. In just a few minutes, Lauren will be headed for her father's apartment in Bronxville, where he and Roxanna will show her to her room, an alcove, really, right off the dining area, where she can camp out until something better comes her way.

Isn't there anything she can say to Alex that will do the trick? He continues to insist that the two of them aren't soul mates and never were, but Lauren swears, right here in the lobby of Alex's building—surrounded by a couple of her carelessly packed suitcases on wheels and three jumbo shopping bags stuffed with books—that they are. She murmurs a few other things as well, keeping her voice down so that the doorman and concierge can't hear the sound of her last-ditch effort to reclaim the guy whom she knows, whom she swears, to be the love of her thoroughly well-intentioned but ultimately ordinary life. Right here in this vast lobby decorated with wine-colored leather couches and matching club chairs, big brassy pots of identical arrangements of slightly dusty silk flowers.

"I *know*," Alex says. He rubs his thumb absently against the dry heel of Lauren's hand before going out to hail the cab that will shoot her straight to her father's doorstep. Where Roxanna, his live-in girlfriend, teetering on the new, high-heeled suede boots he bought her, will greet Lauren with what appears to be genuine enthusiasm as her father looks on approvingly.

Sweetie! Roxanna will say, and the whistle of her sibilant "S" will make Lauren's heart sink even lower.

KOSTA (2013)

Of the old days, Kosta remembered absolutely nothing, and why would he? He was, he explained to Emily, a mere infant at the time his parents had been wrenched away from him in the middle of the night and then, horrifyingly, executed only hours later. Shot to death by Stalin's thugs in a prison courtyard in Leningrad. For no good reason at all except that they were a couple of Jewish doctors—his mother an obstetrician, his father a surgeon—two well-educated professionals whom the madman Stalin feared and hated, though of course he'd never even laid eyes upon them. "Nice, huh?" Kosta said.

"Jesus Christ!" said Emily, and impulsively placed a hand on Kosta's well-haired wrist. She and Kosta had never spoken in person before, and while at first she didn't find herself particularly attracted to him—despite his big, florid, handsome face—she did have the momentary urge to embrace his bulky shoulders, to bend his head benevolently against her and say something soothing. Something akin to "there, there," a phrase she couldn't recall ever having heard in real life but which seemed appropriate under the circumstances. Instead, she shook her head gloomily and sipped her vanilla latte in its environmentally friendly paper cup.

Emily was an unemployed, never-married thirty-year-old, and Kosta, a successful businessman, was a divorced fifty-something; they had not a thing in common, really. He was, however, going to pay her a generous sum of money ($45,000 dollars, to be exact) to write the story of his life, a story he was convinced could be sold to a publisher and then to the movies if Emily did her job right. And so they were sitting together now in a Starbucks in Union Square, with their absurdly expensive coffees and a single, untouched, caramel praline muffin on a brown paper napkin between them. It was nearly four o'clock on a drizzly Sunday in late November, and the place was packed with holiday shoppers, all of whom seemed to have cell phones set out on their tables, waiting, perhaps, for an urgent call from the love of their lives. Though Emily was currently without a lover, she did have a cell phone, a bachelor's degree from Brown (where she'd done a double concentration in English and Art History), a master's from Columbia, and a bad habit of falling for men for whom long-term commitment remained an unappealing concept. Having recently walked away from an unsatisfying job as a book publicist, she had been only too happy to read Kosta's email response to the announcement on her website—one that listed her services as a "ghost writer par excellence." She had yet to ghost-write anything at all, in fact, but she'd accumulated plenty of A's on her papers at both Brown and Columbia, labored over countless press releases, and on her good days, had enough self-confidence to keep her going. Earlier in the week, over the phone, she took a deep breath and tried not to sound anxious as she assured Kosta of her many virtues, including meticulousness and punctuality, and after a brief pause, he'd replied, "Okay, sounds cool."

Here in Starbucks, he pinched off a surprisingly dainty piece from their muffin, and, with his other hand, flicked back his thick, dark ponytail, which reached just past his shoulders. "Not only that," he said, "but after my parents were murdered, my own relatives fucking disavowed me!" Over fifty years had passed since he'd been abandoned, but he seemed newly outraged, as if the cruel facts of his autobiography still pained him. "Those relatives in Leningrad thought it was too dangerous to take me in, so they dumped me at some adoption agency, and eventually I ended up in Jersey City, in the home of two lunatics named Dorothy and Bobby Morrison, adoptive parents who treated me like their own personal servant boy, and beat the crap out of me if I didn't clean up my room properly."

Emily wiped away a tear. She couldn't bear to look at Kosta; she had to look somewhere, anywhere, else. To her left, a pair of homeless guys, their heads bowed, ignored a fat, battered paperback entitled *Embracing Defeat*, which someone had apparently left behind on their table.

"It was a long time ago, but you can see I've still got anger issues," Kosta said. He offered the muffin to her, reaching over and holding it up to her mouth. "Don't you want some?"

"Just thinking about what happened to your parents—what happened to *you*—makes my stomach hurt," said Emily.

"Well, I envy you those loving parents you probably have."

"I do have them, actually. Very much so," Emily admitted. She almost felt as if she owed him an apology for her untroubled, uneventful childhood and adolescence, for the openly affectionate parents, who, to this day, regarded her and her older brother, Jeff, as the shining jewels that ornamented their long and generally happy marriage.

"Well, then, you hit the jackpot, babe! You won the lottery ten times over! Two loving parents and you're good to go. Two lousy adoptive parents and you're permanently fucked."

Under her breath, Emily cursed the execrable Dorothy and Bobby Morrison, they who had treated Kosta so shamefully, bloodying his nose, he told her, sending him to school now and again with a blackened eye, a shiner that would eventually turn shades of green and yellow before fading away completely. But these were details Emily wouldn't learn until a month later, the night when she and Kosta stripped down to their underwear and fell across his unmade bed together, their hearts thumping in perfect synch with one another, their breathing noisy and a little ragged.

Christmas Eve, Kosta grilled a dinner for the two of them on the roof of the building he lived in near NYU. On the grill next to the steaks were half a pound of shiitake mushrooms that had been marinated for an hour in a vinaigrette of his own invention. There was no salad, but there were glass bowls of artichoke hearts and baby carrots, and a hard Italian bread called a *stirato*, pieces of which he warmed in a toaster oven whose innards, Emily noticed, could have used a good cleaning. She had never been to his apartment before, though they had worked together three weekends in a row at her dining table in a walk-up on the Upper East Side. She had several dozen pages of notes transcribed from the oral history Kosta had spilled to her thus far; she wasn't sure, however, precisely where the project was headed. Most of what Kosta had told her involved his miserable upbringing in Jersey City, and the hatred he felt for those unseemly parents who just wouldn't give him a break but who showered upon their own two biological sons an extravagant love which, Kosta claimed, made him want to puke whenever he thought about it.

From the roof, Emily could see the Empire State Building in the near distance, its upper floors lit in a slightly fuzzy red and green in honor of the holiday season. She shivered in her down vest, and rubbed her mittened hands together as Kosta, in his shirtsleeves, tended to their main course, three generously sized porterhouse steaks that he'd bought from a pricey butcher in SoHo. There was a table of metal and frosted glass with three wrought iron chairs arranged around it, and it was here that Kosta hoped they would enjoy their dinner. But the temperature was below forty, Emily was sure of it, and a sudden icy breeze lifted the royal blue napkins he had instructed her to place on the table after she'd Windexed it with a couple of flimsy paper towels a few minutes earlier.

She came up behind him at the grill and touched his elbow. "We're going to have to eat indoors," she said. "I'm sorry, but I'm just too cold."

"What? Really?" He turned toward her, his face rosier than usual in the light of the fire. "Are you sure?"

Nodding, she said, "I'm going inside now. To the bathroom. And then I'll be back, okay?"

"Here's the thing," Kosta said, brandishing a long knife with a six-inch blade that dripped blood from the porterhouse he'd slit open. "The bathroom's down the hall."

"Down the hall from the living room? I'll find it."

"No no," he said, and gave her a smile tinged with discomfort. "I mean down the hall from the *apartment*."

Emily knew it was a commercial building, with only the top three floors rented out to residential tenants, but even so, what was he talking about? "Everyone on your floor uses the same bathroom?" she said, shocked.

For the first time since they'd known each other, he put his arm around her; in his other hand, he still held the knife. "It's just me," he said. "All the other apartments have their own bathrooms. But what I've got is even better, a whole men's room to myself. No one ever uses it except me. It's got three stalls and three sinks, and I pay good money to one of the cleaning ladies who works for the building's management to keep it pristine." The only problem, he continued, was that he had to take the elevator down a dozen flights to use the shower in the ladies' room on the fourth floor. Before seven a.m., and after nine p.m., when all the commercial tenants were gone.

"No way!" Emily said, and imagined Kosta striding along the cold, uncarpeted corridor and into the elevator, dressed in a bathrobe and flip-flops, loaded down with bottles of shampoo and conditioner, and a bar of soap in a covered plastic dish.

"Do you think any less of me because I have to shower in the ladies' room?" Kosta asked. "Listen, the software company I own is worth a couple of million—I could sell it tomorrow if I wanted to. You know, cash it all in and move to the Bahamas or something. My point being that I could move out of here anytime I like, but I choose not to."

"Why would I think any less of you?" Emily said. Still shivering, she snuggled into his embrace. What she *did* think was that this weird shower-and-bathroom situation was the legacy of his wretched early years, and that it could be traced all the way back to the execution of his parents by henchmen in cahoots with a murderous psychopath.

"But do I need a key to get into the bathroom?" she asked.

"No key. And it's perfectly safe, I promise."

"Fine, but can I bring you back a jacket? Aren't you cold?"

"Got my fat to keep me warm," Kosta said, pinching together some flesh at his ribs.

"Yeah, right, you're real fat," Emily teased. "Though, actually, you *are* a big tall guy."

"Always one of the guys in the back row in every class picture, year after year. The one with his head sticking up above everyone else's. Even in kindergarten." The steaks hissed on the grill; behind the high windows of an apartment in an adjacent building, a man stood playing a violin. "I wonder if my father was a big guy as well," Kosta mused.

Of course Kosta had no photographs of him, Emily realized. Or of his mother. This seemed pitiful, to have been denied even a snapshot or two. She tilted her face upward and kissed his lips—what else did she have to give him?

His mouth opened and he returned her kiss. It was dark on the roof except for the full moon and the lighted windows of the buildings all around them. It had been months since she'd kissed a man; the last time was during the summer, on the ferry back from Fire Island, when she and Todd, her boyfriend of almost a year, were deciding whether or not to break up. By the time the ferry docked in Bay Shore, Todd confessed that the thought of marriage had never crossed his mind and that the fact that Emily's thirtieth birthday had recently come and gone was no incentive whatsoever to pop the question. They rode the train back to the city in silence, and just before arriving at Penn Station, Emily told him, in a tiny voice, that the year they'd spent together was long enough. *Long enough for what?* Todd wanted to know, but there seemed no point in responding to his clueless question.

She pulled gently away from Kosta now so she could study his face. It wasn't the face of an older man; it was unlined, and his neatly groomed beard and mustache, along with his ponytail, were still mostly black. He was only a few years younger than her father, who looked so much older. She wondered what her parents would think if they knew about the kiss she'd shared with Kosta. Emily would always be their child; they still referred to her and her brother as "the kids" when they talked about them. "It's such a pleasure to have the kids around," she'd heard her mother tell her father at Thanksgiving, as if she and Jeff were second-graders and the four of them still lived under the same roof. But she wanted, at that moment, for Kosta to meet her parents, to see what it was like to be enfolded by a loving family, particularly a mother upon whose shoulders you could weep after your boyfriend in grad school revealed that the word "fiancée" gave him the chills— and not the good kind, either.

Kosta wasn't exaggerating, Emily discovered as she entered the men's room; the place was immaculate. She couldn't bring herself to sit down on the toilet when she peed, but that was *her* problem and no fault of the cleaning woman, who'd shined up the three black sinks and the pink-and-black granite countertop that surrounded them. The floor, of veined marble, was improbably pristine, the mirror that stretched across the length of the sinks, smudge-less, and the liquid soap she used on her hands was dispensed from a vase-like silver bottle and smelled faintly of honeydew. It was the one and only men's room she'd ever visited and she had no complaints. Even so, wasn't there something just the slightest bit disconcerting about a guy with his very own men's room? Perhaps, if she were to tell her friends about him, she would simply describe him as eccentric.

They ate their dinner in the living room, and Kosta polished off a bottle of merlot with a little help from Emily. Afterward, they settled into a worn leather couch, which Kosta first had to clear of his most recent load of clean laundry. He was indifferent to his own untidiness; there had been books and magazines piled high on the dining table before they sat down to their meal, and even the chairs had a couple of weeks' worth of newspapers adorning their cushions. There were multiple spider plants and rubber plants crowded into every corner, their leaves coated with dust. And if Emily wasn't mistaken, a small puddle of dog pee had greeted her at the entrance to the kitchen, where, on her arrival, Kosta's silky terrier, Calvin, had first expressed his contempt for her.

Kosta clicked on his home theatre-sized TV, and they watched *Law & Order SVU*. The episode featured a woman with multiple personality disorder (or DID—dissociative identity disorder—as the show's resident shrink corrected one of the detectives). "What a freak," said Kosta as the woman affected a harsh Russian accent and then, a moment later, insisted, in a high-pitched voice, that she was an eight-year-old child. Kosta kicked off his cowboy boots and rested his legs against the coffee table. His arm was around Emily again. Calvin looked at her disapprovingly, and climbed into Kosta's lap.

For some reason the dog had been unhappy with Emily from the moment she'd arrived, and so had been locked away all night in the bedroom. Now he was out on probation.

"Say something to me in Russian," Emily requested.

"*Do svedanya*," said Kosta. "It's the only word I know."

Stroking the top of Calvin's head, Emily was rewarded with a growl. "Did you ever imagine the life you might have had if your parents hadn't..."

"Been summarily executed, who knows, their bodies tossed into a ditch somewhere?" said Kosta as Calvin sank his teeth into the fleshy tip of Emily's thumb and she let out a small cry. "Very bad dog!" Kosta grumbled. "Did he break the skin?" he asked Emily.

She sucked the tiny bubble of blood from her thumb. "It's nothing," she said. "As long as he doesn't have rabies, I mean." Sticking her tongue out at Calvin, she thought about the long subway ride home. She knew Kosta had a car, a BMW that he kept out on the street because he didn't believe in paying for parking under any circumstance at all. Her mother had told Emily, more than once, that wealthy people had their own crazy ideas about money—that, despite their vast resources, there were certain things they simply wouldn't spring for. Even so, she wondered if Kosta would surrender his spot on the street and give her a lift home.

He kissed her slightly wounded thumb, took her hand, and led her into his bedroom without a word, using his foot to shut the door behind them. "I can't wait to see you," he said, his voice not much more than a whisper. On the other side of the door, Calvin yipped insistently.

Later, as her fingers examined the wiry salt-and-pepper thicket of hair that covered Kosta's chest, Emily told herself that he was in excellent shape for a middle-aged guy. (Not that she knew much about middle-aged anything.) His stomach wasn't at all paunchy, his arms and legs long and muscular:

when he'd wrapped them around her tightly, she'd gasped, and had to ask him to ease up.

"So you work out at the gym?" she said.

He pointed to a set of barbells on the floor at either side of the tall, army-green file cabinet where he kept his socks, underwear, and pajamas. "Forty minutes every morning," he said. "Hey, not bad for an old guy, right?"

"Not bad at all."

Flat on their backs, lying side by side, they held hands and ignored the scratching at the door. "I count this as one of the luckiest days of my unlucky life," Kosta announced.

Tears sprang to Emily's eyes. *This wasn't a pity fuck,* she wanted to say, but in truth, she didn't know *what* it was. She'd slept with a total of half a dozen men, mostly for the right reasons, she reflected. But was it even remotely possible that she'd slept with Kosta in part because his parents had been murdered by Stalin? Surely this couldn't be true. And yet surely there were worse reasons for allowing yourself to be seduced by a handsome man who had more than twenty years on you and hellish times in his past.

It was after two a.m. when she slipped back into her jeans and snapped her bra into place. Kosta stayed in bed, observing her closely. "Just watching you get dressed is a real turn-on," he said.

She smiled. "So...any chance you can give me a ride back uptown?"

No dice.

"My parking spot is good until next Monday," Kosta explained. Downstairs on the street, he pressed a twenty-dollar bill into her palm as she ducked into the first taxi that came her way. For an instant, closing her hand over the twenty, she felt the smallest bit like a hooker, albeit one with degrees from a couple of Ivy League universities. Kosta was tapping on the window now, and she lowered it. "It's just that finding a great parking spot is like a fucking miracle," he said apologetically. "Forgive me?"

"There's nothing to forgive," she heard herself say, and blew him a kiss, one of those gestures she rarely made use of.

When spring arrived, she'd accumulated more than a hundred pages of notes dictated by Kosta, but she felt less and less confident that these pages would add up to anything resembling a publishable book. Maybe a self-published book, but in all likelihood one that you might download for free on the Internet rather than buy at Barnes & Noble. Though Kosta's life fascinated her—especially his dismal childhood and adolescence, a couple of dissolute years at a community college, a stint in the army, his eventual success as a businessman, and two failed marriages to women he described as "nut jobs," one of whom was an African princess from Kenya—nothing could beat the single, seminal fact of his parents' execution. As she labored at Kosta's story one afternoon, Emily thought of a quotation from Mark Twain that she loved. *There never was yet an uninteresting life. Inside of the dullest exterior there is a drama, a comedy and a tragedy.* If this was true—and she wholeheartedly believed that it was—then why was she having so much trouble shaping Kosta's extraordinary life into something worth reading about? Per their contract, which had been drawn up and notarized by Kosta's attorney, he had already paid Emily ten thousand dollars, a fact she tried not to think about whenever she spent the night in his bed. Certainly she found him a generous and considerate lover, one who knew how to deliver the lightest and most tender of kisses to her eyelids, whose fingers played skillfully along her body, bringing her moments of electrifying pleasure. Happily, there was that particular, necessary spark between them. But just as she was unsure of the book he was paying her to write, she wasn't yet convinced that she and Kosta would, in the long run, add up to anything at all. If prompted by Kosta, she would say that of course she loved him, though she didn't think she would ever say that she felt as if she'd been set on fire, as Kosta claimed to have been. She was attached to him, having been wooed by the story of his life, but she was also, she recently discovered, a little afraid of him.

At the tail end of the evening rush hour a few weeks earlier, as she and Kosta had boarded a packed subway car, he'd accidentally brushed shoulders with a well-dressed, attaché-carrying woman who was trying to exit; when he murmured "Excuse me," the woman cursed at him and gave him a deliberate shove. To Emily's astonishment, he'd shoved her back. And roughly. He and the stranger exchanged fuck-you's, and then the woman took off. It was all over in less than a minute, and none of the other passengers seemed to have taken notice, but Emily's heart was hammering away, and for an instant she couldn't catch her breath.

"What's *wrong* with you?" she hissed at Kosta.

"Are you fucking *kidding* me?" he said. "Didn't you see what she did to me?"

"Uh-huh, but I also saw what *you* did to *her*," Emily said.

The two of them were gripping a pole to keep their balance as the subway car suddenly swayed sharply back and forth. She stared across the car. A guy wearing chipped, oxblood-colored nail polish extracted a slice of pizza from a cardboard box in his lap and bit into it zestfully, then took a swig from a bottle of Pepsi that had been wedged between his knees.

"She deserved it," Kosta insisted. "She left me no choice."

"That," said Emily, "is patently untrue. Haven't you ever heard of turning the other cheek?"

Kosta smiled at her unpleasantly. "Hey, you know what? That's exactly what I did when Bobby or Dorothy used me as a punching bag. I turned the other cheek and prayed for some-one to rescue me. And you know how well *that* turned out."

She couldn't win, Emily saw. They'd been on their way downtown to Kosta's apartment, where she'd planned to make him linguine with scampi for dinner, but she no longer felt like doing anything for him. She couldn't forget the harshness with which he'd shoved the woman, though in all fairness to Kosta, the woman herself had been churlish and rude, and she'd been asking for trouble. Even so. On the other hand... Kosta had been savagely mistreated by his adoptive parents, and was, perhaps, permanently damaged in certain ways. She'd make the scampi, but after dinner, she'd go straight home, cheating them both of some exhilaratingly good sex.

One time, after they had finished making love and Kosta was channel-surfing the TV in his bedroom, they watched *CSI* in silence for a few minutes; on the screen, the coroner extracted a victim's heart and weighed it on a scale.

"How'd you like to do *that* for a living?" Emily said. "Ick."

Kosta stretched an arm to the nightstand, and lit one of his infrequent cigarettes with a cheap, orange plastic lighter. Slouching against the headboard, he noisily exhaled a plume of smoke toward the ceiling. "You know, I've killed a couple of bad guys in my day," he confided, his eyes on the rising smoke.

"You're a real hoot, Kosta," said Emily. She socked him lightly on the shoulder. "Hilarious."

"No, really, I mean it," Kosta said, still staring at the ceiling. "They were drug dealers working for the Russian mob."

"Come *on*. You think I'm an idiot?" Emily said. The back of her neck suddenly felt prickly, and her palms were damp. "Like I'm supposed to believe you're a murderer?"

Kosta seemed affronted. "Not a murderer. I wacked a couple of very bad people, that's all." The TV was still on; there was a commercial for an Internet dating website being shown, and Kosta froze it with the remote. "Obviously," he said, "this isn't going into the book."

"Obviously," Emily echoed, and laughed, though she wished she hadn't. She knew Kosta was pulling her leg, but she was tired of playing along.

"Wanna know the first thing I thought of when I woke up the next morning?"

"Yeah, whatever."

"That I'd done the world a big favor." A length of dead ash fell from the cigarette onto his bare chest, but he didn't flinch.

Barefoot, seated upright on her bed with her laptop, struggling yet again with the opening chapters of Kosta's story, Emily considered the thirty-five thousand dollars that would be deposited into her savings account if, and only if, she could finish the damn book. *The damn book*—there was no other way to think of it. Always a stellar student and hard-working, conscientious employee, she'd never really failed at anything, but this ill-conceived project had fiasco written all over it. It made her sick with humiliation to think of giving up, and even sicker to ponder the thirty-five thousand dollars and how it might have enhanced her life. She'd been fantasizing, recently, of joining Lara, her best friend from Brown, on a leisurely tour of Italy—Rome, Florence, Venice, Milan, Naples. She was thirty, only weeks away from thirty-one, old enough to have accomplished something substantial in her life. Instead, she'd held a succession of disappointing jobs and spent the better part of a year on a project that appealed to the vanity of a middle-aged businessman who had mistakenly convinced her she could turn his rather remarkable story into something of artistic merit. Though this was the man she claimed to love, she'd yet to introduce him to her parents or even to a single one of her friends. She told herself this was because they wouldn't be able to appreciate his generosity and devotion to her (a thick bracelet of pink, white, and yellow gold he bought for her at Tiffany; the surprising, sophisticated meals he treated her to at Nobu; the sweetness with which he said goodnight to her every evening over the phone when they were apart), but would instead regard him merely as the ponytailed weirdo who showered in the ladies' room an elevator ride away from his apartment. (In a moment of weakness and poor judgment, she'd shared the details of both the men's room and ladies' room with her mother and Lara, each of whom reacted with disbelief, followed by uneasy laughter.)

Her cell phone rang; it was her mother, and Emily briefly debated whether to answer it. Loving though she was, her mother had a gift for exasperating her with her pointed questions and her unquenchable thirst for every last detail about her life. Warily, Emily picked up her phone and said hello.

Her mother was calling from her midtown office to ask if Emily would bring Kosta to the brunch she was making in honor of Emily's birthday in a couple of weeks. It seemed to Emily that every birthday in their family had been celebrated with the same tableful of assorted freshly warmed bagels, platters of lox and cream cheese, and her father's soupy, undercooked broccoli quiche. And a Double Chocolate Indulgence cake from Baskin-Robbins that had to be thawed a little in the microwave just to get a knife through it. This, Emily saw, was what her parents would always be most comfortable with—they were, at heart, authentic suburbanites who had been raised outside of Philadelphia, and who, despite their successful medical practice here in the city and their apartment on Riverside Drive, could not fathom the beauty of that miso-glazed black cod at Nobu.

"It's your birthday, sweetheart," her mother said reasonably. "Just bring the guy and let us have a look at him finally."

"Well, I don't know," Emily said, abruptly closing her laptop, as if her mother had snuck up beside her, and over her shoulder, begun reading all about the crap poor Kosta had, in 1960, been subjected to at the hands of the beastly Dorothy and Bobby.

"What's the worst that could happen? If I don't like him, I'll keep it to myself," her mother promised. "Look, we've met all your other boyfriends over the years. What's the big deal about meeting this one?"

"He's not my boyfriend," Emily snapped. "You don't call a fifty-five-year-old man a boyfriend, okay?"

"Wait, he's *fifty-five?*" her mother said, considering this piece of news with astonishment. "When you told us he was middle-aged, I thought you meant forty, forty-one...Emily, what are you *doing?*"

"His parents were executed by Stalin!" Emily shrieked. "Stop criticizing him!" A moment later, she was sobbing. Suddenly exhausted, too tired even to rise from her bed to look for a tissue, she wiped her eyes with the pair of argyle socks she'd worn yesterday and tossed onto the floor before going to sleep.

"*Joseph* Stalin?" her mother said, and Emily could tell that she was impressed.

"Well, not Stalin personally, but on his personal orders anyway."

Her mother cleared her throat. "I'm speechless," she said.

"And...his ex-wife was an African princess," Emily said recklessly.

"Stalin was married to an African princess?"

"*Kosta,*" Emily said, instantly regretting the impatience in her voice. "He's had a pretty incredible life, don't you think?"

After a sleepover at Kosta's, on the morning of her birthday brunch, Emily had her first shower in the ladies' room. With Kosta leading the way, she hurried from his apartment, down the corridor and into the elevator, dressed in his scarlet-and-white-checked bathrobe that swished around her ankles and his enormous fuzzy brown slippers that were meant to re-semble the paws of a bear and that swam on her size-six feet.

When they arrived at the fourth floor, Kosta darted into the ladies' room for a quick look around, then signaled to her that the coast was absolutely clear.

"No worries. There's never a soul in here on the weekends, of that I can assure you," he said. He helped Emily out of his robe and kissed each of her breasts before turning on the water for her. He'd brought his shower caddy along; a selection of two different shampoos and conditioners were available for her choosing, and a bar of Dove for Sensitive Skin that was still encased in its cardboard packaging. "Just for you," said Kosta. "I knew this day would come." He stood guard while she shampooed and conditioned her hair behind the frosted glass, and then, like a limo driver at the service of his passenger, reached politely for her hand as she stepped from the shower. A velvety gray towel awaited her, and before she dried off completely, she couldn't help but catch a glimpse of herself in the mirrored wall, partially misted with steam, that rose above the sinks. Kosta was looking at her, too, and then an idea came to both of them. Pressed against the wall, a damp towel lining her back, she felt the warmth of Kosta's breath on her neck. There was no lock on the ladies' room door; if someone had walked in on them, Emily would have wanted to shoot herself. But it was a quiet Sunday morning in August, and they were all alone in the city.

Kosta's black sapphire BMW coupe was parked directly in front of his building, and he sighed in contentment as they settled into the car. With a touch of a button, the convertible top eased itself down smoothly behind them. They were out of the Village quickly and flying up the West Side Highway, and the smile on Kosta's face seemed joyful. Clearly he loved his new car and the sultry August wind blowing in their faces. Emily held on to her hair with both hands and wished he would put the top up and turn on the air-conditioning, though she wouldn't have dreamed of saying so and spoiling his pleasure. On her lap was the large, extravagant bouquet of flowers he'd bought for her parents; on her wrist was the starkly elegant black-faced Movado he'd given her for her birthday. She could guess how expensive it was and the thought rattled her, though not so much that she contemplated returning it to him. His generosity was lavish; how could you fault a man for that?

"Thirty-one years old," he said. "A mere slip of a girl. Rejoice in thy youth, missy!" They were on Riverside Drive now, only a few blocks from her parents' apartment, and on the lookout for a parking space.

"Cut it out," Emily told him. She didn't like it when he drew attention to the difference in their ages; the truth was, it saddened her.

"Let's see, when I was thirty-one, I was married to my ex, Jeanne, and miserable. And I mean *miserable.* All she could ever think about was this ridiculous—"

"Isn't that a spot over there?" Emily interrupted.

A woman her age was standing in front of an awning watching over her toddler in a stroller. "'You're a grand old flaaag,'" she prompted loudly, and her little boy sang, "'You're a high fly-ing flag!'"

"Fire hydrant," Kosta pointed out. "No good."

As the BMW pulled away, Emily could hear the child in the stroller shrieking, "'And for-ev-er in peace may you waaave...'"

"Cute kid," said Kosta cheerfully.

They'd circled her parents' building four times but there wasn't a single parking spot to be had. Hydrants sprouted cruelly from every open space, it seemed, and Kosta's mood had darkened. "We have a serious situation at hand," he said. "My hopes have dimmed."

Was he talking about a parking space or a malignant tumor?

"We'll just have to put it in a garage," Emily said. "And of course I'll pay for it." She held her breath, and waited.

"You'll do no such thing," said Kosta. "I'll let you out, and I'll meet you upstairs as soon as I find a spot."

"I'm not leaving you," she said, as if he were going off to do battle with a dangerous adversary.

"Git," said Kosta. He handed her the flowers for her parents. "See you later, birthday girl."

She went upstairs and into the warmth of her family, which included her eighty-four-year-old grandmother, two aunts and uncles, and her brother, all of whom seemed disappointed to see that she'd arrived without Kosta. Emily explained that he was looking for parking, and her relatives clucked sympathetically. Everyone was in agreement with her mother when she acknowledged that it was always a problem finding parking on the Upper West Side, even in summer, when much of the neighborhood was supposedly out in the Hamptons for the weekend.

"Why can't this young man of yours just park in a garage?" her grandmother asked. "What's wrong with *that*?"

He's not a young man, Emily wanted to say. *He's set in his ways.*

"He may very well end up in that garage," her father said grimly. "Like it or not, sometimes you just don't have a choice."

It was decided that they would wait for Kosta, even though the assortment of bagels had already been warmed in the oven and would, undoubtedly and in no time at all, turn cold and stony.

Her mother put out large bowls of fat-free vegan potato chips and salt-free pretzels, in deference to those who had to worry about high cholesterol or hypertension. As for Emily and her brother, they who liked their chips relatively oily and their pretzels full of salt, well, tough break.

Forty-five minutes passed and the voice mail and text messages Emily had left on Kosta's iPhone went unanswered.

"Good luck with that crazy boyfriend!" her grandmother called after her when Emily left the apartment to find him.

He was double-parked in front of the building, his face lowered into the steering wheel.

She came around to the driver's side. "Hey," she said, tugging at his ponytail. "I left you three messages."

He lifted his head and gazed at her sorrowfully. "Looks like I'm going to have to give up."

"Thank God!" she said, relieved that he had, at last, come to his senses. "There's a garage a few blocks away, off West End. My father says it'll only cost about twenty-five dollars for a couple of hours, so if you don't want to spring for it, please just let me take care of it, all right?" she pleaded.

"I can't let you do that," Kosta said. "Absolutely not. Listen, I'm going home. Please give my apologies to your parents." Gently, he placed his hand over her arm, the one sporting that lovely new Movado that sat a little too tightly around her wrist. "You understand, don't you?"

Shutting her eyes against his blindness, his mulish refusal to pay the measly twenty-five bucks, she allowed herself to fully evoke, as she never had before, the night of his parents' execution—that young mother and father, younger even than Emily herself, roused from their warm feather bed, the chilly steel of pistols shoved in their faces, Kosta's mother crying out in terror for her baby dreaming in his crib in the room next door, his father shouting *Who are you?* but immediately recognizing those ruthless strangers pounding on their door after midnight wanting only to destroy their innocent, ordinary lives.

How readily Emily imagined all of it, and the long, long way from there to here, to Riverside Drive and this intractable man who, no matter what, refused to pay for a damn parking space. This man who wanted to know if she understood.

Hasta Luego (2001)

Has it really been more than a year? It has, Dave notes with amazement, actually been fourteen months since he moved here to the suburbs of New Jersey, about as far from the coolest place a single, unattached person could find himself. It is 2008 and he is past thirty and no longer particularly confident—as he once was—that the future may hold the shimmering promise of something better for him. At least he's employed and can count on receiving, off the books, $500 in cash every Friday night, considerably more than he ever earned in the days when he and his band, The Dystopians, were in business together. If you could call it that. The gig he has now comes with free room and board, a real bonus, certainly, for someone earning the princely sum of $25,000 a year. The fact that Cheryl and Bill, his sister and brother-in-law, are his employers and that he inhabits a suite of rooms in their finished basement isn't information he likes to volunteer. But he will challenge anyone who might mock him to try living without that guarantee of money flowing in reliably from one week to the next. He and the other Dystopians had done that for years, sleeping in their van while on tour across the country, buying their clothes at a series of musty thrift shops, eating a couple of artery-clogging, fast-food meals a day, and all of it for *what*? For the sheer pleasure of creating and performing the kind of impressively fierce, energetic post-punk that somehow made Dave feel incandescent. Luminous. Transcendent. He hasn't felt that way in ages, and can't imagine the possibility of anything else making him feel that way ever again. He hasn't been in touch with his bandmates in a very long while. What would they think of him living in a McMansion in Westfield, New Jersey, babysitting for the son of his sister's housekeeper every weekday from eight to four? *That is so fucked up, man*, he can hear them saying, and on his worst days, he might not disagree too vehemently.

The child he takes care of is named Milo; at two and a half, despite Dave's best efforts, the kid still isn't toilet-trained. Maybe if his mother weren't so busy keeping house for Dave's sister, Milo might be out of diapers and into "big boy pants," as Dave calls them, trying, unsuccessfully, to render the words alluring. Milo has soaked through his overalls, Dave has just now discovered, and grabs the kid—all twenty-eight pounds of him—and carries him, fireman-style, from the playroom into the bedroom here in the basement. Living upstairs in their own separate wing, Milo and his mother, Marissa, are half a floor above Dave's sister. They were already in place upstairs when Dave was offered his gig and basement suite; frankly, he's happy in the knowledge that Cheryl will never catch even the slightest trace of the weed he smokes every evening after the rest of the household is asleep. Cheryl and Bill are both nearing forty, and are litigation partners at a two-hundred-lawyer firm in Manhattan. They have more money than any two people could possibly need, or so it seems to Dave, but Cheryl is on one of those SSRIs for depression, and despite looking thin and slight—scrawny, almost—she awakens at five every morning so she can work out on her treadmill for an hour before leaving for work. The brother-in-law (as Dave thinks of him) is bad news in a designer suit and a $300 silk tie, someone who berates waiters loudly and at length whenever his meals prove unsatisfactory in even the smallest way, and who often speaks to Cheryl as if she were a slow-witted child, despite her Phi Beta Kappa key and law degree from Georgetown. Smart enough for all that but dumb enough to have fallen for Bill—what's *that* all about? No wonder she's on Zoloft or Lexapro or whatever it is she's taking—Dave can never remember which one, though he's seen the amber plastic pill bottle sitting next to the vitamins in one of the kitchen's numerous, gleaming glass-and-stainless-steel cabinets. It hurts him, knowing his sister is too disheartened to get through the day without it.

"So, little dude, what's with this diaper business?" Dave says now in his bedroom as he proceeds to get Milo out of his overalls and into a fresh diaper and a pair of flannel-lined jeans. It is midmorning; upstairs, they can hear Marissa getting started on her vacuuming. "This is just plain stupid, man," Dave continues. "Every one of your buddies in the play group is, at the very least, wearing these"—he gestures toward a package of Huggies Pull-Ups training pants that he keeps around optimistically—"but you, you're just a big baby."

"Don't care," says Milo. "*Don't* care." Lying flat on his back, he smiles affably at Dave, who thinks, as he always does when he sees that jaunty smile, *damn cute*. He loves Milo's baby-soft, curly hair, his tiny, pure-white teeth, those pretty, hazel eyes inherited from his father, a Dominican guy Marissa hooked up with briefly a few years ago.

"Well, you *should* care," Dave says. "It's embarrassing, you know, when your little"—he almost says "peers"— "friends are way ahead of you. Especially since you're smarter than all of them put together. You're the one with the brains, dude."

Milo is clutching a Power Ranger figure in each hand, one guy all in red with a silver weapon of some sort instead of a right arm, and one guy in a green outfit, with knee-high, gold-rimmed white boots. Milo brings the figures together, smashing their heads vigorously against one another, over and over again. "Brains, dude!" he says. "Ha ha ha."

"Stop smashing their heads together like that," Dave tells him. "How about you put them down and play with something else."

"Somethin' else," Milo agrees. Flipping over and slithering on his stomach down Dave's unmade bed, he flips again, and takes Dave's outstretched hand. They return to the playroom, a large, slightly drafty space softened with plush carpeting. Shoved against one wall are a mini-trampoline and a plastic slide. Along another stand a plastic sink overflowing with toy dishes; a beige plastic refrigerator/freezer stocked with toy food; a matching stove with several toy pots on its burners and a frying pan holding a single fried egg, its center a garish yellow, beside three strips of plastic bacon. All of which has been bought for Milo by Cheryl, who is convinced that without Marissa running the household, she, Cheryl, would be lost. Well, she can think whatever she likes, but Dave knows this is nuttiness. Or fuzzy thinking at best. On the other hand, without Marissa and Milo, he'd probably be temping at one or another of the many soulless corporations with offices in Manhattan, doing the sort of mind-deadening work he had his fill of in the years after The Dystopians broke up. Surprisingly, looking after Milo is far from the worst gig he's ever had. The kid is whip-smart and exuberant—excellent company most of the time—though occasionally he has furious tantrums that can persist for as long as an hour and from which he emerges sweaty and hoarse. When Milo is busy kicking and screaming over something as minor as a favorite sweatshirt languishing in the laundry hamper, Dave usually hooks himself up to his iPod and closes his eyes, opening them every couple of minutes to see if Milo is showing any signs of surrendering to good old common sense. Every job has its downside, Dave figures; dealing with a tantrum every few weeks beats endless hours of proofreading legal documents, doesn't it?

"What are you in the mood for, bro?" he asks Milo. "How about we check out the basket of toys." His voice lacks enthusiasm, he realizes, and to make up for it, he gives Milo a squeeze.

In the next moment Milo is ransacking the big wicker basket, tossing out handfuls of Lego blocks, a couple of olive green plastic dinosaurs with red eyes and splayed toes, a scowling, blond G.I. Joe, and Batman and Robin, both sporting special armor. Nothing suits Milo, apparently; he's walking away from the basket scornfully. "I'm bored," he announces.

"You don't even know what 'bored' means," Dave says. *And besides, it's only 10:30 in the morning, a long way from quittin' time.*

"Do *so*," says Milo.

"Oh yeah? Let's hear it."

"Well, it means the toys are stupid and I wanna go upstairs and see my mom."

"She's vacuuming," Dave says, "and she can't be disturbed. Not until four o'clock, when she's done working and we're done playing. Those are the house rules, bro. Etched in stone."

Milo engages now in some comically exaggerated eye-rolling, a display Dave has never been treated to before.

"Damn, you're funny!" he whoops. "We should get you an agent and put you in the movies." He finds himself fantasizing about a new career for both of them: Milo will be the next big child star in Hollywood and *he* will be his manager, in charge of safeguarding his millions, helping to groom his image, and most important, negotiating and avoiding the pitfalls of fame for a toddler like Milo. (Dave is, in fact, familiar with a few of the perks of, if not exactly fame, then simply being a performer in the public arena, no matter how small: it's easy enough to vividly recall a handful of college girls clamoring for The Dystopians' autographs after a show, then inviting the band for some beers—and from time to time something a good deal more intimate—back in their dorm rooms. But this is ancient history and why bother to think about it now when all it does is underscore just what Dave has been missing.)

"*I'm* not funny," says Milo. "*You're* funny." He studies Dave briefly but intently, then concludes, "You're a silly billy!"

This is a compliment, Dave suspects, judging from the gleeful look on Milo's face. "Thanks," he says. "Not too many compliments coming my way this week or year, if you know what I mean."

Turning back to the toy basket, Milo seizes a floppy-eared baby lion by its stuffed tail and swings it overhead like a lasso. "Bored bored bored," he pronounces.

"All right, I get the picture," Dave says. "Come on back to my room and we'll read some car magazines."

"Yasss!"

Squeezed into a leather lounger just big enough for the two of them, they spend the rest of the morning poring over *BMW Enthusiast*, *Jaguar World*, and *Classic Car*, studying photographs of all the lustrous, brand-new cars Dave covets and will never be able to afford, while Milo points with his small, stubby fingertip as he identifies, in his high-pitched little-boy voice, everything he sees. "XK-E! Mini Cooper! Aston Martin! BMW!" The kid can't read yet but he knows his cars and their emblems and never once makes a mistake, never once confuses a Ferrari with a Lamborghini or a Toyota with a Honda. One of these days Dave is going to take him to a car dealership and have him blow the salesmen right out of their seats. And this is what he's dreaming of now as his head tips forward and he dozes off, somewhere between breakfast and lunch, down here in the well-furnished basement of his sister's deluxe, super-sized McMansion.

He's wide awake, reading lamp blazing, when Cheryl decides to pay him a visit in his subterranean bedroom at 2:35 in the morning. He can't believe his crazy sister is dressed, in the middle of winter, in a one-piece, turquoise bathing suit, her hair concealed under a pale yellow shower cap, just so she can smoke one lousy, forbidden cigarette.

"You obviously don't understand," she tells Dave.

She's right, he doesn't. Doesn't understand how anyone could be so afraid of her husband finding out that she sneaks an occasional cigarette. "That's quite an outfit you're wearing," Dave says, trying not to stare too hard at her bony chest, her skinny, goose-bumped limbs, the hip bones that jut prominently from her bathing suit. Without those waves of her ginger-colored hair to soften it, her face looks angular, exposed, vulnerable. "I especially dig the shower cap," Dave jokes.

"If my hair smells like smoke, I'll never hear the end of it," Cheryl says as she gets comfortable in the leather chair she bought for him on a field trip they'd taken to Ikea when he'd first moved in. He'd been afraid to say how much he liked it, uneasy about letting her know just how grateful he was for the things she was bestowing upon him—a cozy chair, a suite of rooms, a weekly salary. There is, he thinks, something slightly creepy about being on the receiving end of all this from his sister; after all, he's thirty-three, an adult, surely. And then there's the brother-in-law, who clearly thinks him capable of very little and seems to take pleasure in letting Dave know it, making a big show of deliberately and unhurriedly extracting his credit card from his wallet whenever the three of them are out to dinner, never letting Dave pick up the tab even when they're at an inexpensive place like the local diner, the brother-in-law saying, *Don't be ridiculous,* as Dave goes for his own wallet and a couple of twenties and a ten. The guy's easy-to-read message being, *I know it's too much for you to pay even for this, for these undistinguished hamburgers, this oily, grilled cheddar-and-bacon on whole-grain toast, that side order of overcooked onion rings.*

The price Dave pays, again and again, for having allowed his sister to rescue him.

"And in the old days," Cheryl is saying, "when I was at a pack a day, Bill used to say he could still smell the smoke even after my clothing came back from the dry cleaners. Thus the bathing suit, which I'm going to hide in a little bag under the bathroom sink."

"I'd say Bill could use an attitude adjustment," Dave remarks, and drapes a satin-edged blanket around Cheryl's shoulders as she finishes up her cigarette. "You're freezing," he points out.

"That's all right, I'm going to take a nice hot shower in a few minutes. Gotta get the scent of smoke off my skin before I get back into bed."

"How about getting a divorce instead?" says Dave, absently thinking aloud.

"Hey!" Cheryl says. "I never said I didn't love him. Or that our marriage isn't a good, sound one."

"Sound," Dave repeats. "An odd word."

"I meant 'sound' as in 'stable.' "

"Right, and where's the romance in it?"

Cheryl yanks off her shower cap and squeezes it into a ball. "Where's the romance in *your* life, big shot?"

"Good one," says Dave. "You got me."

Fluffing out her hair now, looking more like her familiar self, Cheryl says, "You ever hear from Suzanne?"

"Suzanne who?" he says. He can be as cavalier as he likes, but in truth, it pains him to conjure images of his ex and her sweetly open face, her short, polished fingernails and size 5 feet. "Oh, you mean that girl from Wisconsin?"

His sister throws the shower cap at him, but her aim is wild and the cap flies directly over his head, landing on the floor in a dark nest of yesterday's navy-blue boxers and gray socks.

"Well, thanks for stopping by," Dave says. "My door, as you know, is always open. And remember, *mi casa es su casa.*"

Cheryl rolls her eyes in that exaggerated way, just like Milo, and it occurs to Dave that this is where the kid must have seen it. Cheryl, he knows, has already started a college fund for Milo. And if Dave should ever want to return to school and pick up where he left off—in the middle of his junior year—she would be happy to finance that, too. He wishes he were ambitious enough to want to go back, wishes he could turn himself into that twenty-one-year-old so abundantly assured and confident. So expectant. To be honest, he can't imagine living with that kind of hopefulness ever again.

According to Suzanne, she had always known, with all certainty, that they were meant to spend their lives together. They even shared the same birthday, though Dave was a year older. The day he turned twenty-one, he announced his decision to drop out of Oberlin: over a birthday dinner two blocks from campus, in a substandard Japanese restaurant staffed by Mexican waiters, he told Suzanne that he was leaving school at the end of the semester, that his bandmates wanted to start touring and couldn't wait around for him to graduate. She might have said, as his parents did, later that week, *Are you out of your mind?* But instead she pushed aside her vegetable-and-tofu soup in its chipped ceramic cup and leaned across the Formica table to grab his elbows and say that she was coming with him. "I'll be your number one roadie," she said, "and you know, do the band's laundry and stuff like that." Dave was deeply gratified by her offer to cast her fate in with his, and he had to acknowledge that he'd savored, all semester, the pleasures of awakening to the lovely sight of her in his bed every morning. But by the time they were finished with their spicy yellowtail rolls and beef negimaki and the waiters had bade them *hasta luego*, he had just about persuaded her that being a roadie was no profession for someone as bright and capable as she was. Besides, there was no room for her in the van. And wouldn't it be helpful if one of them, at least, had a college degree? Suzanne had five semesters left, but a year and a half later, she graduated early and moved from Ohio to live with Dave in a tenement apartment on the Lower East Side of Manhattan, a gritty neighborhood where his great-grand-parents had settled after arriving at Ellis Island as children at the beginning of the twentieth century. (This only added to his parents' distress and to their disappointment in him, and all Dave could do was shrug his shoulders, a gesture he found himself resorting to whenever he was trapped in that same tire-some conversation—the one that usually included the words "foolhardy" and "improvident"—with his mother and father.)

The tiny apartment on Eldridge Street had liver-col-ored linoleum floors that sloped, and was jammed with too many CDs and books; an assortment of guitars was propped against the rarely dusted bookcase that swallowed up an en-tire wall. Several months after Suzanne moved in, Dave was stricken with appendicitis and suffered through an emergency appendectomy and five miserable days in Roosevelt Hospital. It was Suzanne who'd been smart enough to keep dragging him back to the emergency room, three days in a row, insist-ing to the ER docs—who kept sending him home without a diagnosis—that Dave was sicker than they thought. He owed his life to her, really, because when, at long last, an attending physician got the diagnosis right, Dave's appendix had nearly burst. In the evenings following his surgery, Suzanne slept in a chair at his bedside, going home to their apartment only to shower and change her clothes. She held miniature Dixie cups of water to his mouth, applied ointment to the cracked and bleeding corners of his lips, brushed his teeth for him, and when he was able to get out of bed, walked him slowly and lovingly to the bathroom. (And if he'd needed help in there, she would have given it, he knew, never mind the embarrass-ment it might have caused them both.)

Now, years later, long after their relationship came un-done, he thinks of himself slumped in the emergency room the night of his surgery, watching while Suzanne, in her de-termined way, went after nurses and interns and attendings, standing her ground, arguing quietly and then fiercely, that her boyfriend needed their IMMEDIATE ATTENTION, GOD-DAMN IT! There had never been anyone so devoted to him, so unconditional in her love. Which was why it was impossible for him to fathom the news—when it was finally delivered—that he was no longer her boyfriend and had been displaced by someone named Ames. Who he'd logically though mistakenly assumed was a guy, but who was, as it turned out, nothing of the sort. Ames, he learned, had once been known as Amy, a name she found soft and saccharine, and she was a fifth-grade teacher in the public school where Suzanne taught in a special gifted and talented program. Their affair had begun while Dave and the band were off promoting their new CD on a month-long, cross-country tour, from which he'd phoned Suzanne, consci-entiously and unfailingly, every single night.

"I go away for a big four weeks and, what, suddenly you realize you're gay?" he'd said in disbelief. "Come on, this is a joke, right?" They had made love for what would be the very last time and were still in bed; Dave wiggled his toes, check-ing to see if he were actually awake, since what he'd just heard seemed to have sprung from a weird, unlikely nightmare.

"Of course I'm not gay," Suzanne said. "I assumed that would be more than a little obvious."

"So...what, then?" said Dave.

"Put it this way, don't you think sexuality is fluid?" Suzanne smiled at him patiently, as if he were one of her stu-dents, though perhaps not as gifted and talented as the rest.

"Fluid?" He thought immediately of semen and saliva and how often he'd marked her body with them. He'd never been greatly concerned with grammar, but he was well aware of the difference between a noun and an adjective, and knew he was on the wrong track here.

Suzanne sat up in bed, searched for her bra, and hooked it in place. "How about this: There are boundaries between gay and straight, right, and those boundaries are easily crossed. So yes, fluid."

There was no denying he considered himself pretty hip—he was a musician, a rock 'n' roller, and he'd done his share of exploring boundaries out there in the world—but he had no idea what the fuck Suzanne was talking about. "You're my girlfriend," he said helplessly. "We've been together for seven years. So don't tell me we don't love each other." He had to wait for her response, which wasn't forthcoming until the turtleneck of her sweater came down over her face and settled on her delicate collarbone.

"Dave, sweet pea," she said, and he must have been deluding himself, but even the way she uttered his name was like an embrace. "We *do* love each other, I think, but I have this thing with Ames, too, and right now it's just something I wanna explore."

"Can't you explore this *thing*"— he struggled not to say the word angrily or contemptuously—"and stay here with me at the same time?"

The answer to this arrived without delay. "I'm afraid not, sweet pea. So what I need from you is to give me a little leeway here and we'll see how things go. And I want you to try and take it easy, okay?" She bent toward him and planted a kiss of tender apology on his cheek. "Now I'm going to get my stuff and get out of here, all right?"

It wasn't all right—it was utterly wrongheaded—but he couldn't figure out a way to stop her. His thoughts were scattered all over the place, his brain jumping from fluid to boundaries to Ames to dim, fuzzy images of Suzanne making love to a woman who couldn't be happy with the perfectly good name her parents had given her.

If tears had been permissible, he might have shed them; instead, he made a visor of his hand and lowered his head, concealing his stricken face from Suzanne's shockingly, peculiarly unfamiliar one.

By the next day, his mind had cleared and he was able to see straight again, and he decided this bi-curiosity of hers was not unlike her yoga phase and her vegan phase, both of which had come and gone with a velocity he found amusing. So the plan was to wait patiently (or, more realistically, *impatiently*) until her interest in Ames diminished, as it inevitably would, and, in the interim, he and Suzanne would check in every couple of weeks, meeting for drinks, texting, talking on the phone, emailing each other. Allowing himself to believe it was just a temporary state of affairs, he managed to live this way for months, forcing himself to date a couple of women here and there while incurably in love with Suzanne. One night, at a time when their relationship had been reduced almost entirely to email, he saw that she had read and deleted his last two letters to her without responding. He discovered he just didn't have the heart to chase after her, surrendering instead to the realization that she and Ames had settled in for the long haul and weren't going to budge from their love nest in Park Slope. And yet, like someone who'd recently lost a lover under tragic circumstances, he still harbored hope that someday he would run into Suzanne and persuade her to return home with him.

Every once in a while on a Saturday, Marissa has something she needs to do for herself and doesn't want to take Milo along. Today, as he has in the past, Dave volunteers to watch him. Marissa is meeting a friend for lunch and a shopping expedition this afternoon, and after Dave gives her a lift into the city and drops her off at Macy's on Thirty-Fourth Street, he and Milo drive to Eleventh Avenue to check out the car dealerships that line both sides of the street. It is spring now, and in the fall Milo will start nursery school. What this will mean for Dave is unclear at the moment; certainly his time with Milo will be cut back and he'll have to look for a part-time job covering the fifteen hours a week that Milo will be attending the Toddle-In Preschool, next to a pizzeria in a small strip mall not far from Cheryl's home. Neither Cheryl nor Marissa has said a word to him yet on the subject, and whenever he allows himself to think about it, he feels both a sickening uneasiness and a vague melancholy: Milo is growing up too fast. Dave can't imagine feeling any more nostalgic for Milo's rapidly disappearing childhood than he does, not even if he were Milo's father. Biological father? Adoptive father? He is, in fact, no father at all. He's the hired help, $500 a week plus room and board, and all-too-easily replaceable. You think he doesn't know that? And the craziest thing: fifteen years ago, when he was a high school senior, he was voted "Most Likely to Succeed." It was one of those small, Upper East Side private schools with an overabundance of bright, driven students, but the only thing *Dave* had been driven to wasn't even remotely connected to dazzling SAT scores or an impressive GPA. His band, the very first one he'd started, was called The Abyss, and their songs—every note and word of which had been written by Dave—must have touched a nerve. Because whenever they played, late at night in obscure clubs downtown in Alphabet City, their fellow students showed up, rocking to the belligerent, pissed-off, clamorous music that was Dave's gift to them. But it hits him now, in a realization that raises hackles all along the back of his neck, that perhaps the award for Most Likely to Succeed had been offered ironically; that really what was meant by the faux-marble-and-gold trophy with his name printed in large block letters in Magic Marker was that he was the most unlikely of all to score big-time. If so, how prescient his classmates had been! What geniuses, to have accurately imagined his life in the twenty-first century, completely devoid of accomplishment, love, sex, and, of course, money.

"Let...me...out!" he hears a voice saying.

"What?" Dave says as he pulls up in front of a Nissan dealership and puts the car in "park."

"Let me out, Dave!"

He turns around to see Milo tugging at the straps of his child-proof car seat. "Oh, sorry, dude." Stepping out of Cheryl's Lexus, he frees Milo and helps him onto the sidewalk. "Hold my hand, okay?" Dave says, and Milo is already pulling him toward the entrance to the showroom. Inside, salesmen in sport coats and ties lounge at their desks, some fooling with their computers, others chatting on their cell phones and drinking coffee from mugs imprinted with the Nissan logo. A handful of customers mills around, opening car doors and peering inside, running their hands across leather interiors and wondering aloud about sound systems and heated seats. Dave can't wait for Milo to shake a few of them up with what he himself can predict will be an astonishing performance.

Thirty-four inches tall, dressed in a sweatshirt emblazoned with a spike-tailed, blue-and-orange stegosaurus, Milo skitters across the showroom's glossy floor, singing out, "Maxima! Pathfinder! Altima! Sentra!" his voice brimming with the confidence of one who knows his stuff and will not falter, that tiny, pudgy index finger of his—the one he'd learned to call "my pointer"—punctuating every word.

And here they come now, two middle-aged salesmen in blazers sauntering over in tandem, followed by a third, this one clutching his coffee mug and spilling a little of it in his excitement, all three of them stupefied with amazement, awestruck, muttering *un-fucking-believable!* as Dave stands there in the middle of the showroom and beams, as proud as if he himself had given birth to Milo in the goddamn delivery room.

"More!" Milo cries, and followed by Dave and the salesmen, he crosses the threshold into the adjacent dealership, where an assortment of Volkswagens awaits him. "Jetta!" Milo shouts. "Beetle! Golf! Passat!" he says, wrapping his mouth around the words, spitting out each of them joyfully.

"This kid just blows me away," a salesman says, shaking his head. Pinned to his sport coat is a badge revealing his name—G. Lucky Winslow. "He should be on TV or something," Winslow says.

"He's still in diapers," Dave brags. "He's just a baby, really."

"I'd put him in that whatchamacallit, *Believe It Or Not* book."

"*Ripley's*," says Dave.

"Right, and they've got a wax museum right here in the city, don't they? Just picture a wax figure of your little boy next to, like, Abraham Lincoln in that stovepipe hat, you know what I'm sayin'?"

"I believe that's Madame Tussauds," Dave says. But he decides not to correct Lucky's assumption about *your little boy*, because what's the harm, really? And in *this* city, anyway, it's not unlikely that a white guy with a dirty-blond beard might just be the father, or stepfather, of a darkly beautiful kid like Milo. And, too, shouldn't Dave be flattered by this case of mistaken identity? Who wouldn't be? Who wouldn't want to be linked to this diminutive car maven who studies *Autoweek* as if it were his own personal bible?

Lucky Winslow confers with his Nissan colleagues and some Volkswagen salesmen, and they agree that Milo deserves a gift. En masse, they approach a locked glass case displaying a VW mousepad; billed black caps, their brims adorned with images of a GTI or the New Beetle; fancy, aluminum shift knobs; and a couple of model cars that can fit in your palm and happen to go for thirty-nine dollars a pop.

"You choose," Lucky Winslow instructs Milo. "You see anything you like there?"

"Beetle hat!" Milo says decisively, and someone goes off to find him a pipsqueak-sized one.

Eyeing the model cars, which, in his opinion, are the obvious—and smarter—choice, Dave rubs his knuckles lightly against the top of Milo's head.

"Carry me," Milo orders.

"Carry you *where*, buddy?"

"McDonald's."

"McDonald's is bad for you, as I believe I've previously mentioned," Dave says, grimacing emphatically for Milo's benefit. "It'll make you fat and stupid, and we don't want that, do we?"

"McDonald's is *good* for me."

"Bad," Dave says. "Trust me on this." He looks around impatiently for the guy who went to find the Beetle hat, but what he sees, instead, is a tanned, raven-haired, attractive woman in a tight-fitting T-shirt that brags, "NOBODY KNOWS I'M A LESBIAN!" Just what he's been looking for, an eye-catchingly pretty woman who wants nothing to do with him. He turns back to Milo, who is still lobbying for McDonald's.

"Dave?"

"Yeah?" he says reflexively; it's a woman's voice and her hand is on his shoulder, and all at once he knows that he can't bear to turn around to look at her.

"Dave, it's me," the voice says. He has no choice but to acknowledge her and the hand that still rests on his shoulder.

"Hey you," he says. He is unprepared for the hug that comes next, for the scent of Suzanne's perfume or moisturizer or whatever it is he's forced to inhale that smells vaguely, tantalizingly, like caramel. As if diving underwater in his sister's backyard pool, he holds his breath for several moments and then has to come up for air. So Suzanne is a blonde now—one more shock for him to absorb—and she is, like her girlfriend in the boastful T-shirt, tanned as well. (A romantic vacation for two in Aruba? he speculates.) If only he felt nothing more than mild curiosity as he looks at her now. Or, even better, mild distaste.

No such luck.

But he is relieved, at least, to see that she's wearing some kind of leotard top and not that public announcement of a T-shirt like the woman he assumes is Ames, who is upon them now and offering her hand to Dave for a good, friendly shake.

"I'm Julia," she says. "Nice to meet you."

"*Julia?*" he says in confusion. For an instant, he feels a kinship with Ames, who he imagines was suddenly and unaccountably cast aside after years of steadfast love.

"So whatcha been doing for the past, what, three years?" Suzanne is saying.

"Oh, stuff...you know."

"The band still around?"

He tells her that The Dystopians dissolved shortly after the two of them had their own private breakup. "Our label sort of dropped us," he confesses, cutting to the chase. He shrugs, as if it were his parents he were speaking to and he were trying, yet again, to shield himself from their disappointment.

"Oh Dave," Suzanne says, "that's *horrible!*"—this last word approaching, in that Midwestern accent of hers, something that might be spelled "whoor-able." And he can't help but feel a pang at the sound of that single ordinary word pronounced by her, as always, in that distinctive way.

"Dave, look!" Milo cries, and Dave realizes, guiltily, that he's forgotten all about the kid. "My Beetle hat!" One of the salesmen has arranged it on Milo, with the brim facing backward.

"Cool," Dave says. He scoops him up from the floor and Milo wraps his legs tight around Dave's waist.

"And who's *this* little cutie?" Suzanne says.

"This," Dave says, "is Milo." Julia and Suzanne are staring quizzically, waiting for further information.

"Is he your son?" Suzanne mouths.

"It's complicated." That and a mysterious sigh are all he will allow himself to give her.

"I see," she says. But of course she doesn't and he wishes he could tell her that she couldn't possibly, not in a thousand years, fathom what is in that sigh. "Well, he's adorable in any case," Suzanne says. And to Milo, "Will you gimme some sugar, honey? Right here," she says, pointing to her cheek. "One little kiss."

Bewitched, Milo obeys, and honors her with a small, shy kiss.

"Thank you, sir," Suzanne says, then nods when Julia reminds her that they need to get busy on the paperwork for the car they've decided to lease.

"Which one?" Dave asks politely. He pretends to listen while Suzanne's girlfriend fills him in on their new Jetta, but all he can think of is finding his way to the nearest McDonald's.

With Marissa up front beside him and Milo asleep in the back, safely tethered to his seat, Dave cruises homeward through the Lincoln Tunnel and onto the Jersey Turnpike. The weekend traffic isn't nearly as heavy as he feared it would be, and his sister's almost-new Lexus LS drives like a fucking dream, and aren't these things to be grateful for?

Whoor-able, he hear himself say softly.

"Wanna see the jeans I found for Milo?" Marissa says. She is bent over and rummaging through the paper shopping bag at her feet. "So cute, and on sale for $10.99, right?"

Whoor-able, he murmurs, caressing the word, as though it were something Suzanne had—in an impulsive burst of generosity and affection—bestowed on him today, a small but priceless keepsake that's his to hang onto for as long as he desires.

End. Of. Story. (2020)

Here is my father on the last day of his exceptionally long life, lying in a rented hospital bed on a steamy mid-August afternoon, claiming to have spotted sixteen beautiful ballerinas dancing on his bedroom ceiling. Not *some* ballerinas, or a couple, but precisely sixteen; he is adamant about that. I am his only child, his only son, and seated in a folding chair arranged at his bedside, I comfort him, promising that the maintenance guys in the condo will make sure to get those dancers safely down from the popcorn ceiling above him. Knowing this, he will be able to exit this world a few hours later with a half-smile on his slackened, soft-skinned face, just before giving Silviana, his caregiver, one last glimpse of his drowsy-looking, greenish gray eyes.

Today, however, the expression on his face is one of resentment and barely contained fury, and I can't believe what I'm hearing from this ninety-six-year-old father of mine.

I have escorted him to the wall of windows in my parents' living room—in an apartment just two floors below my own in this 1970s' sky-scraping high-rise—and gesture to the lights of the city puncturing the pitch-darkness so brilliantly.

"Come on, Pop, you know the difference between breakfast time and dinnertime," I remind him, though this is most likely overly optimistic thinking on my part. "So you're just going to have to trust me when I tell you it's not even close to breakfast time now. It's nighttime. Come on, take a quick look out the window and you'll see."

He is significantly deaf in both ears, and my mother and I

have no choice but to shout to him—often, regrettably, in the most public of spaces.

"Are you listening to me, Pop?" I yell as I cup both sides of his jaw in my hands and do my best to pivot my father's face toward the row of windows.

"Don't you lie to me, Mister!" he says. "And don't think I'm not wise to you and the way you're always trying to pull a fast one on me."

He's calling me "Mister" because he's forgotten my name, and even though this has been going on for months, this memory lapse sometimes brings a momentary gloss of something resembling tears to my eyes.

This is not one of those times.

I think longingly of Silviana, that lovely, soft-spoken powerhouse of a caregiver without whom, I've come to understand, my own life—not to mention my parents' lives—would be utterly out of control. But Silviana is off tonight and won't be back until eleven, and my parents and I are on our own until then.

"*Listen* to me, Marty!" my mother instructs him. "If Andy and I are both telling you it's nighttime and we're getting ready to go out to dinner now, you have to believe us." She is still in her eighties, though her ninetieth birthday is looming, and her eyesight is severely compromised. The worst of it is that she can no longer read, even using the jumbo magnifying glass that was offered to her by an upbeat but misguided assistant in her ophthalmologist's office. Watching my mother raise the magnifier to one eye and then the other so expectantly, then seeing the look of crushing disappointment on her still-sweet face, is as painful as anything I have ever witnessed.

"You people are crazy as loons," my father reports, but allows me to zip him into his golf jacket nonetheless. Their rented condo here in Carnegie Hill, where my parents have been living these past couple of years after more than a half century in the suburbs, in Larchmont, is littered with crumbs today, and I'm down on my knees in the foyer, sweeping together a tiny pile of broken twigs of raw spaghetti with my fingers. Usually my wife, Josie, is in charge of crumb patrol when Silviana is off-duty, but we were enmeshed in a blistering argument a half hour ago, and aren't on speaking terms. Josie will neither be reaping twigs of spaghetti from the floor tonight nor joining the family for dinner at Goldie's Corner Café, my parents' favorite neighborhood restaurant.

"Get up off the floor, please," my mother says. "That's you there on the floor, Andy, am I right?"

"You are correct, sir," I tell her, mimicking Johnny Carson's *Tonight Show* sidekick from long ago. I speak loudly to her, as well, though her hearing is excellent—unsurprisingly, maybe, because as her vision has worsened, her hearing has only grown keener.

I'm eager to get this show on the road; it's been a long day attending to my freshman comp summer-session students in Brooklyn and acknowledging their urge to stay and talk to me after class about their eating disorders, their gender issues, their romantic partners' outrageously selfish demands. Something about me compels these young students to linger at the ink-smeared Formica seminar table in my classroom and unburden themselves—probably they recognize a soft touch when they happen to bump up against one. Like my mother, I've been a soft touch my whole life. Neither one of us has learned how, exactly, to say *Sorry, no can do,* to anyone. Earlier tonight, just before reaching home, as soon as I finished paying for a small bunch of bananas that I bought from a street vendor, the Nepali woman who manages the fruit-and-vegetable stand on the corner across from my condo asked me to *please, please* take her place for a few minutes while she went inside the Japanese restaurant next door to use their bathroom. "Take money from customers and put in your pocket. I trust," Geeta told me, and how could I deny her this urgent, straightforward request? This poor, hard-working, middle-aged woman, scarcely five feet tall, stood outside all day, every day—in the suffocating heat and the freezing rain and the fiercest wind—selling limp tomatoes and droopy red peppers, rock-hard peaches and bruised-looking lemons. Didn't Geeta deserve a bathroom break? How could I possibly say no? Never mind that I was already late for an appointment with my shrink, whose office, conveniently, is just a few long blocks east of my apartment. Happily, while Geeta was peeing in the restroom in Naoki's Shumai Palace, I sold four avocados for four bucks, and two lemons for thirty-five cents apiece to a neighbor who wasn't even interested enough to question me about my new temp job as a street vendor. Afterward, kicking in a twenty-dollar bill for Geeta along with the money I collected for the avocados and lemons, it hit me that this was the most gratifying moment I'd had all week.

When I arrived at the therapist's office, almost ten minutes late and a little out of breath, I found myself seriously annoyed by her greeting.

"To tell you the truth, I could really use a hug. It's just that I've had *such* a crazy day today," Dr. Goodgold informed me, skipping her usual "Hey there, how *are* ya?"

Three hundred and fifty bucks for a forty-five-minute appointment, and this was the welcome I got? Couldn't Dr. Goodgold have waited until I had a chance to get myself out of my blazer and settle into her not exactly dust-free little office halfway between First and York?

What about me? Did it ever occur to you, Doc, that maybe I'm the one who could use a hug? I wanted to kvetch, and then considered the possibility that what Dr. Goodgold could *really* use was a good therapist herself. There she was with her thick, freckly arms outstretched, coming toward me in white snakeskin Birkenstocks on this surprisingly cool July evening.

There was a pleasing scent of coconut that accompanied her embrace, but come on, wasn't it sort of worrisome that my shrink was so hungry for a hug?

Like Dr. Goodgold, I was someone who was technically eligible to receive Social Security benefits and also someone who had, to my complete astonishment, only recently discovered I was married to an unfaithful partner—though unlike my shrink (who, oddly, had confided her life story to me), I believed there was a chance I might still love that wife who so grievously betrayed me. And so I decided, at the beginning of the previous month, and after a lot of silent back-and-forthing with myself, not to kick Josie out from the apartment where the two of us had raised our tall, skinny daughters, Allison and Rebecca, and had lived so peaceably these past three decades. Because what I also discovered was a whiff of hope that it might be possible to love someone while, at the same time, be painfully disenchanted with her as well.

"I've truly had a rough day," Dr. Goodgold reported, but then failed to elaborate. "So how about you?" she finally asked as I folded my blazer into a messy lump in my lap.

I had been a loyal patient for weeks now and was still waiting for Dr. Goodgold to say, *You know what, dude, we're both just a few years shy of Medicare eligibility and we both know all about those shitty spouses of ours who reduced us to bitter tears, so why don't you just loosen up and call me Nancy instead of Dr. G?* But that day would never come and I knew it. Just as I knew there was always that prospect I might wake up one morning and realize I'd fallen permanently out of love with Josie, who hadn't, until she was busted, bothered to keep her jeans properly zipped for the past six months.

Or require that her "affair partner"—the euphemism Dr. Goodgold taught me—use a condom. Not even once!

Josie finally admitted this mortifying fact after I'd questioned her—for nearly an hour, and in a voice that trembled with both rage and sorrow, insisting that, at the very least, she owed me the truth—about the particular landscape of her six-month-long entanglement with some asshole in her 7:30 weekly abstract painting class at the Y. Eli, the abstract artiste/affair partner, was a cardiologist who specialized in bypass surgery. And he, too, was married, with a couple of sons, and an office on the Upper West Side, where he and Josie enjoyed themselves after class on a gray tweed couch across from the glassed-in reception area, and once or twice even on the exam table covered over with that crinkly white paper in the inner office.

You're killing me, I wanted to tell her, just after she'd reluctantly spilled a bunch of lurid details, but I didn't want to give this to her, didn't want her to know the power she wielded over me and my happiness, my composure, my self-assurance. And so I fell back on a handful of *fuck you*'s and worse, and bent my head to hide my stricken face from her that night—the night I caught her, phone in hand in our bathroom, typing a love text to her sixty-three-year-old "boyfriend," when, in fact, Josie was supposed to be in there brushing her teeth with our brand-new Oral-B Pro-Genius supersonic electric toothbrush.

Genius? That would be me—the husband whose greatest gift to his wife was his dumb, blind trust in her. So when Josie would say, vaguely, that she was out to dinner with *friends from work,* or attending, with those very same *friends*, a Q&A at the Brooklyn Heights branch of the public library with the author of some best-selling literary thriller, of course I believed her. Why wouldn't I? Even though she hadn't offered much about that Q&A in Brooklyn or the dinner that followed, except to say it was all "very entertaining."

Maybe next time she would invite me to go along with her and her crew? I'd asked her.

"Okay, maybe," she told me, and headed off to the shower, which was very solicitous of her, considering she was occasionally sleeping with both me and the "affair partner" on the very same night, in the very same borough of Manhattan.

When I mentioned this to Dr. Goodgold tonight, that knowing that Josie had abused my trust again and again had made me feel like a fucking moron, the doc nodded her head and had me repeat, quietly, and with my eyes closed, the uninspiring words "just...this...one...just...this...two...just...this... three..." all the way up to ten and then all the way back to one.

Big surprise: This mantra of hers didn't bring me any sort of peace, even for a moment.

At the elevator, on the way to dinner tonight, my father still insists it's morning and time for breakfast.

"MartyMartyMarty, I honestly don't know what we're going to do with you, sweetheart," my mother says as I usher them into the elevator, whose door slowly wheezes shut. Our fellow passenger, a forty-something woman in shredded jeans, is chatting on her cell phone: "My housekeeper just told me she's having a hysterectomy next week...I mean, what the fuck am I gonna do?" When she sees me staring at her, the woman smiles semi-apologetically and lowers her voice to a loud whisper. "Like I'm really looking forward to getting down on my knees and cleaning my own toilets. Who knows *what* kind of post-op recovery we're talking about after a hysterectomy? It could be, like, two weeks or something before Rosa Maria's back to work. Or longer!"

In some other lifetime, one in which I would feel no obligation to keep my mouth shut, I would have said, *Listen, you spoiled, entitled princess, where's your sympathy, your empathy, your compassion, huh?* But saying nothing and feeling guilty about my silence is my MO right now, with my energy level sinking to zero and my parents so excruciatingly needy.

My phone chirps.

"Text!" my mother announces gleefully, a new habit of hers that drives me crazy.

Pretending instead to be grateful, I thank her and guide my parents out of the elevator and through the lobby, where they take a break while I read my phone. The text is from Josie, a half-dozen short, simple words that, in the old days—before she was caught with her hand lodged so deeply in the cookie jar—the two of us mostly kept to ourselves, neither of us being the soft and squishy kind. Except once a year on our wedding anniversary, when I might present her with a card adorned with a smiling fried egg and a grinning slice of bacon and the words *We're sizzlin',* and Josie would respond with something from Hallmark displaying two love-struck peacocks seated breast to breast and beak to beak behind a vividly colorful rainbow.

I read Josie's text now and then I read it again.

Love you, babe
Truly madly
Unfailingly

Josie is one of those lawyers who has devoted herself to public service—someone with the heart and soul of a social worker, I would have said, until just last month, when it became all too clear she was a woman with a deceptive veneer of goodness and a lot of explaining to do about some of those charges on our shared Mastercard which, in retrospect, I should have examined more closely. But Josie had always taken care of the bills, paying them online and on time, and why would I ever have thought to question her about that $86 box of luxury Belgian chocolate or the $115 limited-edition bottle of Clive Christian men's cologne? Listen, if you can't trust the beloved person with whom you've happily spent thirty-plus years, well then, you're wading in the deepest sort of shit, aren't you?

And yet I feel the weight of my anger diminishing a bit now at the sight of Josie's affectionate text, even though I can still hear that high-pitched, shrieky voice from just a half hour ago calling me an *asshole* and *pathetic* in response to my own name-calling, which included the words *lying* and *fucking* and *bitch* all lined up in a row. If only I could pretend that pair of adjectives and that single angry noun were misplaced, wrong-headed, false in every way.

"Text!" my mother sings out again as the three of us head for the door, and it's a postscript from Josie.

Did you get my last
text, baby? ☺

**I did. And I do
appreciate it.**

This time I decide to reply with an all-purpose joke-of-a-sort we like to use between us.

FINE!!

And I smile when she responds in kind.

Though it's not my usual way, I send her a particularly dopey emoji with an open-mouthed, toothy smile, then deposit my phone back in my shirt pocket.

"What are *you* so happy about?" my father asks me. "And if you want to know why *I'm* so miserable, it's because you and your mother are forcing me to go out for breakfast at this crazy hour. Who eats breakfast in a restaurant? That's just cuckoo." To make sure I get his point, my father adds, in a supremely silly voice, "Coo-koo, coo-koo," a voice that reminds me of the way he talked to Allison and Rebecca when they were babies— when he would use that voice to say, *Hi there, sweet baby dear,* just before asking permission to lift, so gently, one or the other of them from their crib or their playpen or stroller.

We're all outside on Second Avenue now, my father hanging back as my mother and I walk arm-in-arm toward the restaurant, which is only a block away but will take us forever to reach because my almost-ninety-year-old mother isn't what she used to be—a brisk walker, for one thing. And then there's my father, who's busy murmuring angrily to himself. Though she can't see him, my mother stops and yells over her shoulder, "Be cooperative, Marty! Don't be such a troublemaker!"

"Wait right here for a minute," I tell her, and go back to get my father, who, thankfully, doesn't resist when I take him by the arm and lead him to where my mother stands waiting.

But then, when we arrive at our destination, as always, there's the issue of the restaurant's revolving door.

And, as always, I explain to my mother exactly what she needs to do, then install her in a section of the door and give it a push from behind. When she's safely out at the other end, I abandon my father for a minute, rush to join my mother, and enlist a waiter's help to move her away from the door, after promising I'll be back momentarily. Then I return to collect my father, who says, "Where the hell have you been, Mister?"

He's got the hunched old-man-shuffle thing going, and this, combined with the hostile sound of his voice, makes me feel as if I'm in the presence of a stranger—some forlorn, woebegone figure whose connection to me is just too hard to figure out.

"Let's go, Pop," I tell him, and manage to get him into the revolving door and out again.

We are seated at a small table tucked in the back of this quiet, brightly lit café, and a waitress soon comes to take our order, but my father refuses to cooperate. He clasps his arthritis-thickened fingers together, and with a thump rests them on the tablecloth. He stares at me and at my mother as if we've sunk so low in his estimation that we're simply beneath his contempt. He has absolutely nothing to say to the two of us, now and forever.

"I'll have the prosciutto-and-mozzarella wrap thing, as per usual," my mother says happily. She was born the daughter of an Orthodox rabbi and I recognize the pleasure it still gives her to feast on what was once forbidden—it's already there in the inflection of her voice as she announces her order.

I tell the waitress to please make that *two* wraps as my mother reaches out her arm and pats my father's elbow. "What about *you*, Marty? Any thoughts about your dinner, sweetie pie?"

"Leave me alone," he says, pulling his arm from the table. "I'm a deep person and I just want to look into the universe. So I'm asking the two of you to leave me alone."

Fine. I wouldn't dream of distracting someone who just wants to size up the universe.

At the table next to us, a young couple settle in with their snoozing baby; plugged into his mouth is a pacifier ornamented with a big black plastic mustache that sweeps across both sides of his perfectly serene face. I laugh, and start to tell my mother to check out the baby's whiskers before I remember that those days are forever gone for her—she's lucky if she can see her own hand held up to her face.

She asks why I'm laughing, but when I start to explain the mustache, the joke gets lost in translation.

"Your father is a very sick man," she confides, as I break off a piece of a warm baguette and dip it very lightly in a tiny plate of olive oil before handing it to her.

"What?" There's bread for my father, too, but he grunts something mostly unintelligible and brushes my hand away when I offer him some.

Just leave me the hell alone, he mumbles, though without enthusiasm, and so I don't take offense.

Now he is sitting with his arms folded across his chest, his face tilted downward so he doesn't have to look at his family.

"You understand what I'm talking about, Andy, don't pretend you don't," my mother says to me.

We both know my father can't hear us, but we keep our voices low anyway. There's olive oil shining on my mother's fingertips and around her mouth, and I use the cloth napkin in her lap to delicately wipe her face. I think of something she confided to me years ago—late one night as we sneaked a couple of Winstons around the kitchen table when I was home from college for Christmas break my senior year and nursing a newly broken heart: that during the War, in 1945, just after their first wedding anniversary and while my father was stationed in Paris, he'd begun a brief affair with an older woman who lived in the Marais near the Chemin Vert métro stop. That was all he had told my mother, a couple of impersonal facts about the "affair partner," facts that meant nothing to her. And that was all my mother wanted to hear about the affair, nothing more. *What could I do?* I remember her saying, my mother and I clouding the small linoleum-and-Formica kitchen with harshly scented cigarette smoke while my father snoozed in the master bedroom upstairs. *At least he was honest with me and asked for my forgiveness. At least there was that. He told me then—that summer after the War had ended—and I believed him, and still do—that if anyone had asked him to name the love of his life, his answer, then and now, would be me. And really that's all I needed, then and now.* Listening to her, my twenty-year-old self had shrugged, not being particularly interested in either my parents or their marriage. But now, after a thousand years have passed, and as I consider my mother's confidences, it hits me that it's possible the two of us may finally have something in common besides being a soft touch.

"What are you *doing* to me?" she says as I clean the olive oil from the tips of her fingers. "I'm not a baby."

She has always been an uncommonly generous-hearted mother to me, openly loving and remarkably even-tempered, but now she's cranky because she's nearly blind and my father has dementia, and it's just no good for any of us.

Silviana, my parents' five-star caregiver, is home by 9:30, well before she's due back. I'm thrilled to see her there in the apartment, and my delight is shared by my father, who, both Silviana and I have come to realize, has a crush on her. Several times over the past few months, he's leaned his head against Silviana's shoulder and said, "Do people know about us, about you and me?" Hearing this, loud and clear, pisses off my mother, who is aware Silviana is in her late thirties but cannot see that she's blessed with beautifully thick pale hair, eyes that are aquamarine, and a face as sweet as her own—though of course with the added benefit of being a half-century younger.

"What's up, Sil?" I ask her, as all four of us head for the bedroom and my parents' bedtime routine kicks in. "What are you doing home so early?" She and my father are holding hands as the gang walks down the burnished parquet hallway, and my mother's arm is linked in mine.

"Shitty shitty boyfriend," Silviana tells me. "You know." She was born in Romania, where her parents and her seven-year-old son, Alexandru, still live, in a suburb of Bucharest. Someday, when she's saved up enough money to buy a house for her family, Silviana plans on moving back; in the meantime, Josie and I agree, she's the best thing that's happened to my mother and father in years. Because in addition to all the housekeeping she's taken over from my mother, and all the zesty, but not too-zesty, meat-and-potatoes recipes she has in her repertoire, Silviana is an expert at getting my parents into and out of the shower, on and off the toilet, and in and out of the double bed that has served them so well over the many decades of their marriage.

"Hey, that sucks, Sil, but listen, if you ever want me to break Omar's legs for you, just let me know," I joke.

"You very, very funny."

Everyone's in the bedroom, and Silviana is carefully laying out a fresh pair of tattersall pajamas for my father and a night-gown patterned with violet chrysanthemums for my mother, both of which were ordered online by Josie not long before I found out about her and the cardiac surgeon she'd been banging.

"Josie not coming?" Silviana asks. "Not going to help to-night?"

"Tonight's...no good for her...but definitely tomorrow." To her credit, Josie has been a stellar daughter-in-law all these years, and most recently, never complaining about accompa-nying me on these daily visits to the family she married into long ago. Even during those months when she was hooking up with her affair partner, she was still helping Silviana get my mother into her nightgown and slippers, still squeez-ing Colgate Maximum Strength Sensitive onto my mother's toothbrush, still dispensing meds directly into my father's dry, creased palm every night, still patiently standing by with a plastic cup of filtered water so he could knock back a couple of pills for his high cholesterol and blood pressure.

A big-time cheater, but who knows, it's possible a part of me will continue to love her nonetheless.

After all, anything's possible.

When I asked her why, why did she have to fall for this fucking adulterous cardiologist with a wife and family of his own, *why why why*, she explained that she'd mistakenly thought it was love when really it was just a lustful obsession with the guy's graceful hands—the hands of a surgeon, which she loved to watch as he stood beside her painting in their class every week, his sleeves meticulously rolled to his elbows, his easel parked so close to hers. And, in truth, his paintings weren't half-bad, she said, and started to tell me all about what the guy's "art" had in common with Mark Rothko's, especially an untitled Rothko from 1954 known as "Blue, Yellow, Green on Red" and then I just couldn't listen anymore, imagining those surgeon's hands savoring every inch of Josie's stark naked body as *I* once had savored every inch, night after night, when we were young.

My father is in his pajamas now and sitting up in bed against the mahogany headboard while my mother insists on getting in beside him even though she's not yet in her nightgown; she's only half-undressed. She's in her bra and a pair of stretchy black pants with an elastic waistband, and I don't bother to look away anymore; seeing my mother in that big hot-pink bra Josie picked out for her in the lingerie department of Macy's doesn't even make the top ten on the list of things in my life that I find disturbing these days.

"Come, Claire," Silviana says in the soothing voice she uses to keep my parents in line, "time to finish getting into nightgown."

"Why?" my father says.

"Because almost ten o'clock and time to sleep," Silviana explains.

"Don't listen to her," he tells my mother. He grabs her by her bra strap and won't let go.

"Come on, why are you doing this, Pop?" I hear myself say in a voice loud enough for him to catch every word, and now my father has slipped his whole hand under the bra strap; the elastic encircles his wrist like a bracelet. When I try to maneuver it out from beneath the pink elastic strap, he punches my forearm with his free hand, and it's a pretty powerful punch.

"Get. The fuck. Away. From me," my ninety-six-year-old father orders. For forty years he was a high school English and drama teacher, this cultured man who, with my mother alongside him, routinely drove in from the suburbs to Lincoln

Center, to Carnegie Hall, to the Guggenheim, and MoMA. He has never spoken this way in my presence. Ever. Or in my mother's—I'd bet my life on it. They've been devoted to one another for more than seventy years, except for that one surprising glitch in Paris during the War; I'd bet my life on that, too.

"Honey! Why you not be nice to you good son?" Silviana wants to know.

Despite that punch, I'm still trying to ease my father's hand out from under the bra strap, but he's not giving up. It's almost as though this were a fight for his life—that keeping his hand there on his wife's plump, bare shoulder is everything to him.

"Come, honey, be nice," Silviana says, as if she were talking to the seven-year-old she'd left behind in Otopeni, at the outskirts of Bucharest. But even though my father has a crush on her, the look he shoots her is ugly, his eyes narrowed, his teeth clenched menacingly.

"MartyMartyMarty," my mother wails, and maybe there's nothing more powerful in her arsenal. "MARTY!" she tries one last time.

"POP! Let go of the damn bra strap!" Silviana and I are struggling together, but the old guy is hanging on so fiercely, we're making no progress at all.

"Get away from me, you piece-a-shit bastard. You're no son of mine," he growls. "You never come to visit me, not even once."

It's hard for me to talk now, hard to calmly form the words I'm pretty sure I want to say. "Uh, I think you have me confused with someone else, Pop," I decide to tell him.

"Oh no I don't! I know exactly who you are, you creep. So just get the fuck away from me if you don't mind."

Piece-a-shit bastard, get the fuck away from me.

Of course my father has dementia and can't be held responsible for anything at all, *of course of course of course*, but for some reason this doesn't make hearing those words aimed directly at me any easier.

It's been a long, long, interminably long day, and I'm losing myself in all this.

So who the fuck *am I* anyway?

I could swear on the lives of my cherished daughters that I'm a good, decent, sweetheart of a guy and always have been, but those closest to me have clearly told me otherwise today.

So let's see: I'm a sixty-two-year-old guy whose father has, at this moment, brought me to tears, as if I were some miserably misunderstood second-grader who'd been chewed out for crimes of which I'm completely innocent.

Or maybe my wife is responsible for these ridiculous crybaby tears shimmering in my eyes, the same wife who, earlier tonight, referred to me as an asshole.

But I know this isn't who I am: these people so intimately connected to me are profoundly mistaken.

"Honey!" I hear Silviana saying to me. "Oh, honey!" She's removed her hand and mine from my father's, the one still entangled in the bra strap, and her arms are around me now and I'm breathing in the scent of her kindness.

Go home, she's urging me, *go home and be with you wife who love you.*

Less than an hour before my father's death, while my mother is in the living room with Josie and Silviana, all three women lounging on the couch listening to a couple of federal officials making fools of themselves in a clip on MSNBC, my father says, in a whisper, that there's something he needs to tell me.

It's August now, and it's sweltering. There are noisy air-conditioning units in every room, and my father's voice has grown so soft these past couple of days, I can barely hear him.

"Sure, what is it, Pop?"

He's in the rented hospital bed and in hospice care, which

simply means—according to the hospice nurse who blows in and out every few days—that my father has less than six months left on this earth. Inexplicably, one morning near the end of last month, he refused to get out of his own bed, and has been, ever since, in a state so weakened, he's unable to rise from this recently delivered hospital bed even to pee or shower, and has to be hand-fed the only thing he has just enough energy left to eat—the homemade applesauce Silviana has fixed for him in a blender with brown sugar, cinnamon, and nutmeg.

"What can I tell you?" said the young hospice physician who showed up for a house call around midnight several days ago. "He's ninety-six—end. of. story. And that's perfectly okay, guys." She was dressed in tangerine-colored rubber clogs and a white lab coat; ornamenting her lapel was a large round pin that said, "GOD BLESS THE GREAT INDOORS!" She seemed just a bit too cheerful for a hospice-care doc as she chugged down the glass of Arizona zero-calorie green tea Silviana offered her after she examined my father.

"Remember, no worries!" she said. "Call me anytime, you guys."

Six months, six days, six hours, six minutes, no matter how you look at it, this isn't the news my mother wants to hear, and so Silviana and Josie and I have decided to keep it to ourselves.

"What is it, Pop?" I ask my father again.

"How will I ever be able to figure out what time it is?" he murmurs. "I just don't understand what the hands of the clock are trying to tell me," he says, and now it sounds as if he's weeping.

These will be the last words he will ever say out loud, but neither he nor I have any way of knowing this; all I know is that my father is genuinely distraught.

I slowly stroke the back of his hand, from his knuckles to his wrist, as I promise him Silviana will always be here to tell him exactly what time it is, and my father seems relieved.

*   *   *

I'm on a fifteen-minute cigarette break from my station at my father's bedside, smoking my first Winston in many months; the taste is sort of nauseating, and the smoke makes my throat unmistakably sore, but I'm standing here under the awning in front of my apartment building taking one mindless drag after another when Josie texts me and tells me to please come back upstairs. She doesn't tell me why or say I need to hurry, and so I decide to stop and get our mail in the lobby first. While I'm throwing out circulars from Whole Foods and Home Depot, and unsolicited mail from the American Red Cross and real estate brokers wanting to list our apartment, I hear a neighbor beside me at the mailboxes saying into his phone, "Why in God's name would you put money in the meter and then just drive away? For Christ's sake, Sasha, *why*?" he asks, pure anguish in his voice. He's a nice-looking young guy; he can't be more than thirty or thirty-five, and he sounds like a broken man.

By the time I get back to the apartment, my father is gone, and I hate myself for having taken my sweet time sifting through junk mail while upstairs in the living room Josie and my mother watched Brooke Baldwin on CNN, and Silviana, sporting a pair of latex gloves, scoured the bathroom sink with Lysol, as my father, alone in his rented hospital bed down the hallway, departed from this universe, unaccompanied, entirely on his own.

A tearful Josie embraces me, rather seductively, in the doorway, and at least for the moment, as she loops her arms around me and I feel her heat through the thin denim shirt on my back, the slate has been wiped clean and I need no further apology from her, no further acknowledgment of her failings as a wife. *And really that's all I needed, then and now*, I can hear my mother saying in our small suburban kitchen polluted, that night, with the smoke from our Winstons.

Within five minutes, my father's flesh has turned cold and moist; I don't like the feel of it but continue to stroke the back of his hand anyway, again and again, until the hospice nurse arrives and pronounces him officially dead.

I immediately try to summon up a sterling childhood memory or two of my father escorting me excitedly to the 1964 World's Fair, or even a recent screen shot from Josie's cell phone that she posted of him on Instagram on Father's Day this year, but I'm stuck so firmly in the present that nothing comes to me.

Never mind those sixteen alluring ballerinas on the bedroom ceiling, that momentary half-smile Silviana observed on my father's beloved, familiar face only minutes ago, never mind the framed photograph I have of my old man as a toddler, arranged in a wicker carriage in 1923, that two-year-old sporting a sailor suit and casually tilting a baby bottle up to his mouth nearly a century ago, a horse-drawn wagon visible in the background. Never mind all that; like my mother, I just can't see any of it.

All I can see, so vividly, is my father's hand trapped beneath that shocking-pink bra strap; all I can hear, so distinctly, is *Get. The fuck. Away. From me.*

About the Author

Marian Thurm is the author of eight novels and four other short story collections, including the most recent, *Today Is Not Your Day*, a *New York Times* Editors' Choice. She had her first short story published in *The New Yorker* when she was 25 years old. In addition to *The New Yorker*, her stories have appeared in *The Atlantic, Michigan Quarterly Review, Narrative Magazine, The Southampton Review*, and many other magazines, and have been included in *The Best American Short Stories*, and numerous other anthologies. Her novel, *The Clairvoyant*, was a *New York Times* Notable Book. Her books have been translated into Japanese, Swedish, Dutch, German, and Italian. She has taught creative writing at Yale University and Barnard College, in the MFA programs at Columbia University and Brooklyn College, the Writing Institute at Sarah Lawrence, and at the Yale Writers' Workshop.